"Y—— need t— ——————" ——
sai— the quie— —————
his thoughts.

"Your pack needs you."

"And —hat about you? Do you need me?" Eli asked.

Looking him right in the eye, she said, "Like I need a hole in the head."

There were so many things that he wanted to say to th—. The anger that had initially risen up in the face of her own rage was fading, replaced by a raw, intens— knot of regret. "We have a lot we need to talk a——t, Rey."

"Like hell we do. All I need is you back on that moun——ntop, ready to do battle, and not a damn thing more."

"You —ally think we can fight together and not talk about ine elephant here in the room with us?"

"I h—— a few conditions before I agree to *let* you come home."

"Y— came here for me," he pointed out. "What do you want, Reyes?"

Voice —ittle more than a whisper, she kept her gaze lo——— on his and said, "I want the bond broken."

DARK WOLF RETURNING

RHYANNON BYRD

Published in Great Britain 2014
by Mills & Boon, an imprint of Harlequin (UK) Limited,
Eton House, 18-24 Paradise Road, Richmond, Surrey, TW9 1SR

© 2014 Tabitha Bird

ISBN: 978-0-263-91403-0

89-0814

Harlequin (UK) Limited's policy is to use papers that are natural, renewable and recyclable products and made from wood grown in sustainable forests. The logging and manufacturing processes conform to the legal environmental regulations of the country of origin.

Printed and bound in Spain
by Blackprint CPI, Barcelona

Rhyannon Byrd is an avid longtime fan of romance and the author of more than twenty paranormal and erotic titles. She has been nominated for three *RT Book Reviews* Reviewers' Choice Awards, including best Shapeshifter Romance, and her books have been translated into nine languages. After having spent years enjoying the glorious sunshine of the American South and Southwest, Rhyannon now lives in the beautiful but often chilly county of Warwickshire in England with her husband and family. For more information on Rhyannon's books and the latest news, you can visit her website at www.rhyannonbyrd.com or find her on Facebook.

To the awesome readers who have given this
series such wonderful support...

This one's for you!

THE BLOODRUNNERS' LAW

When offspring are born of a union between human and Lycan, the resulting creations may only gain acceptance within their rightful pack by the act of Bloodrunning: the hunting and extermination of rogue Lycans who have taken a desire for human flesh. Thus they prove not only their strength, but their willingness to kill for those they will swear to protect to the death.

The League of Elders will predetermine the Bloodrunners' required number of kills.

Once said number of kills are efficiently accomplished, only then may the Bloodrunner assume a place among their kin, complete with full rights and privileges.

THE DARK WOLF

A Dark Wolf bloodline is the purest of the Lycan race.

They are the most primal and powerful of their kind. Visceral. Predatory.

Creatures of instinct and hunger.

They are the potential for all things good and evil.

And they will forever act with furious vengeance to protect the ones they love.

Prologue

Love sucked. And it hurt. Like a bitch.

Carla Reyes believed this with every fiber of her being, because she'd learned it the hard way. By experience. She bore the internal scars to prove it.

But she wasn't alone. As far as tales of pain and betrayal and heartbreak went, she knew her specific story wasn't all that different from what had happened to thousands—make that millions—of other women around the world. At the emotional level, of course. Obviously, the fact that her mother was a werewolf, which made Carla a half-breed, added a certain edge to the situation. As did the fact that the object of her need was a male so completely and utterly alpha wolf, he'd once made other deadly Lycans literally scurry out of his path.

Now, from what she'd heard, he intimidated everyone he came across, no matter their species. Everyone but *her,* that is. She'd taught herself to feel nothing where Elijah Daniel Drake was concerned. And it had worked for a long time. Until her shields had been blasted to hell and back almost two weeks ago, when she'd been taken prisoner by a rival werewolf pack and overheard their battle plans before making her escape.

Now the time had come for him to make things right. Both for her…and for Eli's birth pack, the Maryland-based Silvercrest Lycans. Failure wasn't an option, because failure could mean the death of not only the pack, but also her friends and their loved ones. And her fellow Bloodrunners meant too much to her to sacrifice because of misplaced pride.

As Carla drove into the star-filled night, she was so tired she could almost taste the sweetness of sleep, but refused to give in. For two weeks, she'd had to struggle through injury and fatigue to find him. Tonight, he felt closer—within her reach—and she knew this was it. She was currently making her way across Louisiana, and within a mere matter of days, her search would finally be over.

Then she was going to do what she should have done the moment he'd abandoned her. She was going to end the pain once and for all. Break the connection, like a bone fracturing beneath the force of a brutal, crushing blow.

She was going to make him cut her loose…and be free.

After that, things would be…easier. She would get on with her life, and find a way to forget that she'd ever even known Eli Drake.

Were there risks with her plan? Of course. Weren't there always when it was something that mattered?

Her life as a Bloodrunner—a hunter of rogue wolves who had taken a liking for human flesh—was nothing but one continual risk after another. And now, thanks to Silvercrest enemies who were planning to attack the pack, which was already weakened after catastrophes it had suffered at the hands of Eli's own father, an inevitable war was on its way. A bloody battle on a scale she knew might very well wipe out every person she'd ever loved and cared about. Her band of brothers, in the truest sense of the word.

They needed Eli and his fellow mercenaries on their side. Needed the mercs' strength and expertise to help train the members of the pack who were willing to fight. But once he'd served his purpose, she was making this happen. Ripping him from her heart and her thoughts for the final time. For forever…

Even if it killed her.

Chapter 1

Two days later...

Eli Drake blinked his bleary eyes, unable to believe what he was seeing.

Shit. Had he drank so much he was hallucinating? If so, his pickled mind couldn't have come up with a more stunning, confounding vision. The hole-in-the-wall, small town Texas bar where he and his crew had landed for the night was a decent enough place to settle for a few hours while they tossed back some liquid therapy—and after the last assignment they'd taken, they'd definitely needed it. Hell, they could have drowned themselves in whiskey and beer for days on end, and it wouldn't have been enough to wipe out the horror of what they'd seen in that little South American village.

So, yeah, the woman who'd just walked into the bar *had* to be a by-product of his inebriation.

Only…as far as he could recall, he'd only had two whiskeys. For a man his size, even if he had been human, that wouldn't have been enough to make him start seeing…imagining… *Damn it*. He couldn't even get the words out within the privacy of his own mind.

Maybe it's a stress vision? I probably just need a break from my shitty day job.

Yeah, that was a better explanation than the alcohol, and extreme stress *had* been the riding theme of his life these past few weeks. Months. *Years*.

Squeezing his eyes shut, Eli focused on forcing the vision away. He didn't need crap like that screwing with his head. Sure, he was going to have to face her soon enough, considering he and his men were finally headed back to the mountains where he'd grown up, to his hometown of Shadow Peak, where the Silver-crest Lycans lived. But he wasn't ready for it now. Not tonight.

Facing Carla Reyes again after three years of banishment was something that would take battle armor and a heavy duty, steel-lined cup to protect his balls.

Fate, however, apparently didn't give a damn.

When the Lycan to his left softly swore under his breath, his deep voice rough with appreciation, Eli choked back a biting curse. Christ, he wasn't imagining things if others could see her, too. She was really there. In the flesh. Carla-Fucking-Reyes.

His next indrawn breath confirmed it, his dick hardening with ridiculous ease beneath the fly of his jeans. The soft, sleepy, feminine moan that followed made him look down, and he was momentarily surprised to find a woman straddling his lap, her face planted against his chest. He'd completely forgotten she was there, but then, it'd been a while since she'd spoken. He couldn't recall her name, but she wasn't in any shape to remind him. She was out cold, a line of drool slipping from the corner of her pink lips.

Hmm... Classy chick.

With a jerk of his chin, he signaled Kyle Maddox, his second-in-command and the guy who'd spotted Carla, to deal with the comatose blonde. But it wasn't the woman on his lap that had Kyle's attention, his nostrils flaring as he pulled in the Runner's scent. Eli knew the moment his friend pegged her as a half-blood Lycan, his dark brows slowly rising on his forehead.

Eli gestured again to the blonde in his lap. "Take her."

Kyle snorted as he moved to his feet and lifted the woman into his arms. "And do what with her?"

Keeping his gaze locked on Carla, Eli said, "Just make sure she gets somewhere safe for the night. I don't want one of these assholes in here taking advantage of her."

"She's definitely a local girl, so I'll talk to the servers. Maybe one of them can take her home with them."

"Good," he muttered, impatient for Kyle to get the hell away from him before Carla reached the table. "Just do it."

Carla had spotted him in the crowd and was headed his way, her gaze sliding toward the nearby group of Lycans standing at the bar—Sam, James, and Lev— who were watching her with unmistakable interest. Even Kyle, who had moved over to join them with the blonde in his arms, had his full attention focused on Carla. She looked exhausted, but gorgeous. At five-six, she was just tall enough that she didn't look like a child when standing beside a man of Eli's height, but was still…petite. Lithely muscled and battle-scarred, but somehow still incredibly feminine. Big brown eyes flecked with green and framed by thick lashes. Slim, delicate nose. Waves of thick, silky hair the colors of sunshine and honey and gold, the soft bangs falling across her brow. She was, quite simply, stunning. The most perfect, alluring, sensual female he'd ever known.

And, Jesus, that mouth of hers had always been his undoing. Full, sexy, sweet. Velvety and pink, like the petals of a flower. He wanted to devour her. Kiss her until he drew blood, which wasn't surprising. From the moment she'd hit adulthood, this little half-breed had always drawn the hunger of both the man *and* the beast inside him. A hunger that was as visceral and dark as it was insatiable. How he'd fought it for so many years, when he'd been living with the pack, he didn't know. He should have been given a damn medal for not falling on her like a rabid, sex-starved animal the instant she came of age—but he'd somehow kept himself under tight control, his fears for her safety the only thing that had a chance in hell of keeping him in line.

He'd been a goddamn saint when it came to Reyes… until that last week before his banishment.

As if they were some kind of penance for his sins, the memories of her from that week still woke him in the dead of night in a sweat, filled with an aching need that was primal, savage, and raw. So powerful he could taste it in the back of his throat. Here he was, three years later, and he still dreamt about her every night he didn't drink himself into a stupor.

Studying her expression, Eli wondered if she was about to make him pay for the carnal things that had happened that week. Is that why she'd tracked him down? To tell him she'd rather see him dead before letting him return to the pack? Because that was definitely hatred he could see burning in her beautiful, narrowed eyes.

Shoving his emotional reaction to her presence to the back of his mind, he focused instead on simply watching her…waiting. Eating up the sight of her in the tight jeans and T-shirt and battered hiking boots.

At a quick glance, you would never guess she was a hunter of deadly werewolves. Certainly, the clueless humans in the bar, who had no idea they had shapeshifters in their midst, would have never guessed she was both battle and weapons trained. The Silvercrest Lycans would be surprised to know that much of that training had come from Eli himself, since it'd been in secret. Every aspect of their complicated "friendship" had been private and secret and forbidden.

God, he'd been so drawn to her. Though he was older than her, she hadn't been a typical giddy twenty-two-year-old when their relationship had developed. She'd been sweet, but reserved. Eager for friends, and yet, wary to trust. But she'd trusted him. Past tense.

Eli had never told a soul about them, and he could only assume that Carla had done the same. Though not for the same reasons.

He moved to his feet when she reached the table, fighting the powerful urge to pull her into his arms, and the next thing he knew her tiny fist was launching toward his mouth. *Whack!* Damn, she'd hit him so hard it jerked his head back, the coppery taste of his blood instantly filling his mouth.

Softly laughing under his breath, Eli lifted his hand

and wiped the blood from the corner of his lip as he brought his gaze back to hers.

"What the hell is so funny?" Her soft words vibrated with fury.

"Nothing," he murmured, thinking he'd come close to getting what he wanted. Someone's blood had been drawn, just not hers. And not in the way he'd hoped for.

Contempt clouded her expression. "You never could just give an honest answer to a question, could you?"

"Insults and accusations already?" he drawled, sliding back into his chair. The worst thing in the world he could do was let her know how the sight of her affected him, especially when he could feel his own angry frustration with fate and life and her blatant hatred building inside him, desperate for release. "That didn't take long."

She drew in a sharp breath at his snide tone, the skin around her eyes tightening as she took the seat across from him and asked a passing server for a Scotch. It was clear from the look on her face that she hadn't meant to launch into the topic of their past. She was irritated with herself that she had, and seemed determined to get to the point of this strange, unexpected visit. "You know about your dad?"

"That he's dead?" He lifted a hand, rubbing his stubbled jaw. "Yeah, I heard about it."

As soon as the words left his mouth, a painful mix of emotions flashed through her eyes before she managed to bank them. "And you didn't think to come home?" she asked in a careful tone.

Brows drawn together, he tried to reason out why she thought the death of his psychotic father would herald his immediate return. Had the entire pack thought he would come crawling back the moment he learned that dear ol' daddy had staged a bloodthirsty coup that resulted in the death of the pack's entire governing body, the League of Elders? An attack that would have led to Stefan Drake's total control of the Silvercrest Lycans, if not for the help of the half-breeds his racist father had tried so hard to turn the pack against.

The League of Elders might have banished Eli for the unsanctioned kill he'd made on one of the rapists who'd attacked his sister three years ago…but they weren't the only reason he'd stayed away. Hell, they weren't even at the top of the list. No, his reasons for staying away had far more to do with… Well, with things he spent a lot of time trying not to think about. Things he was still trying to figure out how to deal with.

And every damn one of those things had to do with the woman sitting across from him.

Voice low, he finally responded to her question. "Once I heard that you and Eric and Elise were all right, I didn't see any reason to rush home. But I didn't plan on staying away forever, Rey. I was coming back."

"When?" she asked, as the server set her drink on the table.

"Now, if you can believe it. That's where we're headed."

"Bullshit." She gave a bitter laugh. "You know what I think? I think you were waiting for *me* to come to *you*. And here I am," she offered with a sharp smile, spreading her arms wide, and he couldn't help but notice the way the cotton shirt stretched tight across her mouth-watering breasts. Then she leaned forward, bracing her palms flat on the rickety little table with its scarred surface and dirty ashtray, and lowered her voice. "But I'm not here to beg for myself, Eli. I just need you and your ragtag little group to come back with me and do what you do best."

Hoping to rile her into hitting him again, like some kind of masochist—though he was pretty sure he just wanted to feel her hands on him—his lips curled in a cocky smirk. "You have no idea what I do best. You only got *part* of the show, if you'll recall."

"Not interested," she grunted in response to his silky, suggestive tone, before taking a drink of her Scotch. She winced as she swallowed the smoky alcohol, then wiped her mouth and shot his cocky expression right back at him. "And let's face it, Eli. The only thing you've ever done well is kill."

"Ouch, Reyes. If I didn't know better," he murmured, clucking his tongue, "I'd say you don't like me anymore."

She rolled her eyes. "Just get your band of Merry Men together and let's get out of here."

"Merry Men?" he snorted. "I'm no bloody Robin Hood."

She smirked. "Yeah, what was I thinking? The idea of giving something to the less fortunate is probably a little sappy for a guy like you."

"A guy like me?"

Lifting her brows, she said, "You know, the big bad mercenary who doesn't give a shit about anything or anyone, except for how much they can pay him. I hear you've cultivated the reputation well."

Irritation burned through his veins, not easy to hide. But he managed with a lazy grin and a slow drawl.

"You shouldn't believe everything you hear. A lot of men will lie when it suits them."

"Oh, God." She suddenly started to laugh so hard it made him scowl. Wiping the tears from her glittering eyes, she finally managed to splutter, "D-don't I know it."

Hell, he'd walked right into that one.

A fraction of his control began to slip, his hands flexing as he fought the urge to reach out and grab her, yanking her into his lap. "You're pushing it, Reyes."

Her laughter faded, and she kept her gaze on the Scotch as she swirled it in her glass. "If you're uncomfortable with my attitude or reactions," she murmured, "then I gotta tell you that I don't really care. I'm not here to make you feel better, or to talk about the past." She stopped swirling her drink, her dark gaze lifting, locking with his. "I'm here because your family needs you. You do recall that you have a brother and sister, right? And I can only imagine they have a hell of a lot to say to you right now, considering you haven't been returning their calls." She pushed back from the table and gave him a look that would probably scare a lot of men into doing whatever the hell she wanted them to. "Now get off your ass and let's get out of here."

"No," he rasped. "Not until you answer a few of *my* questions."

"Like we have the time," she started to argue, but he cut her off.

"We have as much time as we need, because I'm not going anywhere until you fucking spill." He took a deep swallow of his whiskey, and waited for her to bring her chair back to the table, before asking, "You came here alone?"

"Of course." At the look on his face, she said, "What? You thought someone needed to come with me and hold my hand?"

His jaw got tighter. "Why now?"

She glared back at him as if she couldn't understand what his problem was. "War isn't enough of a reason?"

"From what I've understood from Eric's messages, the Silvercrest have been in trouble for a while now."

"With no help from you, huh?"

He narrowed his eyes. "Like I said, I was planning to head back."

"Right. How kind of you."

"Why *now,* Reyes? Why *you?* You didn't rush out and try to track me down months ago, when this all started. So tell me the truth. Why— Now?"

She held his stare, and he could tell she was planning on just waiting him out, until she let herself really look him in the eye. Whatever she saw there, whether it was anger or his sheer determination—it made her frown deepen. Forcing the words out between her quickening breaths, she told him, "It was the right time. I felt…raw. And I suddenly *knew* I could find you. When I was in danger, the bond started to pull at me—"

"So you feel it, too?" he cut in sharply, interrupting her explanation. His heart started trying to pound its way through his chest with hard, violent beats, and it was all he could do to stay in his damn chair in his relaxed pose, instead of surging to his feet and grabbing her shoulders, demanding she tell him *everything*.

Still scowling, she cast a wary look toward the hand still holding his glass, as if surprised it hadn't shattered in his brutal grip. Her chin lifted in assent.

"I've wondered about that." He tossed back his

drink, slamming the empty glass onto the table, while his thoughts churned. He felt pain, frustration, loss. But mostly rage. A deep, seething rage for everything that had happened, and why.

He cleared his throat, his hooded gaze locked in hard and tight on her face, trying to read her expression. The bond should have enabled him to feel her emotions as easily as his own, but it didn't, because it was only half-formed. He'd realized that right from the start, though it'd taken time to sort out exactly how the partially formed bond would affect him. And it'd kept him up at nights, wondering if Carla was being affected in the same way.

When he couldn't get a damn thing from the look on her face, Eli lowered his gaze to the table and heard himself saying, "For what it's worth, I didn't even realize the bond had taken hold until almost a week after I left. By that time, I was already in South America."

When he looked up to see her reaction to his confession, she turned her head to the side and laughed again. The sound was hollow and heavy, sounding as exhausted as she looked. "Well," she murmured. "I guess it's good to know I'm not the only one stuck in this hell."

His jaw tightened, but he forced out a slow breath, not wanting to rise to her bait. And she was definitely baiting him, spoiling for a fight. Damn it, he was handling this all wrong, but it was like a train wreck he couldn't stop from happening right in front of him. He was pissed at how badly he wanted her. At how fucking sexy she looked. How angry she was at him.

Knowing he needed to change the subject, he asked, "What were you in danger from?"

Her mouth flattened with irritation, as if she hadn't meant to let that bit slip out either, her reluctance making him even more suspicious. He could feel it in his gut, the fact that there was something she didn't want to tell him. "I'll sit here all damn night and wait you out if I have to," he threatened in a low voice. "But you're going to answer that question."

She took a deep breath, her nostrils flaring a little, and he felt the pull down in his lower body get even tighter as he wondered if she could scent him the way he could scent her. Not just on a Lycan level, but one that went even deeper. And if she could, was it affecting her, making her hungry for something only *he* could give her?

Her head dropped back on her shoulders, then dropped forward, and he could have sworn he heard her give a soft growl. Then she lifted her head, looking right at him, and nervously licked her lips. "I know Eric's been leaving you messages at a number he had for you, asking you to come home. Didn't he tell you about Elise?"

Because he was so often in places where cell phone coverage was nonexistent, and hadn't had a permanent base since leaving the pack, Eli had used a couple of different messaging services for both work and his family. It was one of those numbers that Eric had been calling.

Answering her question, he said, "I haven't heard from Eric the last couple of weeks. He sounded pretty pissed off in his last message, because I hadn't returned any of his calls. But I wasn't in a situation where I could talk to him," he explained, which was only partially true. "What is it you think he should have told me about Elise? Is she all right?"

"Two weeks ago, Elise was kidnapped by Sebastian Claymore."

He shot forward to the edge of his seat. "Was she hurt? What the hell happened?"

From what he'd been able to piece together from Eric's messages, Eli knew that a Lycan named Roy Claymore had assumed control of the Whiteclaw pack, and Sebastian and Harris Claymore were his nephews. Eric's last message had mentioned something about Harris being under suspicion for hassling their sister, Elise, and that had been enough for Eli to know he needed to get his affairs in order so that he could head back, even though he'd known it would mean facing Carla. Elise had already been through too much not to have her brothers there looking out for her. He just hadn't realized the situation would escalate so quickly. Had thought he still had time to make it back, before he was needed.

"She's fine, Eli. She made it out of there that same day, and she wasn't…they didn't hurt her."

"Eric mentioned that the Runners were having trouble with the Whiteclaw, but said he'd go into more detail when I got in touch with him. What exactly did the Claymores want with her?"

"It's a long story, and not one for someplace this crowded. She was scared, but she wasn't harmed. I made sure to give them a hard enough time that it kept them busy."

"You were with her?" he asked sharply, while the mother of all headaches started pounding in his temples.

"I was taken as well," she murmured, clearly not

wanting to make a big deal out of it. "They were able to sneak up on us, and we were taken back to Hawkley together."

They'd taken his woman and his sister to Hawkley, the Whiteclaw pack's hometown? A place where they would have been surrounded by those bastards?

Oh, hell, those sons of bitches are gonna die.

There were about a million questions he wanted answers to, but Eli scraped out the most important one first: "Did they touch you?"

The idea of her in danger—a danger he hadn't been able to sense because of the weakness of their bond— was too much for him, making his inner beast seethe for release. His gums ached from the heavy weight of his fangs, the tips of his fingers burning as his claws prickled beneath his skin. He couldn't believe he was a fraction away from shifting in the middle of a goddamn human bar, but that's how this woman had always affected him, making him do things he'd never thought he would otherwise do.

Instead of tensing up and getting riled by his demanding tone, her posture had relaxed, one lightly muscled arm hooked over the back of her chair. "That isn't something that should concern you."

"Did they touch you?" he asked again, his voice now little more than a snarl.

Cocking her head a bit to the side, she studied him through her lashes. After a heavy silence, she finally said, "I would have been raped if I hadn't managed to get free. As it was, I just got knocked around a bit."

He wanted to roar at how casual she sounded about that, when it made him want to go for the blood of every Lycan who'd hit her, gleefully ripping them apart, one painful piece at a time. "How did you get away?"

"I knew that when the Runners realized we were missing, Wyatt would—" She paused suddenly, giving him a strange look. "Uh, when Eric left you messages, did he happen to mention that Elise and Wyatt Pallaton are bonded now?"

"I didn't know it'd happened, but Eric thought it was headed that way."

He could tell she was trying to figure out how he felt about his sister permanently attaching herself to the male who was Carla's Bloodrunning partner, but he didn't know. Until he saw the two of them together, he wasn't forming an opinion. If Pallaton treated his sister right and made her happy, he'd have no issue with him. If he didn't, Eli was going to kick his ass. It was as simple as that.

Reaching for her glass again, she said, "Anyway, I knew Wyatt and the others were coming, but there was no way they would get to her if I didn't create a distraction. So that's what I did."

"And afterward?" he pressed, sensing that she was leaving out a hell of a lot. He had a strong suspicion her distraction had required her to put her own life at even greater risk to save his sister's, and it made him both grateful and viciously angry.

She downed the last of her drink, and set the glass back on the table. "While I was making my escape, I heard some things that compelled me to steal some money and a car and come after you."

"To drag me back home. For the pack."

She gave him a look that would have wilted a lesser man. "It sure as hell isn't because I want you there."

"What did you hear?" he demanded, noticing the discoloration on her cheekbone as she turned her head and the light caught it. It was a healing bruise, and based on how many days since she'd gotten it, he knew it must have initially been brutal. Lycans had accelerated healing abilities, and though she was only half wolf, her body healed much faster than a human's. Given the look of her face now, Eli imagined she'd been more than knocked around a little, and he was looking forward to paying back the ones who were responsible. In blood and pain and death.

"Before I left Hawkley," she finally replied, bringing that dark gaze back to his, "I overheard some of the Whiteclaw soldiers talking about their plans for the Silvercrest. They haven't managed to secure the number of soldiers they were hoping for from other packs, so they've come up with a new plan. One even deadlier than we'd feared. Since you said Eric didn't go into a lot of detail in his messages, it sounds like there's a lot you need to be brought up to speed on. But you can believe me when I say we need a miracle, Eli. Unfortunately, the only thing we've got on our side, other than my guys, is you."

He knew who she meant by her "guys." There were five men who made up the Silvercrest's Bloodrunning team: Mason Dillinger, Jeremy Burns, Brody Carter, Wyatt Pallaton, and Cian Hennessey. Actually, he needed to make that six men, since his brother Eric was now working as a Runner, though the last Eli had heard, his brother wasn't partnered up yet the way the others were.

At his silence, she added, "You were always rumored to be the most ruthless wolf the pack had ever seen. Jeremy told us you tore the male who attacked Elise into pieces. That's the kind of man we need."

For a moment, he was surprised that Jeremy knew what had happened, since his father had purposefully kept the Runners ignorant of Elise's attack. The only reason Carla had known was because Eli had told her. She wouldn't have been able to share that confidence with any of her fellow Bloodrunners without giving away their secret relationship, but that didn't mean that the truth hadn't eventually been leaked by someone else. For all he knew, Elise herself had been the one to finally share the horrific story. Or perhaps Eric, since he was now one of them.

Not that it mattered. Regardless of how Jeremy had learned what he'd done, what she'd said was true. Eli *had* ripped that bastard to pieces, and he didn't regret it. But it bothered him that Carla might think of him as some kind of monster, and he couldn't stop himself from asking her if that's what she'd meant.

"Are you calling me a monster?"

"No." She slowly arched her brows. "I'd only use that term if I was talking about your personality."

He let that slide, knowing she was willing to say anything to make the canyon between them even deeper.

"So how did you find me?"

She shifted a little uncomfortably in the chair, but she didn't refuse to explain. "It was like the thing with the Whiteclaw jolted me out of a fog, and I suddenly knew that it would work. That if I wanted to, I'd be able to pinpoint your location. So instead of making my way back home with the others, I stole a car. Grabbed a map from the glove box. Called Wyatt and told him I was coming after you."

Staring at her beautiful face, Eli felt a confusing wave of emotion sweep through him, piercing and sharp. He'd heard that in times of danger, a bonded mate could use the connection that created the bond to locate their other half. And if the distance was too great, they could use a map to help feel the "pull" that would take them in the right direction. From the sound of it, it'd taken Carla several weeks to find him, which seemed longer than he would have expected. But, then, their bond wasn't complete, which meant it probably didn't pull as strongly as others.

He refused to acknowledge how much that little fact irritated him. He hadn't had any right forming a bond with her in the first place, much less to be angry that it wasn't as powerful as it should have been.

"You need to come back," she said, the quiet words breaking into his thoughts. "Your pack needs you, and Elise and Eric need you."

"And what about you? Do *you* need me?"

She didn't try to shy away from the question. Looking him right in the eye, she said, "Like I need a hole in the head."

There were so many things that he wanted to say to that. The anger that had initially risen up in the face of her own rage was fading, replaced by a raw, intense knot of regret that was making him break out in a sweat. "We have a lot we need to talk about, Rey."

"Like hell we do. All I need is your ass on that mountaintop, ready to do battle, and not a damn thing more."

Eli gave a frustrated shake of his head. "You really think we can fight together and not talk about the elephant here in the room with us?"

"That's exactly what I think, because I have a few conditions before I agree to *let* you come home."

"You came here for me," he pointed out, scowling as he picked up on one of his guys snickering under their breath. It sounded like Sam, and he knew the jackass was enjoying hearing him get his ass handed to him by a woman. "What do you want, Reyes?"

Voice little more than a whisper, she kept her gaze locked on his, and said, "I want the bond broken."

His muscles pulled so tight he was surprised he didn't shatter, a feeling of dread coiling through his insides that felt remarkably similar to fear. "It can't be done."

"It *can*."

"What the hell are you talking about?"

"Come home with me, Eli. Fight for your pack. And when the blood clears, you and I can erase what never should have happened in the first place." She leaned forward in her chair, her eyes bright. "We can finally end this nightmare, once and for all."

"You really think you can do it?" he scoffed. "Break an unbreakable bond?"

"Yes." She gave him a slow, determined smile. "I plan on breaking the hell out of it."

Chapter 2

Carla knew the instant he realized she wasn't bullshitting him, his belligerent expression slowly giving way to shock.

It was because of Eli's supercharged bloodline and her own powerful alpha genes that they'd ended up in this mess. At least that's what her friend Jillian believed had been the cause of her problems, landing her with a bond that was, but wasn't. One that was only partially fixed in place, thanks to the crappiest timing in the universe. Or…maybe the luckiest, depending on how you looked at it. In Carla's case, a partial bond was better than a full, *un*breakable one.

As it was, she'd been able to manage without him. Oh, her heart had been battered and bruised for…well, for a long time after he'd abandoned her. But she'd been able to go on, functioning without him.

The only thing she hadn't been able to do was crawl into bed with another man.

Eli, from the look of things when she'd walked into the bar and found him with a scantily clad blonde passed out in his lap, hadn't been suffering that particular symptom. And, God, did that tick her off.

After all, it wasn't like a guy who looked like him would have trouble getting any woman he wanted in his bed. A man too gorgeous to be real—and certainly for his own good. Chiseled, rugged, and massive. Tall and broad and ripped with muscle. Golden skin. Ice blue eyes rimmed with dark, stormy gray. Thick, inky black lashes. He'd always worn his hair short when she'd known him but it was shaggy now, curling around his neck and ears. Messy in that way that movie stars spent a fortune trying to achieve, while Eli probably just ran his hands through it and let it dry. Unfair, how beautiful he was. A dangerous, primal predator who could slay with nothing more than a sarcastic twist of that bold, sensual mouth.

He was so breathtakingly masculine, and so impossibly lethal. To the heart as well as the flesh. And she knew that lesson better than anyone.

Taking a deep breath, she tried to calm down, knowing he could no doubt sense her every emotion. But it was difficult when inside she was seething with rage. She hated feeling this out of control. It wasn't something she allowed, given her occupation. Anger made you stupid, and a hunter couldn't afford to make careless mistakes.

Neither could a woman.

The silence that had settled between them was just about to the point where she wanted to snap at him to say something already, when the tall guy she'd seen him sitting with earlier approached the table. Thankfully without the blonde Eli had dumped in his arms. "I hate to interrupt, but we need to get out of here. They're closing soon."

Eli nodded, then moved to his feet in a rippling display of muscle that his jeans and T-shirt did little to conceal. As she stood, as well, the rest of the group who'd been standing nearby at the bar joined them, looking between her and Eli as if they were waiting for him to make the introductions.

Sounding more than a little pissed off, Eli said, "Carla, this is Kyle Maddox, Sam Harmon, James Bennett, and Lev Slivkoff. Guys, this is Carla Reyes. I, uh, know her from home."

Carla almost winced in sympathy for the gorgeous jerk, since he'd sounded so awkward there at the end, as if he didn't know what to say about her. He'd obviously never mentioned her to any of his friends or coworkers or whatever a badass Lycan called the other badass Lycan mercenaries that he fought with. Something buried deep inside her gave a stupidly pained cry at that fact, but she refused to pay any attention to it. She wasn't going to let a little hurt make her act like an idiot in front of him.

"It's nice to meet you," she murmured, shaking their rough, battle-hardened hands. They were all tanned and tall and dark, except for Lev, whose shoulder-length mane was as golden as hers. And while the others had dark, midnight-colored eyes that nearly drowned out their ebony pupils, his were an interesting mix of green and blue that could barely pass for human.

They were all pretty much stunningly attractive,

oozing the kind of raw sex appeal that probably made most women drool when they saw them—but Lev was definitely the best looking of the bunch, reminding her of a badass Russian enforcer she'd once met during a hunt. When he grabbed her hand, she almost laughed, thinking he was going to kiss the back of it, like something out of a movie. But he didn't. Instead, he turned it over and licked the inside of her wrist with a rough tongue, right over her pulse. Her startled gasp was drowned out by Eli's guttural snarl, and the next thing she knew Lev had released her hand and was stumbling into the guy named James, who had a wicked scar on his throat, because Eli had just given Lev a violent shove.

"Don't be a jackass," Eli growled.

"He loves me, really," the Lycan drawled, though there was something in his rich, masculine scent that told her he was more. They all were. She just didn't know what that *more* was, and there was no way in hell she was asking when she wasn't sure she wanted to know the answer.

Carla kept a careful eye on the group as they settled their bill at the bar, not quite sure what to expect from them. They were eyeing her with open looks of curiosity and friendly smiles, but she was still a bit wary. Not physically, but emotionally. The last thing she wanted was for one of them to blurt out a question about her relationship with Eli. And they looked nosey enough to do it.

"Since the men and I are heading back with you," Eli rumbled, "we should find a motel for the night, then hit the road first thing in the morning."

She'd just started to ask how quickly he thought they

could reach Maryland, when the sound of screeching tires and loud voices came from the bar's front parking lot.

"What was that?" she asked, though no one was paying her any attention. They were all focused on the one named Sam, who had made his way over to one of the front windows and was peeking outside. "Shit," he muttered. "It looks like we've got a problem."

Eli grabbed her arm and jerked her behind him. "Who is it?"

"I can't tell yet," Sam replied, while the remaining customers, along with the staff, started pouring out the back entrance. It apparently wasn't the first time this place had seen this kind of "problem," and given the look of the clientele, Carla doubted it would be the last. "But we've got three pickups with beds full of armed bad guys," Sam was saying, "and they're stopping by our trucks. So my guess is that they're here for us."

"Were you followed here?" Lev asked her.

"What? No! Of course not."

"Then they're definitely here for us," the one named James murmured in a deep, gravelly voice.

"Don't be so sure," Eli muttered. "She has a knack for dragging trouble in her wake."

"I do not!" she snapped, poking him hard in the back of his shoulder.

Sam scratched his head as he sauntered back over to the group, a funny expression on his handsome face as he looked at Eli. "I've never seen him like this," he seemed to be saying to the other guys. "He's always so blasted nice to women. Why's he keep riling this little thing?"

James shrugged. "Beats me."

"All of you, mind your own damn business," Eli growled.

Kyle flashed a smile. "I don't know about you guys, but I'm starting to get a good idea of the problem."

Lev threw back his head and let out a lusty laugh. "This is gonna be priceless."

Eli slowly looked from one man to the next, his powerful frame drawn tight with tension. "Shut up about her," he said in a low voice, "or I'll break your heads before those idiots out there even get a chance."

As she moved back to his side, Carla thought he looked and sounded more than ready to thrash the next guy who teased him, but they didn't seem to care.

"You don't have to get so testy," Sam drawled, his dark eyes shining with humor. "We like her."

"I'm afraid the feeling isn't mutual anymore," she muttered, reaching back and pulling the gun she'd stolen off one of the Whiteclaw soldiers from the waistband of her jeans.

"Oh, God," Lev murmured, clutching his heart when she opened the clip, checking her ammo. "I think I just fell in love."

At her startled look, Sam laughed. "Lev has a thing about women who can handle a weapon."

"Mmm. That I do."

Kyle snorted. "He has a thing about *all* women."

The blond arched his tawny brows at the grinning merc. "And you don't?"

Kyle winked and blew him a kiss. "Don't go sounding jealous, honey. You know I love you."

This time, Lev was the one who snorted. "You just like the way I fill out my jeans."

Carla looked at the four laughing idiots and wondered what on earth she'd gotten herself into. What was Eli doing with these clowns? She'd come here for warriors, damn it. Not a collection of frat boys who enjoyed ribbing each other.

Though, to be fair, these mercs didn't look anything like any frat boy she'd ever seen. They would have made even the college ball players look puny.

Ah, now I get it, she thought a few minutes later, after they'd decided how to handle the situation and she, Eli, and Kyle had made their way out the back entrance and around the left side of the building. The customers and staff had thankfully scattered, no doubt heading into one of the other bars farther down the road, since there wasn't much of anything else around. There'd been a small group of human thugs lying in wait for the mercenaries just outside the exit, but Lev, Sam, and James, who'd gone out first, had quickly taken care of them, before going right. Then the three mercs had engaged the armed gunmen causing havoc in the front parking lot, while Eli and Kyle stayed with her in the shadows.

These guys might act like a bunch of frat boys, but they sure as hell didn't fight like them. Relief swept through her in a warm rush as she watched them, making her breathe a bit easier. If she was going to have to endure the seven circles of hell by being close to Eli, she at least wanted to know it was for a good reason. And protecting the ones she loved was as good a reason as there was.

Wyatt was worried about her, and had tried talking her into coming back during each of their conversations since she'd started this journey. It was a testament to how much she meant to all the guys, since they knew Eli and his men were needed—but they apparently cared about her even more. She really was like the little sister none of them had, aside from Eric, and she should have realized how they would react to her heading off on her own. There was probably going to be hell to pay when she finally made it back to the Alley—the place that the Bloodrunners called home.

But at least it would have been worth it. These mercenaries might be even more of a joking, smartass group than the Runners, but they were seriously skilled when it came to combat. Bullets sprayed from the humans' guns as they scattered around the remaining cars in the lot and shot wildly into the night, unable to pinpoint the mercs' locations as the guys quickly took down one assailant after another. She could sense Eli and Kyle's need to join the fight and help their friends, but knew they were sticking close to her in order to provide protection.

Eli Drake had always been the most overprotective male she'd ever known, and that obviously hadn't changed. She knew he didn't want to leave her side, but when it looked like four of the thugs were going to slash the tires on the two shiny, badass black trucks she assumed belonged to the mercs, he told her to stay with Kyle, and headed off to deal with them.

"You know, we don't have to hide over here," she murmured, as soon as Eli had left. "I'm perfectly capable of helping in a fight."

"I'm sure you are, honey. But I think Eli would probably castrate me if I let anything happen to you. And I'm kinda partial to all my body parts."

That probably would have been the end of it, if another truckload of men hadn't come barreling into the lot. Someone must have called for reinforcements, and this time the truck stopped near the side of the building where she was waiting with Kyle. No longer willing to stand this one out when the mercs were so outnumbered, she lifted her weapon as she moved toward the cover of a nearby grove of pecan trees and started firing on the armed gunmen who were shooting into the parking lot.

Carla had managed to take out five of the humans, before she felt a sharp burn cut across her left side, just beneath the edge of her bra. It felt like acid had been poured onto her skin, but she kept firing, until the last gunman in the truck fell. Then she slumped against the thick tree trunk Kyle had pulled her behind, listening to the fighting still taking place out in the parking lot. There wasn't as much gunfire now, and she knew things were winding down. They needed to get out of there while they still could, before the cops showed up and things *really* got complicated.

"You're gonna be in so much trouble," Kyle predicted, his low voice holding the soft, melting edge of a Southern accent. "Eli told you to stay out of it."

"I didn't even get my claws out," she huffed. "All I did was fire some bullets."

"He's still gonna be pissed."

Ignoring him, she took another look around the side of the tree and watched as Lev finally caught one of the few remaining gunmen for questioning, his big hand fisted in the front of the guy's bloodied shirt as he pulled the Hispanic-looking male close to his face and spoke to him. The human was apparently being stubborn, because Lev gave him a frustrated shake that probably jarred the thug's brain loose. She could see his lips moving, and a moment later Lev tossed him aside, not even bothering to watch where the guy landed as he turned and started making his way over to where she stood with Kyle.

"What the hell is their problem?" Kyle asked, as soon as Lev was within hearing distance.

"They work for Julio Varga. Seems ol' Julio thinks Eli slept with his woman when we were staying down at their compound last month."

All this because Eli screwed the wrong woman? she thought, her lip curling in a disgusted sneer. "Why doesn't that surprise me?"

Kyle clucked his tongue at her in admonishment. "He didn't touch her, honey." Jerking his head toward a smirking Lev, he added, "It was this jackass who couldn't keep it in his pants."

Lev's grin got wider. "Not fair, man. She caught me when I wasn't wearing any."

"You could have tried a little self-control," Kyle muttered.

"I did," Lev protested. "But then she got on her knees and—"

"Enough!" Carla waved the hand still holding her empty gun, cutting him off. "I don't want to hear this."

Waggling his brows, the golden Adonis sent her a crooked smile. "You sure, pretty wolf? It's good stuff."

"Then maybe over a beer sometime," she relented, finding his boyish charm kind of endearing. He was like a big freaking teddy bear, once you got past the serious sex appeal. "But not in the middle of a fight."

Before either male could say another word, the gunfire abruptly ended, and Eli was suddenly standing right in front of her. His face and arms were spattered with blood, his shirt and hair damp with sweat, while all those acres of hard muscle flexed beneath his skin as he breathed in a harsh rhythm. And the expression on his face was as darkly furious as his tone. "What the fuck, Carla? Did you or did you not hear me tell you to stay out of it?"

"Oh, I heard you," she murmured, trying to ignore the fire in her side. "I just don't take orders from you."

His nostrils flared, and he fisted his massive hands at his sides. "If you had, then you wouldn't be bleeding."

"Shit! She got shot?" Kyle moved to get a better look at her, and his eyes went wide when he saw her blood-soaked left side. "Damn it, woman. Why didn't you tell me?"

"Because I'm fine. It's just a graze." She lifted her brows when she looked at Eli. "And I didn't know you found the sight of a little blood so upsetting."

One of the mercs choked off a laugh, though she couldn't tell which one. She was too busy keeping a careful eye on Eli, since he looked like he wanted to throttle her.

"Come on," he finally muttered, gripping her right arm and dragging her with him as he headed toward those massive black trucks that sat on the far side of the lot.

"Wait, I need my car!" she yelled, looking toward the little VW she'd picked up for almost nothing the week before. It looked a little sad, but damn it, that car had character. She couldn't just leave it there all by its lonesome to turn into a rust bucket.

Eli flicked a dismissive look over the car. "That piece of shit stays here."

"Oh, no, it doesn't!"

"It's not even yours," he argued, obviously noticing the Georgia plates.

"Is too!" she shot back, wishing he wouldn't walk quite so fast, since her head was starting to get a bit woozy. "I bought it off a guy in Atlanta last week for a hundred bucks."

He stopped and gave her a look that set her teeth on edge, as if he thought she'd gone out of her mind. "You bought a stolen car off some random guy?"

She clenched her teeth, having already figured that part out for herself. No way the human would have sold it to her for that amount if the transaction had been legit. He'd probably just been looking for some quick money to pay for his next fix. And it's not like they'd dealt with any of the legal paperwork. She'd just needed to ditch the car she'd stolen off the Whiteclaw and find something a little more fuel efficient, since it'd become apparent that tracking down her so-called "other half" was going to take more time than she'd hoped.

So, yeah, the car was most likely hot. But she'd still paid money for it!

"What if I take the keys inside and leave a note to let them know she's up for grabs?" James offered, speaking up for the first time since they'd come outside.

"Fine," she muttered, figuring it was better than nothing. "But please get my bag out of the trunk first."

James nodded as he took the keys she'd dug out of her pocket, the pain in her side burning like holy hell as she moved. But she refused to groan, not wanting to give Eli the satisfaction. Instead, she glared at him as he pulled a set of keys from his own pocket.

"Are you even sober enough to drive?" she asked with a scowl.

He wasn't looking at her, but she could swear he was rolling his eyes at the question. "We're not human, Rey. It would take a hell of a lot more than what any of us have had tonight to put us over the limit." Then, in a lower voice, he muttered, "And you should know I wouldn't put you at risk like that."

Five minutes later, she was sitting in the front seat of one truck, one of the guy's T-shirts balled up and pressed against her side, while Eli drove and Lev and Sam sat in the spacious backseat. Kyle and James had piled into the other truck, along with everyone's gear. Since Eli refused to stay in the town they'd just been attacked in, in case this Varga guy decided to send more men after them, they had to drive for nearly an hour before they found a cheap roadside motel that had enough rooms for them all. Unfortunately, she hadn't been paying close enough attention when they were checking in, the blood loss making her a little dizzy, because it wasn't until the keys were handed out that she realized they were one key short.

Which meant they had five rooms, instead of six.

Son of a freaking bitch!

"Eli," she started to growl, before stumbling and nearly face planting against the cracked concrete walkway that led to the rooms. *Damn it!* Her lack of decent sleep the last two weeks, combined with the stress of finally facing Eli again, not to mention the blood loss, was getting to her. She was thankful the other Runners weren't there to see her like this. They never would have let her live it down.

Kyle had grabbed her before she collapsed, his hold

careful, as if he was afraid of hurting her. Did she really seem that fragile? "I think one of us should carry her," he said, glancing at the others over the top of her head. "She's looking a little pale."

"I've got her," Eli grunted, his heavy arm wrapping around her shoulders as he pulled her out of Kyle's hands and jerked her against his side.

"I don't know, boss man. You sure you don't need any help?" Kyle asked from behind them, sounding both concerned and like he was trying not to laugh his ass off. She wasn't sure what he found so freaking funny, but if it turned out to have anything to do with her, she was going to kick him. Hard.

"Kyle?" Eli muttered, as he opened the door to one of the rooms and all but shoved her inside.

"Yeah?" Kyle asked from the sidewalk.

"Piss off." Eli slammed the door in the merc's smirking face, then turned around and shoved a hand through his hair, his narrow gaze immediately connecting with hers. Carla had sat down on the foot of one of the beds, her left side now completely covered in blood. She'd felt a wave of relief when she'd seen that there were two beds in the room—but the look on Eli's face as he pinned her under his dark glare completely shredded it. He still looked like he wanted to throttle her, but there was something even darker than anger in his unusual eyes, and it had her pulse kicking up. She wasn't afraid of him, but that hungry, visceral look made her nervous as hell.

Needing a distraction, she said, "I could have paid for my own room, you know."

His response was dry. "My mistake. I wasn't aware

you'd be flush with cash after escaping from a kid-napping."

She lifted her chin. "I didn't run empty-handed. I stole a wad of cash off the Whiteclaw. There's still enough left to pay for my rooms and my meals on our way back."

"Don't worry about it. We've got it covered," he murmured, slipping two packs she hadn't even noticed he was carrying off his shoulder. She was glad to see that one of the bags was hers. The blood on her skin was starting to get sticky, and she was trying to work up the energy to head to the shower so she could clean it off, when he set his bag down on the desk, opened it up, and pulled out a first-aid kit. He came over to the bed she was sitting on and started taking things out of the kit—antiseptic wipes and some ointment—setting them on the comforter.

Carla knew she should object when he grabbed the chair in front of the desk and dragged it over, sat down, then took a pair of scissors from the kit and started cutting her ruined shirt off. But she just couldn't find the energy. If he wanted to help her, fine. It didn't mean anything, and it sure as hell wasn't going to lead to anything.

"Your men, they seem pretty loyal to you," she said to break the uncomfortable silence. As well as to get her attention focused on something other than how freaking hot he looked. Eli had always worn the post-fight look well, and it looked even better on him now, with his shaggy hair and fierce expression. There were more little lines crinkling at the corners of his eyes than the last time she'd seen him, but they only added to his rugged appeal. It was one of those unfair imbalances in the universe, how things that made a woman look aged usually only a made a man look more attractive. And Eli wore that "lived in" look well.

She didn't think he was going to bother giving her any kind of response, but he surprised her when he tossed her ruined shirt aside and said, "They're a good bunch of guys. We've been through a lot together."

She didn't have time to be embarrassed about sitting there in nothing but her jeans and bra, because he opened one of the wipes and started cleaning the oozing wound. Her breath hissed through her teeth at the sharp sting of pain, but she forced it to the back of her mind and asked, "How did you all meet?"

He tossed the wipe into the nearby trashcan, and shot her a wry glance. "How about I tell you that story when you don't look like you're about to pass out?"

"I'm fine. I've had worse than this and survived." *Both physically...and emotionally.*

He frowned, as if he'd heard her thoughts. Or maybe he just didn't like the idea of her getting hurt. He never had liked her being a Runner, thinking it was too dangerous. But she'd never had any intention of leaving her job to make him happy. The way she'd seen it, if he'd truly cared about her, he would have learned to accept her and see her for who she really was: a woman *and* a warrior.

But, then, he'd never really cared about her, had he?

Trailing his rough fingertips just under the graze, he said, "You'll heal with rest, but the bra needs to come off or it's going to keep rubbing against the wound during the night."

Carla looked him right in the eye and gave him her best *as if* look. "Not—Happening."

"I wasn't asking, Rey."

Gritting teeth, she muttered, "You always were a bossy, manipulative jerk."

He snorted as he shoved the chair back and knelt in front of her, his big body so close she could feel his delicious heat like a physical touch against her chilled skin. "And yet you used to love spending time with me," he offered huskily, his mouthwatering scent settling on her tongue like a gift. "What do you think that says about you, princess?"

God, he was so damn good at pissing her off. "I'm *not* a princess."

His sensual lips curved in a way that would have made any other woman whose heart he hadn't shredded light-headed with desire. "Sure you are, Rey. All those big bruisers in the Alley think of you as their little sister, which makes you the princess of the group."

"They think of me as their equal," she snarled, wondering why he was goading her on purpose. Then she felt her nipples tightening in the cool air, and realized he'd managed to cut her bra off while she'd been growling at him. *Argh!* She must be woozier than she'd thought if she hadn't caught on before he'd bared her to his dark, heavy-lidded gaze.

He was staring at her naked breasts, *hard,* and she blushed clear to the roots of her hair, trying to cover herself with her right arm, her blood nearly boiling when she caught the crooked smirk on his lips.

His hot gaze flicked up to hers. "After everything that happened between us that last night we were together, modesty is a little pointless now, don't you think?"

"It was dark in your room that night." Not to mention it was three years ago, and he'd been drunk off his ass.

"Yeah, but I'm a pure-blood. My night vision is even better than yours." He flicked his tongue over his teeth, and his lips twitched into a wicked grin. "My sense of taste, too."

Lust shot through her in a burst so primal and potent it made her shudder, and it took every ounce of strength she possessed not to pant…or throw herself at him. "I would have thought you were too wasted to remember anything from those particular *minutes,* Eli."

He slowly arched one of his dark brows. "That night wasn't the only time I had your taste in my mouth, Rey."

She blushed even hotter when she realized he was talking about the time he'd licked her juices from his fingers after they'd been inside her. He'd made her come with his hand during their last "sober" interaction together. It'd been two days before the drunken night at his house in Shadow Peak, and they'd met in the woods, as they so often had, carefully avoiding the prying eyes of the pack.

A bitter laugh sounded inside her head as she thought about that telling fact. She should have known then that she was nothing more than his dirty little secret. Something he was too ashamed to admit to. But she'd been blinded by love and faith and foolish dreams. Dreams that had lived inside her heart for too many years to fight them.

With perfect clarity, Carla could still remember the first time she'd ever set eyes on Eli Drake. She'd been no more than twelve, and he'd been…well, the most beautiful man she'd ever seen. He should have detested the sight of her, given his father's virulent hatred of humans and half-breeds, but he hadn't. Instead, he'd grinned at her that day that they'd passed on a small street in Shadow Peak—but it'd been years before they'd ever spoken to each other. Ten, to be exact. And she could still recall the details of that night as if it'd happened only yesterday.

Her mother had always had...issues. And she'd had dismal taste in men. After a string of abusive relationships with Lycan males, Nicole Cates had vowed to only date humans. But the relationships never lasted. The only lasting relationship Nicole had ever enjoyed was with a bottle.

Carla was the result of a short-term affair her mother had had with a human named Antonio Reyes, and he'd disappeared from her life as quickly as he'd entered it. To her family's surprise, and disgust, Nicole had decided to keep the child, thinking a baby might help her find some stability. But it was Carla who'd become the caretaker. Nicole's family had made it clear they wanted nothing to do with their pathetic daughter and her half-human offspring, and so the two of them had been on their own. Though she'd had the support of her fellow Bloodrunners when she'd gotten older, no one from the pack had ever helped her and her mother, until the night she'd first spoken to Eli, less than a week after she'd turned twenty-two.

She could still feel the hot slide of angry, frustrated tears slipping down her face as she'd struggled with her mother's limp body that night, the salty taste of them on her lips. She'd had a call that Nicole was passed out on a sidewalk outside one of Shadow Peak's bars. Too embarrassed to tell the other Runners, she'd left the Alley and gone up to town to handle it on her own. As she'd tried to get Nicole on her feet, shame had burned in her belly at the thought of the girls she'd gone to school with seeing her mother like this, knowing how horrible they would be. The derogatory names they would call them. The same names she'd heard her entire life.

And then, out of nowhere, Eli had walked out of the darkness and taken her mother from her arms, carrying her home while a stunned and wary Carla had walked beside him. She'd been amazed to realize that he not only knew her name and where her mother lived, but that she was Bloodrunning partners with Wyatt. Afterward, they'd talked out in her mother's backyard, and it had been the beginning. Of their friendship. Of her love. Of…of everything.

Eli Drake had been her hero that night, coming to her rescue at a time when she'd desperately needed him. But now he was her nightmare. The thing in the world that could hurt her most. That could break her.

Her mother had always warned her that a Lycan male would destroy her heart if she wasn't careful. How awful to learn that Nicole had been right.

Shattered by the memories flooding through her, Carla closed her eyes, determined to block them out— to block *him* out—hoping it would help her find some measure of control. *Huge mistake.* The sudden touch of his tongue to the sensitive skin over her ribs made her gasp, then whimper, and she flushed with mortification. God, she couldn't have sounded more needy if she'd tried, and his hands flexed against her hips, holding her tighter.

"What the hell do you think you're doing?" she choked out, when she felt the delicious rasp of his tongue gliding higher, until he was licking the flesh of her blood-smeared breast that she hadn't managed to cover with her arm. Her breath seized in her lungs, her eyes shocked wide as she stared down at him, too stunned to do anything more than shiver as she watched him lick another smear of blood off her tingling skin, taking the crimson fluid into his mouth, like it was his *right*.

"Christ," he groaned, the hungry sound vibrating deep in his chest. "Like I could ever forget that taste."

"Eli?"

Pulling his head back, Eli looked up at Carla's flushed face, and thought *To hell with it*. He needed this. No matter how dangerous it was to his sanity, he *needed* it. *Craved* it. Would have sold his damn soul for it.

Not giving himself time to change his mind, he leaned in close again, wanting her mouth this time, but she jerked back from him, turning her head to the side, her chest heaving. He started to tell her to stop acting like a fucking child and just give him what they both needed after being apart for so long, then stopped when he caught sight of the tears spilling over her pale cheek.

Shit.

"Rey," he breathed out, feeling like he'd just been gutted. In all the time that he'd known her, he couldn't ever recall seeing her cry. Not since the night that he'd helped her with Nicole.

Her throat worked as she swallowed. Then she turned her head to look at him and licked her lips. "From the moment we first realized there was something between us, you told me to wait, so I waited," she whispered unsteadily. "To give it time, so I did. And do you know what I got for it? *Nothing.* Except your lying ass disappearing without a single goddamn word."

He wanted to look away from those tear-soaked eyes that were making him feel like the biggest son of a bitch who had ever walked the planet, but couldn't. "I was banished," he heard himself scrape from his tight throat. "What did you expect me to do? What the hell would I have said?"

Years-old fury flamed beneath her tears, so bright it made him wince. "Maybe *Come with me*? Did that ever cross your pea-sized brain? If you ever meant a single damn word that you said to me, you would have asked—"

"I had no idea where I was going," he bit out, the familiar rise of frustration nearly strangling him. There'd been no goddamn right answer where she was concerned. No matter what he chose, what he did, she would have ended up hurt. He'd simply tried to choose the path that would be easiest for her. And...*fuck,* maybe easiest for him, as well—at least when it came to his emotions—which just made him sound like a coward. "I didn't have a home to offer you, Rey. No security or protection. How could I have asked you to give up everything you'd ever known for that kind of life? To leave your friends and family?"

"*You* were my family," she whispered, digging that knife even deeper. "At least I thought you were. Fool that I was. You just wanted to screw the girl who'd never bedded down with a Lycan, didn't you? Was it a bet between you and your friends? Did you all laugh about it behind my back before you left?"

"You know that's not true," he growled, wanting to

shake her. "I didn't want anything to happen to you. I was trying to take care of you!"

She gave a bitter laugh. "And what a stellar job you did. I'd hate to know what it's like to be someone you *want* to hurt."

"Carla, I—"

"Stop!" she pleaded, wiping the tears from her cheeks with the back of her free hand. "Please, just…stop. I don't want to hear another lie from you. I just want you to leave me alone."

Shit! This is so screwed up.

Moving to his feet, Eli stared down at the top of her golden head, and wanted to roar with frustration. "I wish I could make you understand, but everything I've done…the reasons…it's complicated, Rey."

She didn't say anything. She just turned and crawled up over the bed, then curled into a ball on her side, telling him without words that she was done listening to his bullshit.

"Sleep fast," he muttered, moving to sit on the foot of the other bed. Elbows on his parted knees, he dropped his head into his hands, squeezing his skull, and kept talking. "We're getting an early start tomorrow. And I still have questions, so be ready to start answering them."

There was no response, but he hadn't expected one. He listened until her breathing evened out, then moved back to his feet and stripped down to his fitted boxers. He pulled the covers over her small, curled up form, forcing himself not to look at her too closely because he knew he'd never be able to stop once he did. Then he turned out the light.

Lying down on his bed, Eli put his hands behind his

head and stared up at the watermarked ceiling, wondering what in God's name he'd been thinking. He'd actually thought he could get his head together before he and the guys reached Maryland and he had to face her again. What a jackass idea. Even if it'd taken months to get back, it still wouldn't have been enough time to sort out this messed-up situation.

And he could no longer say for certain if he was still trying to protect her…or if it was his own miserable hide he was worried about. Especially seeing as how she wanted rid of him. Wanted to break the tenuous bond that tied them together, severing that final connection.

Turning on his side, he stared at her delicate shape beneath the soft streams of moonlight filtering in through the blinds, and pulled in a deep breath of her warm, intoxicating scent. This woman had been under his skin for years, and he wasn't sure if staying away from her anymore was the right answer…or the wrong one.

All Eli knew was that it was killing him, not being in that bed with her, holding her against his body, where he wanted her.

And where she'd always belonged.

Chapter 3

After a horrible night's sleep, and a scalding shower that'd barely made her feel alive again, Carla had changed into one of her last clean pairs of jeans and a T-shirt. There was only so much cash she'd been willing to spend on clothes from the money she'd stolen off the Whiteclaw, and so her wardrobe was limited at best. Life would have been a lot easier if she'd had her stupid wallet on her when she'd been kidnapped, but hey, at least she'd had her cell phone. And she'd thankfully had another bra and pair of panties in her pack for this morning, as well as a hairbrush. So while she wouldn't be winning any beauty contests at the moment, it was nice not to have bed head.

Eli had woken her up with a touch on her shoulder about thirty minutes ago, just after six a.m., and told her he would be waiting outside the room while she got ready. He didn't mention anything about their argument from the night before, and neither did she. In fact, she didn't even look at him. She could forgive herself for her momentary lapse last night, but that was her only pass. From now on she needed to stay sharply focused. She had her eye on the prize—being free of him once and for all—and she wasn't going to let her stupid hormones ruin it for her.

No matter how crazy desperate for him those little suckers turned out to be.

And I doubt going without will kill me, she thought dryly, running her brush through her hair. *If that were the case, I'd have dried up and died a long time ago.*

A glance in the mirror over the dresser showed that she was still sporting a few yellowish bruises, had dark circles under her eyes, and the tight pinch of fatigue in her facial muscles. She might be only twenty-eight, but she felt eighty. Damn near looked like it, too. But what the hell? It's not like she wanted him to be attracted to her. Zipping up her pack, she tossed it on her bed and joined him outside.

As they walked to the crowded diner next door, where they were meeting the others, he asked, "You ever hear from your mom?"

Nicole had finally given up on the pack a year before Eli's banishment and left Shadow Peak, claiming she needed to find a place where she could make a new life for herself. "No," Carla replied in a flat tone, wondering if her mother had ever managed to succeed with her dream. If so, she was obviously too content there to worry about contacting the daughter she'd left behind.

He didn't say anything more, and the guys kept the conversation light when they joined them for a quick breakfast. Afterward, they all headed back to the room she and Eli had shared to discuss the situation in private. Once everyone was settled, Eli explained to her what the men already knew: that his father had had a maniacal plan to take over the Silvercrest. A bloodthirsty plan that had resulted in a significant loss of life, had shattered the pack's sense of safety, and left an entire group of teens—as well as most of the residents in Shadow Peak—emotionally traumatized. As a result, the town had been left without its leaders, and the Bloodrunners were now handling all elements of security for the pack.

Since it was up to Carla to bring them up to speed on the rest, she explained everything that had happened with the Whiteclaw pack over the past weeks, starting with how Eli's brother, Eric Drake, had met Chelsea, the human he'd recently married, while she was searching for her younger sister, Perry. Making a bad choice, Perry had gone chasing after the wrong guy and ended up falling in with the Whiteclaw pack who lived to the south of the Silvercrest, and who were now controlled by a man named Roy Claymore. With the Runners' help, Eric had been able to prove that the Whiteclaw had partnered up with the Donovans, a corrupt local Lycan family, on a number of illegal activities, the most horrific being one that involved human girls. With the Donovans' support, the Whiteclaw had been drugging the girls and pimping them out for Lycan gang rapes. The drugs not only acted as an aphrodisiac on the girls, but also impaired their memories of the attacks. And Claymore was using tapes of the assaults to later blackmail the participants into aiding the Whiteclaw.

She then told them that the Runners had managed

to close down a strip club in Wesley, a human town not far from the Silvercrest's territory. The Whiteclaw had been using the club to find the girls, and closing it down had only increased Roy Claymore's power hungry desire to destroy the Silvercrest and take their land. Something Claymore felt would be easy to accomplish, given the state the pack had been left in after Stefan Drake's failed bid for power.

Later, after an attack that some of the Whiteclaw and Donovan wolves had made on the Runners in the Alley, they learned that the Whiteclaw had also developed a "super soldier" drug that not only made them violently strong, but also camouflaged their scent. Which meant they were damn difficult to defeat.

The atmosphere in the room had been grim during her telling, but the group's tension only increased when she explained about the plans she'd overheard before making her escape after her and Elise's kidnapping.

"The Whiteclaw were hoping to blackmail the other packs in our region into helping them by providing foot soldiers. But they haven't secured the kind of numbers they were hoping for, so they came up with a new plan. They've used a sizable portion of the money they've made from the gang rapes to purchase help from someone in your line of work. A man named Jack Bartley."

"Son of a freaking bitch," Kyle muttered.

"You know him?" she asked.

"We've gone up against him before," the merc explained. "He's human, but he's a maniac. Has a small army under his command, and they'll do anything for the right price."

"He's human?" she murmured with surprise.

Kyle grimaced. "Well, most of him is. It's rumored

he has shifter blood somewhere in his family tree, which is how he knows of our existence."

"You were right to be worried," Sam murmured. "Bartley and his men will spell bad news for your pack."

She wanted to argue that they weren't *her* pack, they were Eli's, but bit her tongue instead. She didn't need to make herself sound any bitterer about the pack's longstanding treatment of the Runners than she probably already had.

"When you went up against him, did you win?" she asked.

"Yeah," Eli muttered from his position against the wall, his muscular arms crossed over his chest. His dark brows were knitted with tension. "But it was at a cost. We lost one of our best men. A guy who would often come and work with us when he needed to earn extra money for his wife and kids. Bartley got his hands on him during the op, and by the time we found him, all that was left was a bloody pile of tissue and bone. They'd skinned him alive."

"Jesus."

Holding her worried gaze, he said, "He can be stopped, Rey. We just need to outthink him."

"Can you do that?"

He jerked his chin toward his men. "These guys can."

"So these different drugs—the ones they were giving the human girls and the ones that they use on themselves to improve their abilities—are still in production?" Kyle asked from his seat on the foot of the bed. Lev had positioned himself up by the pillows, his back braced against the cheap headboard, while Sam had his shoulders propped against the door and James sat in the desk chair. Carla sat on the foot of the other bed by herself.

Answering Kyle's question, she said, "As far as we know, production has been halted. We have a Fed named Monroe dealing with the drug labs out west, where it was all being made. Monroe's sister is married to one of the Silvercrest males, and the Fed is someone we consider a friend. But there's still the problem of the drugs they have stocked in Hawkley."

"Why did they target my sister?" The quietly spoken question had come from Eli, and she took a deep breath before turning her head to look at him again.

"They wanted to make a dig at the Runners, and saw Elise as an easy mark. We never should have let her stay up in town by herself, because it drew their attention."

He made a low sound of agreement, but she could tell he knew there was more to the story. Things she wasn't telling him. But he didn't push, and she wondered if he was dreading the explanation as much as she was dreading having to be the one who gave it.

"It's getting late," he suddenly muttered, pushing away from the wall. "We can talk things over some more when we stop for lunch, but right now we need to get on the road."

Fifteen minutes later, they had their gear stowed in the backseat of the truck James and Lev were driving, the rest of the group loaded into the other one, and were heading back down the highway.

With Sam and Kyle in the front seat of the truck she and Eli were in, Carla didn't speak to him during the journey, though she'd carried on some light conversation with the two mercs. For such ruthless badasses, they were nice guys who even managed to make her laugh a few times, while Eli glared out his window, lost in his own thoughts. The hours went by faster than she'd thought they would, and before she knew it they'd reached a little town the men had stayed in before, where they planned to stop for the night.

They ate together at a great little diner that made killer fried chicken, then grabbed rooms at a local motel. Six of them, at her insistence, which had caused the men to slide curious looks between her and Eli. He went off with Kyle to meet up with a local weapons dealer they'd done business with on several occasions, hoping to score a small arsenal that they could take back to the Alley with them, and refused to let her come along. So she was left sitting alone in her room, with nothing but her thoughts for company. It was still only nine and she was too wound up to sleep, so when Lev knocked on her door and asked if she wanted to grab a drink at the pool hall around the corner, she was glad for the distraction.

They ordered a pitcher of beer, picked out their cues, and before she knew it, she'd laughed her way through three games and they were starting on their fourth.

"No, no. You're going at that shot all wrong," Lev drawled, coming up behind her and leaning over her back. "You've got to move this hand here, and this one here," he told her, rearranging the placement of her fingers on the cue.

"Thanks," she said with a smile, when she made the shot. "That was—"

"Slivkoff!"

She jumped as Eli's guttural shout silenced the noisy

pool hall, the back of her head connecting with Lev's chin. He swore as she quickly turned to apologize. "Sorry!"

"No problem," he murmured, casting a funny look over the top of her head. She couldn't tell if he was about to laugh…or run for cover.

Sensing Eli was close, she turned and found him rounding the pool table, heading right for her. Once again, the scowl on his gorgeous face matched his tone as he growled, "What the hell do you think you were doing?"

Huh. Was it just her, or did he ask that question *a lot?*

Squaring her shoulders, Carla slowly arched one of her eyebrows. "What did it look like I was doing? Lev asked if I wanted to play some pool."

His nostrils flared as he stared her down. "And that meant you had to rub your little ass in his groin?"

Lev started to argue that point, but she lifted her hand to silence him. Setting her cue on the table, she took a deep breath, crossed her arms over her T-shirt covered chest, and tried not to let Eli see how furious he'd just made her as she carefully said, "Considering the bimbo blonde who was passed out in your lap last night, I don't think you can cast any judgments here, Eli."

He opened his mouth, then obviously changed his mind about whatever he was going to say, because he snapped it shut again. A muscle was starting to pulse at the edge of his jaw, his pupils were nearly blown, and his teeth were clenched so hard she was surprised they hadn't cracked. Carla recognized the signs of him struggling with his temper, and couldn't help but shake her head at his outrageous display of jealousy. After ditching her when he was banished, he didn't have any freaking right to get pissed about anything that she did!

"We're getting out of here," he finally muttered, jerking his head toward the door. "Now."

She could have argued with him, but since he'd already ruined her fun, she didn't see the point. Instead, she gave him her snarkiest smile and said, "Sure thing, *boss man.*"

Lev was grinning like a jackass when she turned to tell him goodbye, so she socked him in the shoulder, which just made him laugh. Turning her back on the goofball, she wondered if he'd set this whole thing up just to make Eli jealous, and if so, why?

Whatever Lev's reasons were for asking her to play pool with him, it had definitely put Eli in a bad mood. Not that he'd been anything but irritable the entire day. But now she could feel him seething behind her as she headed back to her room, his glare all but drilling holes in the back of her head. Not to mention her ass. When she reached her room, he managed to push his way in behind her before she could slam the door in his face, which had been her intention. After the way she'd broken down in front of him the night before, the last thing she wanted was to be alone with him.

Instead of moving deeper into the room, Carla leaned back against the door after she'd shut it, and crossed her arms over her chest again. The graze on her side from the bullet was no longer hurting, thanks to her healing abilities. It'd already scabbed over and probably would have been gone in a day or two, if she weren't so run-down at the moment.

"Did you get the guns?" she asked, watching him

pace along the foot of her queen-size bed, his big hands braced on his hips. He was dressed like the badass mercenary he was, wearing black boots, a faded pair of jeans that perfectly molded his muscular thighs, and a black T-shirt, its short sleeves stretched tight around his powerful biceps. Wherever you looked, his tall body was hard and sinewed and ripped. Even his hair-dusted forearms were mouthwatering, with heavy veins and ridges of muscle pressing against his scarred, golden skin. Then there were his thick wrists. And those big, masculine hands...

"Yeah, we got them." He sounded distracted, and she could sense his agitation and his...*hunger*. She just couldn't tell who or what it was for. Her? Food? A fight? Or some woman she didn't even know? The bond wasn't strong enough to give her any definitive answers—just annoying enough to mess with her head.

Pushing her bangs out of her eyes, she went for the safest topic she could think of to take her mind off her nerves. "I noticed that both of the trucks were missing from the parking lot. Did the guys go out somewhere?"

"Yeah," he muttered without even looking in her direction. "They're out finding women."

"Ahh."

He stopped in the middle of the floor and shot her a piercing look, the lamp on her bedside table casting a soft spill of light over his right side, while his left was bathed in shadow. Voice low and rough, he asked, "Given their agenda for the night, why do you think Lev was here with *you?*"

"How would I know?" she snapped, throwing her arms out wide in a gesture of frustration. "Maybe he just liked the idea of spending time with a woman he knew wasn't going to have sex with him?"

He didn't make any verbal response to her outburst. He simply folded his arms over his broad chest, the black cotton stretching tight across his solid pecs, and glared at her.

"The truth is I don't know what he was thinking, Eli. I just know that you're acting like an ass."

Moving with the slow, predatory precision of a hunter, he lowered his arms and came toward her, his heavy-lidded gaze so hot she felt scorched. "You keep pushing me like this, Rey, and I'm gonna start thinking you want me to do something about it."

She shook her head. "Am I even meant to know what that means?"

He came even closer, until she had to tilt her head back in order to hold his gaze. "It means that if you think you can get my attention by flirting with my men, you're going to end up getting a hell of a lot more than you bargained for."

Pushing off from the door, she jabbed her finger in the middle of his chest. "Back off. You have no claim on me, so stop the act. I'm not buying it."

"You think it's an act?" he rasped, the softness of his voice giving her chills.

"I know it is!"

He had her backed against the door before she even knew it was happening, pinning her there with his big, muscular body, his rigid erection pressed hard against her stomach. Cupping her jaw, he tilted her head back even more, and put his face right over hers, so close their noses were nearly touching. "This feel like an act to you, Rey?" he asked huskily, his warm breath coasting over her lips.

"Don't even think about it," she warned. Though the effect was kind of ruined by her quickening breaths and flushed cheeks.

His eyes were still angry and hot, but the corner of his mouth kicked up in one of those deliciously wicked, crooked grins that had always made her melt. "Baby, I can't seem to think about anything else."

"Try—harder," she sniped. "Because I'm seriously not interested in being your sloppy seconds, Eli."

It seemed to take him a moment to figure out what she was getting at, and then his expression darkened. "I didn't touch the blonde," he told her, biting out each word.

A harsh, humorless laugh jerked up from her chest. "Oh, really? So she just happened to pick your random lap to pass out in last night?"

That muscle started to pulse in his jaw again, the day's growth of stubble looking damn good on him. "What she was doing there isn't any of your business."

"Exactly!" she yelled, shoving hard at his shoulders. "So get the hell away from me!"

Catching her wrists, he pinned them against the door on either side of her head, the tight tips of her breasts pushing into his muscular chest as he pressed even closer.

"Tell me you don't feel *this* the same way that I do," he said against her lips, rubbing them softly with his. "Tell me and I'll leave you alone, Rey."

"Damn you," she moaned.

He laughed roughly, the low sound deep and dark and sumptuous, like he was suddenly feeling happy and hungry all at the same time. "That's what I thought, baby."

And then, before she could blink or scream or draw her next breath, his mouth covered hers and his hands left her wrists, laying claim to her body. His touch was aggressive, *greedy,* as if he'd wanted the feel of her under his hands for too damn long to control himself, while his kisses were…mouthwatering. Slow, deep, and deliciously intimate, his tongue stroking and rubbing, while he ate at the shivery, needy sounds that she made. He'd only just started this…this…whatever *this* was, and she was already lost, sinking into the moment like a weighted body being pulled deeper and deeper into the sea. Drowning…no longer even trying to resist. She only wanted to fall deeper because she'd been just as desperately starved for the feel and touch and taste of him. She didn't even remember moving her hands when he released her wrists, but they were fisted in his shaggy hair, the silky strands so warm and thick against her fingers. She pulled him tighter against her, lost in the slick, explicit kiss that made her think of his powerful body moving and thrusting into hers. It was that intense. That raw and hungry and achingly erotic.

When he pulled his head back and suddenly buried his face against the side of her throat, Carla gulped at the cool air, her lungs starved. He was rolling his hips against hers, one hand shoved up under her shirt and bra, molding her heavy breast, his thumb and forefinger pinching the throbbing nipple, while his other hand gripped her hip, jerking her against him. She crawled up his hard, rugged body and wrapped her legs around his waist, giving him what he wanted. He notched the thick, heavy ridge of his erection against her jeans-covered sex and thrust against her, stroking her clit at just the right angle, and she cried out as her head shot back, hitting the door, the husky sound of her shout echoing off the room's dingy walls.

"Need it in my hand," he growled against her throat, breathing hard, his voice little more than an animal's primitive snarl. His mouth was directly over the place where he'd started to mark her all those years ago, and she wondered if he even realized. "I need it *now,* Rey."

In a distant part of her mind, she knew this was... wrong. Foolish. Dangerous. To her heart and her pride. She wasn't meant to fall into his arms...or crawl up his body, holding him as if she wanted to crawl right inside of him. Claim him. Keep him. *Forever.* She knew that, damn it, but it didn't matter. When he was touching her, the hot, drugging scent of him filling her head, his exquisite taste on her lips, nothing else mattered but him. Needing him. Wanting him. *Getting* him.

"Please," she heard herself beg, too desperate to even care that she was pleading with him. With the monster who had broken her heart. "God, Eli. *Please!*"

His lungs worked hard as he ripped at the buttons on her jeans, his mouth hot against her skin. His tongue stroked across her racing pulse point just as he shoved his hand into the front of her cotton panties, the fabric already drenched with her juices. His fingers delved, separating her slick folds, searching out the small, sensitive opening. He circled it, before pushing inside, working that long finger deep into her tender, clutching tissues while his thumb found the tiny knot of her clit and started playing it...stroking it...faster and faster. He pushed in a second finger, forcing her body to stretch and take it, and her hips rolled, needing them deeper. Needing to be full of him.

"Jesus, Rey. You're just as tight and soft as I remember," he groaned, each roughly spoken word laden with something, with some unnamed emotion, that made her want to scream at him for breaking her heart and destroying what they'd had. "I've fucking dreamed about this so many times."

"Eli," she gasped, sinking her nails into his shoulders, the pain in her heart momentarily forgotten as he used his fingers to drive her wild, thrusting them hard and deep, stretching her in a way that felt so good she could feel tears gathering at the corners of her eyes, her throat shaking. She needed him inside her. Not just his fingers, but the thick, engorged shaft she could feel him grinding against her hip. Needed him on top of her, his body hard and heavy and hot against hers, while he shoved all those brutal inches inside her until she was clenching around him, milking him, lost in the most mind-blowing climax of her life.

Her sex was creamy and swollen and ripe, ready for whatever he wanted to give her. Fingers. Tongue. Cock. She was aching and desperate for every part of him, same as she'd been every night that she'd dreamed of him since he'd left her. Even years before then, when she'd wanted nothing more than for him to make her his, always waiting…and waiting. But he was fighting it. She could tell. Resisting with everything that he had, and it frightened her to think of why. Why she wasn't enough for him. Why he'd always struggled against their connection with such ferocity.

Fight back! Resist! Damn it, she should be tossing the rejection she could feel coming right back in his face, but she...she couldn't. As he touched her between her legs, his rough fingers stroking through those slick, plump folds with such perfect skill, making her gasp... arch...shiver, the only thing she was willing to fight for was *more*.

But as with everything else when it came to this man, she was destined to lose.

One moment his fingers were buried deep, bringing her to the cusp of a shattering orgasm, and in the next she was empty, his palm pressed tight against her sex, cupping her, holding her...and she could feel the smooth, hot slide of his fangs against her vulnerable throat. *Ohmygod!* Did he want to bite her? What on earth was going on with him?

His body was pressed so rigidly against hers, and she sensed his...pain. A visceral, devastating, burning agony. He cursed hoarsely, and she felt the first tremor that rocked through him, followed quickly by a second, until he was shaking so hard in her arms it made her teeth chatter.

"E-Eli?" she stammered through lips that were salty with her tears.

He quickly set her on her feet and pushed away from her with a choked roar, his eyes hooded and bright as he clenched his teeth. His dark brows were drawn with an emotion she could have sworn was anguish. Something had stopped him, but the bond was too weak and his emotions were too intense for her to read him clearly. Which was perhaps a good thing. Whatever had caused him to pull away from her, she had a feeling she wasn't going to like it.

"What the hell, Eli? Are you—"

"Don't! Don't touch me!" he snarled, stumbling back

from her when she started to reach for him. His gaze darted from side to side, reminding her of a trapped wolf desperate for escape.

She crossed her arms over her middle, determined to hold herself together. "What's wrong?"

"Nothing," he scraped out, sounding as if a brutal set of hands was crushing his throat. "Just...just go to bed, Carla. It's late."

"No. I want to know—"

"Just get in the damn bed!" he barked, brushing her aside so he could rip the door open. "And lock this damn thing behind me!"

He slammed out of the room then, and she reached out and slid the lock into place with a shaking hand, her thoughts reeling, and her body... *Oh, God.* Her body was vibrating...awakened. Misery crashed over her like a cold rain, and she shivered even harder, somehow making it to the bed. For the second night in a row, she crawled onto a lumpy mattress and curled into a ball, trying to block out everything until she was nothing more than molecules of air. Weightless. Floating. No pain or fear or emotions.

Carla tried to reach that feeling of nothingness with every ounce of her will, but it never came. As she lay there in the cold, depressing room, she just kept wanting and longing and aching...for things she would never have.

Chapter 4

Her life since setting off in search of Eli Drake had been the worst kind of hell, and Carla had never been so eager to return to the Alley as she was now.

She'd skipped breakfast that morning because, well, rejection apparently killed her appetite. Exhaustion weighed heavily on her shoulders, and while she knew it was unforgivably stupid to have let her body do the thinking instead of her head, she was simply too tired to beat herself up over what had happened with Eli. Learn, regroup, and move on. That needed to be her motto, because if it wasn't, she'd still be curled up in that crappy motel room bed, wishing for things that were useless. And oh so obviously bad for her.

As far as wake up calls went, the way Eli had walked out on her *again* had been a bruiser. But she was tough. She could take the hit and keep on going.

What she couldn't do was let him get too close to her again. Work together? Fine, so long as she wasn't alone with him. But kissing? Touching? Losing her head over him because her body craved him like he was freaking manna from heaven? Uh, no. That was *not* a part of her game plan. She would give herself last night as a freak moment of insanity after missing him as badly as she had, but no more. That'd been her last freebie. There wouldn't be any others.

When they'd climbed into the truck that morning, both of them taking the backseat again, Eli had turned to her and asked, "Are you okay?" At her questioning look, he'd stiffly explained his concern. "I wasn't thinking about the bullet graze last night. Did I hurt you?"

"My side is fine," she'd murmured. He'd caused her pain, just not physically.

As if he'd read her mind, he'd said, "I wasn't rejecting you, Rey. I was—"

"It doesn't matter," she'd cut in, watching the clouds through her window as the wind blew them across the sky like puffs of dandelion seeds. "I don't care."

"That's a damn lie. If you didn't care, you wouldn't be hurt. And I'm sorry as hell that it happened, because I didn't mean to hurt you. Not last night, and not before. That was the last thing that I... *Damn it*, I was trying to pro—"

Her head had whipped to the side so quickly her hair smacked her in the face. "If you say you were trying to protect me, I will get out of this truck and I won't get back in it. Understood?"

"We need to talk about this," he'd argued.

"No, we don't need to do anything, because the time

for talking was last night. Now you can just forget that anything ever happened."

He'd muttered something under his breath that she didn't catch, but didn't say anything more when Kyle and Lev hopped in the front, the blond merc taking the first stint behind the wheel. She'd balled up a sweatshirt Kyle offered her, using it as a pillow, and slept.

Then, when they'd stopped for lunch a little while ago, she made sure to catch Eli alone before they entered the restaurant, and told him, "I don't know what your problem is, and I don't care. I just want you to know that what happened last night—that's it, Eli. It doesn't happen again. You don't get to keep making me feel like a fool."

She hadn't waited around to get his reaction, heading inside to join the others. He'd come in a few minutes later, and passed on ordering anything, which had garnered some interested looks from his friends. Lev had lifted his brows at her, as if to say *What'd you do to him?* She'd shrugged in a *I have no idea what his problem is* kind of way, but the merc didn't buy it, his sea-colored gaze filled with curiosity. Too drained to worry about any of it, she'd sucked down a few spoonfuls of soup and resumed her nap once they were all back on the road.

Or at least she'd tried to. Unfortunately, sleep eluded her for the second part of the day, and it wasn't just Eli's brooding presence that had her feeling so restless. It was the entire situation.

After so many days like this, cooped up in a vehicle, Carla was thankful her mother had never been the family vacation type. She was ready to chew her own arm off because she was so…so on edge. She felt trapped, like there wasn't enough air in the cab for her to get a deep enough breath. And what air there was smelled like Eli, which did nothing to help her relax.

Needing to eat more often than human males because of their high metabolisms, the guys decided to stop for a late afternoon snack once they crossed into Maryland. They found a popular diner, and despite her foul mood, she bit back a grin at the reaction the mercs received as they walked to their table. The humans there might not know what the tall, good-looking mercenaries were, but they sensed there was something different about them, the way a vulnerable animal might sense the nearness of a beautiful, mesmerizing predator; the instinct to run battling against the desire to soak up the stunning view.

When they got back in the truck, Kyle said they needed fuel and pulled into a nearby gas station, while Sam pulled in behind him.

"I'm gonna grab some sodas for everyone to have on the road," Lev said, getting out just as Kyle started pumping the gas.

Sitting in the backseat with Eli again, she knew she needed to make use of their privacy. There were things she needed to tell him before they reached the Alley in a few hours, and now was the perfect time.

Turning toward him, she asked, "Are you nervous about tonight?"

He hadn't spoken to her since trying to explain himself that morning, remaining silent, his rugged jaw clenched tight, even when she'd stopped him outside the diner at lunch, telling him that last night would never have a repeat. He'd spent the day in a dark, dangerous mood, and now was no different. Keeping his gaze focused out his window, he responded to her question with nothing more than a slight shake of his head.

"I called Wyatt this morning, so they know to be expecting us at the Alley."

This time, he nodded, still not looking at her.

Carla sighed, forcing herself to just get to the point. "Listen, Eli, there's something I need to tell you before we get there, and now seems like the best time."

He must have picked up on something in her tone, because he finally turned toward her, his dark eyes difficult to read as they connected with hers.

Rubbing her damp palms across her jeans, she said, "It's about Elise, and I think you should know because...well, coming back is going to be hard enough for you as it is. I don't think you need any more shocking revelations thrown in your face."

His head cocked a bit to the side, his gaze sharpening. "What are you trying to tell me?"

She wet her lips, then slowly exhaled. "When Wyatt found El in Hawkley, he had a confrontation with Sebastian Claymore before he killed him. Wyatt told me that Sebastian admitted he was one of the wolves who raped Elise the night of her attack. It was him and Harris, and the one you killed—some guy named Danny. He was helping them make the gang rape drugs."

He was breathing hard by the time she was done, and he lifted one of his big hands, shoving it back through his dark hair as his gaze skittered from one thing to the next—the front window, side window, the inches of leather seat between them that felt more like miles—his thoughts seeming to shift just as rapidly. A flush covered his cheekbones, seeming brighter for the way he'd paled, his tanned skin bleached of color. He worked his jaw a couple of times, cleared his throat, and spoke in a voice so rough, she almost couldn't make out the quiet, guttural words. "Wyatt killed them?"

"Yeah. Well, he killed Sebastian. I think he said that Cian killed Harris. But there's more."

He kept his gaze locked on the back of the driver's seat as he waited, his profile rigid.

"It was Roy Claymore who planned the whole thing. He used Elise as a test run for the rape drugs, which is why she was conscious during the attack, but couldn't describe what they looked like to anyone. He, um, was also the last one to rape her."

His head finally turned her way again, his dark, deadly gaze locking her in its grip as strongly as any physical touch could have held her. "And no one gutted the bastard?"

Understanding his frustration, she said, "They couldn't get to him that day in Hawkley because of his security detail. But Wyatt put a bullet in Roy's head. It didn't kill him, but it would have caused him a lot of pain. With men like Eric and Wyatt gunning for his blood, he has to know his days are numbered."

His head went back and he shoved the heels of his hands against his eyes, the muscles in his arms bulging beneath his tight skin as he worked his jaw like he was grinding his anger between his molars. The seconds stretched out, heavy with the tension and fury she could feel pulsing off him. Then he scraped out, "They blame *me*," and she realized he was struggling with a hefty amount of guilt in addition to the blistering rage.

Not knowing what to say, she bit her lip, fighting the urge to reach out and stroke the broad, straining shoulder that was closest to her. He didn't deserve her comfort, damn it. But that didn't mean she wasn't dying to give it to him, fool that she was.

"Eric—he hasn't tried to contact me since the kidnapping." His expression was anguished when he looked at her, making her chest tighten. "What other reason would he have for that? They blame me for not coming back sooner and helping to keep those sick bastards away from her."

Unable to stop herself, hating this burning need inside her to try and make him feel better, she said, "They don't blame you, Eli."

"Like hell they don't," he growled, every ounce of his surly aggression directed at himself.

"I'm sure there's another explanation. Since Eric knew I was coming after you, I bet he was just afraid of letting it slip if he left you a new message."

His dark brows pulled together in an even deeper scowl. "Why would that matter?"

"Can't you guess?" A wry grin tugged at the corner of her mouth. "He was probably afraid you'd run at the sound of my name and never be found again."

He didn't smile at her lame attempt to lighten his mood. If anything, he looked even angrier. "Is that what you think I would have done? You think I would have *run* from you?"

She shrugged as she focused her attention back on the mundane scene outside her window, noticing that Lev and Kyle were finally paying the cashier inside the small convenience store. "It doesn't matter what I think. I just wanted you to know before we got there."

The guys were heading back to the truck, so they dropped the conversation. But Carla could feel him seething beside her, and knew Roy Claymore was going to have more than one pissed off Lycan coming after him when the war finally hit.

Lev took the wheel again for this last part of the journey, and Eli murmured directions to the merc when they finally neared the mountains. Following Eli's instructions, Lev turned off of the main highway, onto the two-lane private road that wound its way up the mountainside, leading to Shadow Peak. Tonight, though, Eli wouldn't be directing Lev up to the town. Instead, they would turn off the road before they reached Shadow Peak, taking the smaller dirt path that led to the Alley.

The radio was playing softly in the background, the sky lit with the burnished colors of a brilliant sunset, while the wind rushed through the thick forest that lined the road, rattling the trees' leafy branches. It was a stunning setting, and Carla was seeking comfort from the view outside her window, glad to almost be home, when one of the massive trees suddenly crashed across the road just ahead of them, blocking their way. A sick feeling of dread immediately settled in her stomach, her nerves strung as tight as a bowstring. Lurching forward in her seat, she gripped Kyle's headrest and peered through the front windshield.

"This is bad," she whispered. "We're about to be attacked. The rogues working with Eli's dad did the same thing to my friends last year. It's a freaking ambush."

"Well, this time it's not my fault," Lev rumbled, trying for a bit of levity to break the tension that was so thick you could barely breathe through it. "Because I haven't slept with *anyone* from around here. *Yet*."

Kyle shoved the blond merc in the arm while Eli said, "It's the Whiteclaw."

"I think you're right," Carla murmured. "We have scouting groups scouring the mountain, keeping a close eye on all the Silvercrest's borders and roads. But if they're taking the drugs that mask their scent, it's possible that they slipped by the scouts without detection. Especially this far away from the Alley and Shadow Peak. The patrol routes are tighter the higher you get up the mountain. But they're taking a risk by attacking this close to the main highway."

"You think this is because of Eli?" Kyle asked. "Because we're here to help with the war?"

"I don't know," she said. "They might have caught wind that he was returning. Or this might just be a random attack. Who knows what they're thinking?"

"There isn't time to call for backup from the Alley. By the time the guys get here, this'll be over," Eli muttered, his voice more guttural than she'd ever heard it, as if his wolf was prowling just beneath his surface. But it would be a while yet before he could take the complete shape of his inner beast. The moon had yet to rise, still hanging low in the sky, which meant they could manage only partial shifts, releasing their deadly fangs and claws while still retaining their human shapes. They would be stronger, but not as strong as they would be in their standing wolf forms. If the Whiteclaw were doped up on the "super soldier" drugs, she and the mercs were going to be in a shitload of trouble.

Eli rolled down his window and sniffed the fresh mountain air, while Kyle used his cell phone to connect with James and Sam, who had to be wondering what was going on as they waited behind them. "I can't pick up any scent," Eli said in a low voice. "There's no telling how many are out there."

"We're still too close to the main highway to use any of the guns," she added. "If the noise drew any state troopers up here, we'd have an even bigger problem on our hands."

"Carla's right," Kyle agreed, his Southern drawl more raw-edged than usual. He definitely sounded like a man who was more than ready to kick some Whiteclaw ass.

"We need to get out of the trucks," Lev said, all traces of humor gone, his gritty tone sharp with menace. "We're sitting ducks in here. They're probably waiting for us to try moving the tree. But something tells me they're not going to wait much longer."

"Come on," Eli grunted, grabbing her hand and pulling her out on his side of the vehicle. "You stay behind me."

"Eli—"

"They're coming," Kyle cut in with a quiet growl as he came around the front of the truck, his attention focused on the road. The truck's headlights illuminated the fallen tree and the dense woods that lined each side of the two-lane road. "I can see them coming out of the woods up ahead. Doesn't look like they're armed with guns. They want blood on their hands."

Still holding her hand, Eli yanked her closer and put his face right over hers, his rough breaths brushing over her skin. "I mean it, Carla. You stay behind me."

Hating that he'd never been able to see her for who she was, she gave him a slow, tight smile, releasing her claws and fangs just as he'd done. "Not—gonna—happen."

Before he could argue, the Whiteclaw reached them, coming in fast and hard from the front, as well as the sides. Even if Eli had wanted to shove her behind him, he was suddenly too busy fighting off three attackers at once. There was no doubt the Whiteclaw soldiers had taken the drugs, their blows feeling like a freaking truck was hitting her as Carla blocked and kicked to avoid getting cut by the two who had targeted her.

Then the strangest thing happened.

Without any planning or verbal direction, she and Eli went back to back and began working together, moving in perfect synchronization as they engaged the seemingly endless wave of assailants. They fought so well together, it was insane. If she kicked a Lycan away, Eli twisted and slashed the male with his claws. When he swept a soldier's legs out from under him, she swiped her own claws across the bastard's throat. It was a primitive and deadly dance, and yet, there was a kind of savage beauty to it that the Lycan part of her soul could only appreciate, despite her fear.

She might not be afraid of the Whiteclaw, but she was *terrified* by the connection she so obviously shared with the male fighting at her side. She didn't even share this level of intuition with Wyatt, and she and the Runner had been partners for seven years!

When she and the pure-blooded mercenary both turned in the opposite direction and dug their claws into one of the Whiteclaw, pinning the soldier between them as their claws pierced him front and back, Eli growled, "Reyes, what's happening here?"

"Don't know. Just go with it and worry later," she muttered, pulling her claws from the Lycan's chest. A second later, Eli grabbed the male's neck and twisted, then tossed his lifeless body to the ground.

"Are they here?" he grunted, strands of sweat-dampened hair sticking to his gorgeous face as he turned his head to the side and caught her gaze.

"Are who here?" she wheezed, more breathless from the surge of lust that had just slammed into her than she was from the fight. God, he'd never looked hotter than he did at that moment, with his fangs and claws dripping with blood, his tall body rippling with power as his hard muscles flexed beneath his skin, his sensual lips parted for his rough breaths.

"The ones who hurt you in Hawkley," he growled impatiently. "Are they here?"

Angry with herself for being so freaking mesmerized by him, she gave him a cold look. "Why? You want to compare stories? Because you've hurt me more than any of the Whiteclaw managed to."

He flinched, jerking back a bit, as if her sudden verbal blow had physically struck him. His face paled and he looked away from her as he cleared his throat. "I just wanted to know so I could kill them for you," he told her, his deep voice stiff, even huskier than it'd been before.

Oh. She swallowed thickly, her throat too tight to give him a response. She didn't know the bastards' names, but she would easily recognize their faces if she saw them. The fact that Eli wanted to kill them for her made her feel like an ass for being such a bitch to him, but damn it, what did he expect? That she'd just sweep three years' worth of heartache under the rug and crawl back into his bed until he grew bored and bailed on her again? Thanks, but no thanks. And, seriously, he was the one who'd walked out on her last night!

Sam and James were fighting a group of Whiteclaw to their left, Lev and Kyle on their right, as four more soldiers came out of the woods, heading straight for her and Eli. Despite the awkwardness of the words they'd just exchanged, they still fought just as well together as they had before, Carla's smaller size enabling her to get in shots that Eli and his men couldn't make because of their height. The scent of Whiteclaw blood filled the balmy air, but despite the mercs' savage skills, only a few of the enemy had fallen, their drug-enhanced bodies capable of sustaining even the most brutal of wounds—which meant that death by decapitation or the severing of their spinal columns was the only way to take them down and ensure they stayed there.

By attacking at twilight, before she and the mercs could fully shift into the stronger, deadlier shape of their beasts, the Whiteclaw's drugs had put their men at a distinct advantage.

"Stay sharp! We've got more coming!"

The shouted warning came from James, just as a fresh wave of Whiteclaw soldiers emerged from the trees. She and Eli took on six of them at once, and though she could feel the moon rising, and knew it wouldn't be long before they could use its power, she feared it wouldn't be soon enough. There were simply too many of them.

Damn it, she couldn't fail. Not like this! Not when they were so close to the Alley they were practically on its doorstep. She used her upper arm to wipe the sweat from her eyes, and cast a desperate look at Eli, her emotions in chaos at the thought that they might die here tonight, together.

"More coming in at our backs!" Lev called out, heading around the front of the truck.

"Don't attack!" she shouted, her voice almost weak with relief from having caught the scent of the approaching group. "They're Silvercrest scouts. They'll help us!"

Over a dozen familiar-faced scouts joined them a handful of seconds later, her relief so sharp she wanted to freaking cry. With the numbers now in their favor, they were able to defeat those Lycans who didn't retreat, and the battle ended within moments.

Charles Decker, one of the scouts from Shadow Peak who Carla and Wyatt had been working closely with, came over to where she'd just leaned back against the side of the truck bed, her hands braced on her knees as she pulled in deep breaths of air. She'd retracted her claws and fangs as soon as the fighting was over, her fingertips and gums still burning with heat.

Retracting his own claws, Charles shoved his sandy hair back from his face and gave her a concerned frown. "That was brutal. We were heading back up to town after checking on the south border when we heard the fight. I'm sorry we didn't get here sooner, Reyes."

"No worries, Decker. You came just when you were needed."

"Everyone good here?" he asked, casting a worried look over the mercenaries as they each peeled their bloodied shirts off, then used them to wipe the sweat and blood from their arms and faces. She quickly pulled her gaze back to Charles, pretty sure her temperature had just risen from the sight of all those broad, muscular shoulders and chiseled abs. When it came to doing a body good, milk obviously didn't have anything on mercenary work. And the way Eli and his men had fought was beyond impressive. Though she'd handled herself well, it was clearly the mercs' incredible skill that had enabled them to survive.

Replying to Charles' question, she said, "We're a little scratched and bruised, but alive, thanks to you and the other scouts."

Charles jerked his chin at Eli as he came to stand beside her, but that was as far as the greeting went. If the scout recognized Eli, he didn't say, and she wondered, as she often had since she'd gone in search of him, about what kind of reaction Eli would receive from the Silvercrest. Eric and Elise had had a tough time of it after Stefan Drake's failed coup, since there were many who chose to blame them for the twisted things that had happened because of their father. Recently, though, it seemed that more of the townspeople were swaying in the Drake family's favor, since Eric and Elise were now so closely tied to the Bloodrunners, and it was the Runners who were working so hard to keep the pack alive.

Nothing like a little self-preservation to make even the most bigoted of idiots become accepting.

Still, there were many in the pack, like Charles, who had made the firm decision to give the Runners their full support simply because they respected them, and Carla was thankful as hell for each and every one of them.

"We'll take care of the bodies," Charles was saying, his words drawing her attention back to his friendly, freckled face. "You go and get on up to the Alley. I know Wyatt's been worried about you."

Fighting the urge to ogle Eli's mouthwatering chest from the corner of her eye, she managed to give the middle-aged scout a grateful smile. "Thanks, Charles. And say hi to your wife for me."

Charles said that he would, and left to give the scouts their orders. One of the wolves, a thirty-something Lycan named Mike who worked as a mechanic up in town and was hot as sin, smiled at her, showing his interest, but she simply gave him a brief nod and turned her attention back to the mercs. She didn't do wolves. Full stop. Other than Eli, the only men she'd ever been involved with were human ones, when she was younger. Nice enough guys who had had no idea she was only half their species, which had meant the relationships were doomed from the start, though a few had lasted for several months. Thanks to her upbringing and her mother, Carla had never trusted a Lycan male enough to get down and dirty with him. The one time she'd taken a chance, he'd left in the middle of the act and then disappeared from her life.

She didn't think she could ever forgive Eli for that. Even if he hadn't wanted to take her with him, he'd at least owed her a damn goodbye.

"Who the fuck is that?" Eli demanded in a low rasp, one of his big hands wrapping around her upper arm.

Her eyes shot wide as she turned her head to look at him. "Excuse me?"

He stared down at her with a scowl, looking ready to commit murder. "The guy with the chick hair who was smiling at you. Who is he?"

"Ohmygod, are you serious?" she asked, laughing. "*Chick* hair?"

"Who. Is. He?" His voice was soft, but knife-sharp, his gaze storm-dark and hard.

Thinking he had this jealousy act down pretty well, she gave him a bland look. "That's just Mike. He's a mechanic in Shadow Peak. Don't you remember him?"

His gaze cut to Mike, then back to her again. "Yeah, I do now," he muttered, shaking his head as he dropped his hand from her arm. "That guy was always an asshole."

Tucking the windblown strands of her hair behind her ears, she shrugged. "Well, he's been nice enough to me."

He turned his head to the side, his chest expanding as he pulled in another deep breath and rubbed the back of his neck. Tension poured off his tight frame, his massive shoulders bunched, as if he carried the weight of the world on them. She was getting ready to open the door to the truck and grab a shirt from her bag so that she could wipe her own face and arms clean, when he growled, "You let him touch you, he's a dead man. We clear?"

She choked back another shocked burst of laughter, unable to believe his freaking audacity. "You are unbelievable, Eli."

He leaned in even closer, his incredible scent playing havoc with her senses as the tip of his nose nearly brushed hers. "He might not be able to scent my bond on you, but it's there, Carla. And that means that until something changes, you're *mine*."

"And you care about this *now*?"

His gaze burned so hotly it made her feel scorched,

her skin misting with heat that had nothing to do with the warm evening air. "You're damned right I do," he snarled, sounding every bit like the possessive lover she'd always longed for him to be. Too bad it was only an act.

She licked her lips, studying him through narrowed eyes. "You'll understand how ridiculous I think that sounds, considering you haven't cared what I do, or who I do it with, for a long time now."

Frustration sharpened his bold, masculine features. "Just because I wasn't here doesn't mean I didn't care. I told you, my reasons for staying away were—"

"Yeah. Complicated," she scoffed, her lips curling in a bitter, humorless smile. "I heard that lame excuse the first time you spouted it. No need to repeat yourself."

"Christ, Carla. It's not an excuse."

"Well, it's sure as hell not an answer. Until you're ready to give me one, don't think you have any right to so much as even mention that *ridiculous* bond to me."

His nostrils flared as he sucked in a sharp breath, his shoulders so broad he damn near blocked out the glittering stars that were beginning to light the skies. The weather had started to warm since she'd gone off to find him, and as the wind whipped through the forest, it tousled his dark hair, making him look so damn sexy and...touchable. And, God, did she want to touch him. Despite her anger and resentment, she had a sickening feeling that she would go to her grave with this incessant ache for his scent and his heat and the hard weight of his powerful body covering her, holding her, trapping her against him as if he never meant to let her go, still plaguing her. It would be a longing she could never satisfy or kill, slowly eating away at her, until she was nothing more than an empty, desolate shell.

She was cursed, damn it, and the unfairness of it all made her throat shake, her eyes stinging as tears gathered.

He opened his mouth, the fury in his beautiful gaze dimming beneath what she could have sworn was stark concern when he spotted her glistening tears. But whatever he'd planned to say was drowned out by Kyle's deep voice shouting, "Yo, boss man! Should we start digging?"

He pulled in a deep, rasping breath, his eyes narrowing a fraction before he seemed to force himself to turn away from her. "They're going to deal with the bodies for us. As soon as we've moved that damn tree, we can get out of here," he called back, the muscles in his back flexing beneath his tanned skin as he headed toward the felled oak. With Charles and the other scouts helping, it didn't take the group long to shove the massive tree to the side of the road, and when Eli turned and started back toward her, he seemed determined to pick up where they'd left off. But she wasn't having it.

"Let's just get out of here," she murmured when he reached her, turning and opening the back door to the truck. "We can talk later. But you've kept your family waiting long enough."

Chapter 5

Carla knew, from her phone conversations with Wyatt, that extreme changes had been taking place both up in Shadow Peak, as well as in the Alley, since she'd left to find Eli. Fully aware that war was coming, the Runners had made the young and the elderly their first priority. They'd initially thought to bring everyone into the Alley itself, but when it became clear that there simply wasn't enough room, they'd used one of the nearby glades as a sort of base camp they were calling Alpha One.

Mobile accommodations had been purchased and brought up the mountainside with rented big rigs, and the security was top notch, thanks to the volunteer scouting patrols. Every willing Lycan was going through combat training with the Runners, as well as working the patrols in the woods, with extra patrols being run around the clock for Alpha One. In her mind, she pictured the clearing looking like some kind of survivalist camp from an apocalyptic zombie film, but knew that Wyatt and the guys would have created something that was not only safe, but also comfortable.

As for their loved ones, the Runners had brought them closer to home. In fact, many of the couples now had parents or grandparents staying with them, in addition to their siblings.

She'd explained all this to Eli and his men over one of their meals, as well as the fact that two of the empty cabins in the Alley had been set up for their use. Carla herself would be staying with Elise and Wyatt, in their spare bedroom, since she'd agreed to let the soon-to-be mothers from town, three of who were due any day now, to use her place. She wasn't exactly comfortable with the idea of people she didn't know that well staying there, but their safety was more important than her feelings. The four Lycan females with newborns were already staying in the last free cabin, so there'd been nowhere else for the women to go.

To say that things were going to be damn crowded was a serious understatement. But since they expected the brunt of the attack to come in Shadow Peak, no one was willing to risk leaving anyone there who couldn't fight.

A few minutes later, they reached the Alley, which had gotten its name from a pure-blooded Lycan who'd once referred to the Bloodrunners as nothing more than a bunch of "back-alley mongrels." But despite the negative connotations of its name, Bloodrunner Alley was a stunning place, built in a secluded, slightly sloping glade and surrounded by the wild, natural beauty of the forest. And thanks to some hard work, they had all the modern amenities, from power to hot water and high-speed Internet access, just like they did up in Shadow Peak. The mercenaries would be comfortable there, and accepted, though she wasn't holding her breath on how things would go for them with the pack up in town until she saw it for herself. Wyatt had told her that public opinion had started to take a dramatic swing in the Runners' favor since she'd been gone, and she was looking forward to witnessing the change.

Carla had called Wyatt when they'd finally climbed back into the trucks, debriefing him on the ambush so that no one would be shocked by their fresh-from-a-fight appearance. The mercs had all pulled on clean shirts before driving up, but they still looked like serious badasses who had just been in a brutal battle. Make that gorgeous badasses, and she almost snorted at the thought of so much testosterone descending upon the Alley as they parked and exited the vehicles. God only knew the place was already drenched in it, thanks to Wyatt and the guys. Now it would be practically swimming in the stuff, and she was thankful as hell to have the other women there with her. Carla knew she might not be the girliest of girls, but she treasured her female friends as dearly as she did her Bloodrunning brothers.

Standing back a little so that she could watch Eli's reunion with his family, her stomach tight with nerves, her eyes actually watered when she spotted Elise hurrying toward the group, the female Lycan's bright blue eyes focused on her brother.

"Eli!" she cried, running toward him, her red hair streaming behind her. She threw herself into his arms, burying her face against his shoulder. "You're home," she cried, hugging him tight as he wrapped his arms around her. "I can't believe it. I've missed you so much!"

"Hey, baby girl," he murmured against her hair, holding her with one arm so that he could throw the other around Eric, who had just joined them. He gave his brother a hard hug, slapping him on the back in that way that guys did.

Eric's deep voice was gruff with emotion. "It's great to see you, man, but I hate that you had to come back to this shit."

"I'm just glad to be home," he said in a low voice. "I stayed away for too damn long."

Though Elise was a redhead, and Eric and Eli were both dark-haired, there was no mistaking that they were all related. She'd never seen the three *dark wolves* together before in the same place, and it was a stunning sight to behold, if not a little intimidating. Created when two exceptionally pure-blooded Lycans produced offspring, a *dark wolf* bloodline was the most powerful that there was within their world. As well as the most deadly.

The Drake siblings were like werewolf royalty, their blood as blue as the original werewolf king himself. A fact that only solidified her belief that Eli had never planned on revealing their relationship to the pack. Royalty didn't marry from the lower classes. The partial bond between them was no doubt a result of lust and too much alcohol, and she was surprised he hadn't shown more enthusiasm about breaking it. When his fangs had touched her throat the night before in her motel room, he'd certainly run fast enough, as if the idea of completing the bond was something he abhorred.

Yeah, like I didn't see that one coming, she thought bitterly, trying to keep her emotions from showing on her face. If Wyatt was watching her from the growing crowd, he'd see right through her, and there were some things she'd rather keep to herself.

When Jillian came forward, pulling Carla into a crushing hug, she took a shocked breath as the happy news she'd just gleaned from her friend's scent crashed into her. "Jilly, you're pregnant!" she squealed, her troubles momentarily forgotten in the excitement.

"I know!" the beautiful blonde said with a bright smile as she pulled back to see Carla's face. "Don't be mad, but I made Wyatt promise not to tell you over the phone. I wanted it to be a surprise."

Carla knew that Jillian and Jeremy had started trying to conceive before she'd left, and had even started converting the spare room in their cabin into a nursery, and she couldn't have been happier for the couple. If anyone deserved to get everything they wanted out of life, it was those two. Their past had been as pain-filled as her and Eli's, but on a public scale, and there'd been a time when no one had believed they would ever reconcile. But all of the doubters had been proven wrong.

Jillian came from an extraordinary line of witches called Spirit Walkers, who had long-served the Silvercrest Lycans as their holy women, or healers. As witches, Jillian, her mother and her sister, Sayre, couldn't shape-shift like the rest of their pack. But they were formidable in other ways, their powers growing stronger as they aged. Which meant that if Jillian and Jeremy had a daughter, she was going to grow up to be a serious little ass-kicker, and Carla couldn't help but love that idea.

"I'm so excited for you, Jilly. You and Jeremy are going to be the best parents ever, and we're all going to spoil that little hellion like crazy."

Jillian laughed, obviously of the same mind that any child of Jeremy Burns would be a troublemaker. But an adorable one, without doubt.

Introductions were still being made all around them, thanks to Eli, and Carla figured she should make her way over to Wyatt, who she'd finally spotted standing near Brody. Her partner looked as if he was still trying to decide whether he wanted to hug her for making it back or strangle her for taking off without him in the first place. She couldn't even work up any attitude to throw back in his face because she knew she'd feel the same if the situation had been reversed. Wyatt wasn't upset because she was a woman and he didn't think she could handle herself. After all the years they'd worked together, he knew she was as capable as any of the male Runners. But they were like family to each other, and she hated that she'd worried him.

Jeremy came up and wrapped his arm around his wife's waist, and Carla was about to murmur that she needed to go and talk to Wyatt, when Jeremy muttered, "Well, this should be interesting."

"What should be?" Jillian asked, but Carla had already seen what had caught Jeremy's attention. Lev had come to stand on Carla's other side, his heavy-lidded gaze focused on Jillian's younger sister, Sayre, who was talking to her mother and Brody's wife, Michaela. The mercenary was eyeing Sayre like he'd just found something good he needed to taste, and Cian—a badass, gorgeous, womanizing Irishman and the only single Runner left besides herself—looked ready to kill.

Lev's interest she could understand. Sayre was an incredibly beautiful eighteen-year-old witch with blue-gray eyes and curly, strawberry-blond hair. So, yeah, it was understandable for men to get a little lust-eyed in her presence. What everyone in the Alley was still trying to figure out was why the Irishman kept getting so pissed off about it. And he was definitely pissed.

"What's his problem?" Lev murmured to their small group, when he noticed how Cian was watching him.

"He's a little, um, protective where she's concerned," Jillian explained a bit awkwardly, as if she didn't really know what to say.

Lev looked Cian over with a careful eye, then frowned. "Isn't he a little old for her?"

Jeremy snorted. "And you're not, Slivkoff?"

"I'm young where it counts," the merc rumbled, which made the women who'd heard him laugh. Lev smirked while Jeremy just shook his head.

"You're gonna be trouble, aren't you?" Jeremy muttered.

"Naw," Lev drawled, his blue-green eyes twinkling with mischief. "I've promised the boss man to be on my *best* behavior."

Carla snickered under her breath, thinking Lev's "best" was probably a far cry from anything that could be considered good.

"So what the hell happened down on the road?" The question came from Mason, who had walked over to join them just as Eli slipped in between her and Lev, the warm breeze whipping Mason's reddish-brown hair around the rugged angles of his handsome face. "I know Wyatt got a phone call, but I'd like to hear exactly how it went down."

While Eli gave a detailed account of the ambush, Carla stepped away from the group, needing to put some distance between her and the sexy merc. Wyatt must have been waiting for her to separate from the group, because he headed right for her, hugging her so tight that he lifted her clear off the ground. "So glad you made it back in one piece," he rumbled, ruffling her hair when he set her back on her feet.

"You're not getting rid of me that easily," she teased, trying not to let him see how emotional she was. But he always had been able to read her like a book.

His voice dropped, and his gaze sharpened. "I know you didn't want to get into it over the phone, but now that you're back, we're having that talk."

"Sure thing, *Dad*," she drawled, rolling her eyes.

Wyatt shook his head and snorted. "It's good to see that your little road trip didn't kill your smart-ass streak."

"As if anything ever could."

He laughed, then snagged Elise's hand as she walked by him, pulling her into his side. The next thing Carla knew, they were surrounded by everyone, and Wyatt was shaking hands with Eli, who had resumed his place beside her. Jillian started talking to her again, and Carla turned to give her friend her full attention. She was still busily chatting away with Jillian a few minutes later, when she heard something off to her right that caught her attention.

"I'll stay with Carla," Lev had drawled, sliding her a sexy smile and a wink when she quickly turned her head to look at him. "She needs someone watching out for her."

The group had obviously started talking about the

sleeping arrangements, and she wondered what Lev was up to, seeing as how she'd already told them where they would be staying.

"The hell you will," Eli muttered, looking ready to take Lev's head off.

"No one's staying with Carla because Carla's staying with me and Elise," Wyatt pointed out in a dry tone, shaking his head in a way that said he clearly thought they were all acting like children. "And until I know what's going on, neither of you are setting foot in our place."

Eli frowned, glaring at Wyatt, which just made her partner smirk. Pall, as she often called him, knew damn well he'd just made it more difficult for Eli to get her alone.

"Eli, come on," Eric murmured. "I'll show you and your men down to your cabins."

Eli turned his head, watching her with a hooded, smoldering gaze, and she sucked in a sharp breath, stunned that he was being so obvious. It was clear to everyone there that he didn't want to leave her. Idiot male wasn't even trying to hide that scalding burn of possession in his incredible, thick-lashed eyes. She could feel the curiosity and confusion among her friends ramping up until she wanted to scream.

"Come on," Eric repeated, placing his hand on his brother's shoulder. "This is not the time or place, man, to get into it." Confusion creased Eric's brow. "Whatever the hell *it* is," he added under his breath.

Though Eli remained silent, the other mercs told her they'd see her soon, their grins knowing and full of mischief, as if they were loving the tension between her and their friend. Then they headed toward the opposite end of the Alley, following along behind the Drake brothers. Carla wondered if the other women thought it was as impressive a sight as she did, the six tall, powerfully built men moving in ways that made it clear they were anything but human. The tense set of Eli's broad shoulders as he spoke with his brother drew her attention, and she bit her lip, wishing she could read his thoughts.

The moment they were out of earshot, all eyes turned to her. Her closest friends, the ones Carla considered her family, were waiting for an explanation. And they weren't exactly patient, their low voices crashing into each other like storm-tossed waves as they gathered around her, demanding to know what was going on. Only Jillian stayed silent, the look of concern in her brown eyes letting Carla know that her friend was worried about how she was handling everything.

Not well, Jilly, she tried to say with her eyes. *Not well at all.*

"Everyone be quiet," Wyatt finally cut in, placing his hand on her shoulder as he looked over the group. "This is between Carla and Eli. When she's ready to spill the story, she'll let you know. Until then, leave her alone about it."

She blinked, amazed by his loyalty, even though she should have become accustomed to it by now. They might fight like cats and dogs sometimes, but he'd always had her back when it counted.

"Yeah, I guess we should probably head home for the night," Jeremy drawled with a sheepish grin, after Jillian nudged him. "But it's good to have you back, Reyes."

"It's good to be home," she replied, knowing she'd never meant it more than she did in that moment.

"I'd like to say good-night to Eli," Elise said, squeezing Wyatt's hand and giving Carla a brief smile before she headed toward the cabins at the far end of the glade. God only knew what Elise was making of this thing between her and Eli, but Carla trusted El not to go blabbing to him about the questions everyone had just bombarded her with.

There were hugs and murmurs of good-night as the others headed back to their respective cabins, and then Carla pulled her bag, which James had brought over for her, onto her shoulder. Listening to the crickets chirping all around them, while an owl hooted in the distance, she walked with Wyatt over to the cabin he shared with Elise. "If it's okay with you," she said around a yawn, after he'd shut the door behind them, "I'm going to head on back to your guest room and crash."

"The room is all set up for you," he murmured, "but you're not running off just yet."

Carla lifted her brows. "I'm not?"

Shaking his head, Wyatt folded his arms over his chest and sat on an arm of the brown leather sofa that was placed perpendicular to the fireplace. "I might not make you talk to the others right now, but you're not getting off *that* easy."

"Meaning you want the story tonight," she said dully.

His expression was concerned, but kind. "I can't help you if I don't know what's going on, Carla. You're going to have to trust me. We've been through too much together not to rely on each other when we need to."

She shot him a disgruntled look as she let her heavy bag slip to the floor. "You didn't trust me with the truth about Elise."

"Because I didn't think I could have her." His dark eyes were piercing as they studied the strain on her face. "The situation isn't the same."

"It doesn't matter whether I can have Eli or not. I don't want him."

With a snort, he said, "Come on, Reyes. Lying is just wasting our time."

She shoved her hands in her pockets and scowled. "Lie? Truth? None of it matters, Pall. We would be a disaster just waiting to happen."

"You sure that isn't your mother talking?"

Wyatt knew the story of how a sixteen-year-old Nicole Cates had been seduced by an older male who'd sold her lies about how he could feel a bond building between them, while maintaining she was still too young for him to claim with a mating bite. Too naïve to know any better, she'd fallen for his deception and had given him her virginity, only to learn that he'd been using her. And her luck hadn't improved as she moved on from one abusive Lycan lover to another, until she'd finally sworn off pack males for good, drowning her sorrows in cheap booze and clueless human lovers. A weekend-long affair in Annapolis had resulted in Nicole's pregnancy, though Nicole and the man were virtual strangers. All her mother could tell her was that he was Spanish and his name was Antonio Reyes. Carla had taken the name Reyes for herself once Nicole had made it clear that she cared more about her alcohol than her daughter.

Giving Wyatt the short version of her and Eli's history, she said, "We knew, before he left, that there was a life mate connection between us, and we…bonded. If he'd asked, I would have gone with him when he was banished. But he…" A wry, pain-edged smile tugged at the corner of her mouth, and she shook her head a little as she stared into the empty fireplace that was on her left. "Well, he obviously didn't. Instead, he crushed my heart into useless little pieces. So no matter what my body might want, I *can't* trust him." She brought her gaze back to her partner. "And if I can't trust him, what's the point?"

Wyatt worked his jaw, looking as though he wanted to put his fist through something. Something, say, like Eli's face. It was at times like these that Carla was reminded why she loved this guy so much. He was the freaking family she'd never really had. The one she could always count on.

"So he's the reason you never date anymore?" he asked.

She nodded, swallowing the bitterness in her throat. She hadn't dated anyone in the last six years. Half of that time she'd been completely mad over Eli, and the other half completely destroyed because he'd left her.

Wyatt looked curious, and more than a little confused. "I don't sense the mating bond on you. Why is that?"

"Because it didn't fully take." When his eyes went wide, she gave a sharp laugh and held up a hand. "And no, I'm not explaining any more than that. Suffice it to say that there was an unexpected interruption. Then the next thing I knew, he'd been banished and was gone."

He winced. "Christ. Talk about shitty timing."

With another wry twitch of her lips, she murmured,

"In case you hadn't noticed, that's pretty much the theme of this story."

"I didn't even know you knew Eli Drake."

Shaking her head again, she said, "I didn't while growing up. Just *of* him. We never spoke until he helped me with my mom one night after she'd gone on one of her benders and I got a call from town to come and collect her. She'd passed out on the sidewalk."

His dark brows drew together in a frown. "When was this?"

"I'd just turned twenty-two."

"Where the hell was I?"

"You had joined Jeremy and Mason on a hunt for a rogue that had traveled into our territory." She'd planned to leave it at that, only to hear herself adding, "But the truth is that it wouldn't have mattered if you were home that night, Pall. I was too embarrassed to have asked you for help."

A fresh wave of irritation darkened his rugged face, and then he sighed, looking resigned. He knew her too well to expect her to have acted any differently. "Did you know he was yours? I mean, six years ago, on the night that he helped you with your mom?"

"Yes. I realized then, but I...I didn't know that he felt the same. Not for a long time." Pushing her hair behind her ear, she stared into the empty hearth again and quietly said, "As lame as it sounds, we spent the next three years being 'secret' friends. We'd meet for runs...for walks...to hunt or to train, and I'd...I'd have to bathe like crazy after every meeting so that none of you would be able to catch his scent on my clothes."

The memories of those bittersweet nights swept through her in a wrenching rush of emotion, and she dug her nails into her palms as hard as she could, needing that bite of pain to ground her. Keep her from falling apart. She'd never trusted easily, thanks to her upbringing. But she'd *wanted* to trust Eli. Wanted it so badly that she'd been shattered when he'd left without a word, confirming her fear that she'd never been anything more than a dirty little secret he'd used to amuse himself.

Getting back to her explanation, she looked at Wyatt and said, "I always worried that he was too embarrassed to let anyone in the pack know we were friends because of my bloodline." Her voice started to shake, so she took a deep breath and tried to steady it. "I know now that that's exactly how he felt. But at the time, I felt so right when I was with him, I just didn't care."

"You deserve better than that, Reyes."

Her throat worked as she gave a hard swallow. "I actually asked him about it a few weeks before he left, and he told me that it wasn't true. That he would never care about something like that. But it doesn't change the fact that he abandoned me. That after sharing a close friendship with me that he didn't want anyone to know about, then finally admitting that he wanted me and making a partial bond with me on the night before he was banished, he just walked away from me without a single word. Given all that, I can only assume he was lying when he said my bloodline didn't matter."

Stroking his jaw, Wyatt sighed. "Or maybe he wasn't, and there was another reason for his silence. I wish I could give you all the answers, but this is something the two of you need to work out for yourselves. Just know that Elise and I are *always* here for you. Eli might be her brother, but you're family to us, too. And that's never going to change."

She was mortified to feel the sting of tears burning behind her eyes. "Thanks," she scraped out, his show of support meaning more to her than he could ever guess.

"And a word of advice?"

She'd started to pick her bag up, but let it drop back down to the floor at his serious tone. "Do I have a choice?" she asked dryly, sliding him an exaggerated smirk.

Wearing the stoic expression he was so well-known for, he said, "If you want him, don't waste the time you've got with him blaming him for the past."

She couldn't hide her surprise when she gaped at him. "You think I should just forgive him? What the hell, Pall?"

"I'm not thinking about *him,*" he said in a low voice, his dark eyes kind. "I'm thinking about you, honey. And if he's your mate, you're never going to be whole without him."

Her heart was pounding so hard that it hurt, and she pressed a trembling hand to her chest. "He won't even tell me why he didn't take me with him."

"Just give it some time."

"I *can't,*" she muttered, panicked…and determined to do whatever it took to kill the pain inside her. If she didn't, she was terrified it would hollow her out, leaving nothing but hatred in its wake, the same as it'd done with her mother. "I've already given him too much. I'm done."

Wyatt looked at her as if she wasn't making any sense. "Carla, that isn't how these things work. You can't just turn them on and off."

"Not with a full bond. But that isn't what we have."

"And you think you can keep going like this?" he asked, his tone and expression making it clear that he thought she was on the ragged edge.

She shook her head. "No. And I won't have to. I've talked with Jillian, and she—"

Lifting one of his hands to stop her talking, he moved to his feet and said, "Wait a minute. Jillian knows about you and Eli?"

"Yes," she admitted, her voice tight. "She...suspected that something wasn't right with me, and after she moved to the Alley to live with Jeremy, she finally asked me about it. I told her the truth because I...I wanted her help."

His dark gaze looked wary. "Her help with what?"

"I want her to undo it."

He blinked, staring at her as if she'd lost her mind. "Christ, Reyes."

"Can you blame me?" she grumbled defensively.

The groove between his brows deepened. "What did Jillian say? Can it actually be done?"

Wetting her lips, she said, "She had to research it, but she finally found a way she thinks she can make it happen. But I needed Eli here for it."

"And does he know this is what you want?"

Exhaling a rough breath, she rubbed her arms as she turned her head to the side. "Yeah, I told him the night I found him."

His voice became eerily quiet. "And what's the cost?"

She shot him a surprised look from the corner of her eye, her heart still beating to a pounding, painful rhythm. "The cost? You know Jillian wouldn't charge me anything. There isn't any cost."

"I'm not talking about money," he muttered, taking a step toward her. "The whole idea of something for nothing—that's not how nature works. So what's the cost to *you?*"

"It doesn't matter," she shot back, narrowing her eyes. "It could be the greatest risk in the world, and I would still do it."

His own eyes went wide. "Jesus, Carla. You hate him *that* much?"

She opened her mouth, trying to force the words from her tight throat. But they wouldn't come. Shaking…shivering, she locked her watery gaze with Wyatt's compassionate one, and stopped trying to speak. It was too late anyway. She didn't need to say anything to make him understand.

The salty tears that suddenly spilled over her cheeks told him everything he needed to know.

Chapter 6

The moment Eli stepped into the kitchen the following morning, every set of eyes turned toward him. Kyle, Sam, James and Lev had already started in on plates of toast and eggs, but he could see that some had been set aside for him to eat when he joined them.

Leaning back in his chair, Sam gave him a slow once over. "I hate to say it, but you look like shit, boss man."

Yeah, and he felt like it, too. Ever since Carla had detailed for him and the others what the Runners had been dealing with here, he'd felt the sickening slide of guilt working its way through his system. There'd been so many times, since he'd caught news of his father's death, that he could have picked up a damn phone and called home to check on his family. But he never had, because there'd been a part of him that hadn't really wanted to know, so that he could keep going through the motions of living without giving a damn. Because giving a damn sucked.

But after seeing the relief on Eric's and Elise's faces last night, he felt more than guilt. He felt like a pathetic bastard who'd let his family down in the worst way. More than his skill in battle, they'd needed him there just to give them support, and he hadn't been. He'd failed.

When it came to the people he cared about, that was apparently the way he worked.

Which means I'm nothing more than an asshole, he muttered inside his head, grabbing his plate and mug and taking a seat at the table.

"We spoke with Mason and the other Runners earlier this morning," Kyle said, his arms crossed on the sturdy tabletop. "We would have dragged you out of bed to join us, but you were sleeping like the dead."

He choked back a curse as he took a hefty swallow of his coffee, irritated that he'd overslept. But after two sleepless nights and the fight against the Whiteclaw, his body had finally demanded some downtime. Setting his mug down, he looked at Kyle. "What did you learn?"

"They have it on word that at least fifty battle-trained Lycans could be coming from various packs, ready to fight beside the Whiteclaw soldiers. They reckon that total number could be anywhere between two hundred to two fifty. Then you have to add in the mercs that Bartley's brought with him."

"And how many do we have fighting for the Silvercrest?" he asked, taking a bite of his eggs.

"Currently trained? About half that."

Lev whistled under his breath. "And those are shit numbers."

"Could be worse, if the Whiteclaw were a larger pack," James offered in his gravelly voice. "They're thankfully on the small side. But they've spent time training their men to fight, which is why they have the higher number."

"Did you talk to any of the Runners about the day-shifting option?" During one of the meals they'd shared with Carla while they'd been on the road, she'd relayed the story of how his father had taught many of his followers the act of day-shifting. It was a skill that had previously only been known to those who sat on the League of Elders, but Stefan Drake had used it as a way to give his followers an advantage over the Runners, and now the Whiteclaw were attempting to do the same with their "super soldier" drugs.

"I talked to the one named Brody about it," Sam said, after taking a drink of his coffee. "He told me they'd had a meeting about it, since its whole purpose is to be used during times of war. But given how things went down with your old man, and the younger Lycans who are still trying to get their heads on right after all his brainwashing bullshit, they believe it's safer to avoid going that route."

Eli scrubbed a hand over his stubbled jaw. "Yeah, I can see where they're coming from. Sometimes the cure can be even deadlier than the poison."

The group sat in heavy silence for a moment, until he looked round at his men and asked, "So what's our play? That can't be the only thing you've come up with."

Kyle placed his hands behind his head and rocked

his chair back on its hind legs. "We've been brain-
storming some ideas that we'll run by you tonight,
after you've had a chance to settle in."

He swallowed the bite he'd just taken and grimaced.
"Why not just tell me now?"

"Because you look like you need a break at the moment, and we're still putting our heads together. Just
take some time to get things sorted out today, and let
us deal with crunching these ideas into something that
might work. Then you can listen to everything we come
up with and tell us it's all wrong tonight."

He laughed, which was what he knew Kyle had been
going for. It sucked that he'd lost touch with his family
for so long, but he had to admit that he was a lucky son
of a bitch to have found these guys. They were like a
second family to him, and he was going to miss them
when all was said and done.

He couldn't say exactly what he'd be doing when
this thing with the Whiteclaw was over, but if he survived it, Eli was determined to stick close to the ones
he'd left behind.

Whether they want me here or not.

"When I spoke with Mason this morning," Sam
added, "he asked if some of us can help with the training. They've been working with any volunteers they get
from the pack on weapons training and combat skills."

"If they want our help, they've got it. But I think
we need to be careful until we have a better bearing
on how involved they want us. I don't want to step on
any toes around here."

In a dry tone, Lev said, "You're not exactly Mr.
Popular with this group, are you?"

"I don't have a great history with the Runners,"

he admitted with a grimace, "but I'm hoping it'll improve."

"It better, if you want to keep your little lady love," Sam murmured.

James shoved Sam in the shoulder so hard it nearly knocked the guy out of his chair. "Come on, Sam. Don't you remember us warning you that the boss man would be out of sorts this morning?"

Shaking his head, Eli couldn't help but smirk at their antics. "You're all a bunch of jackasses."

They laughed and gave him an even harder time as they finished off breakfast, then cleared the table, making plans to meet up again later that afternoon. After the guys headed out, Eli grabbed a quick shower, then threw on a pair of jeans, his boots, and a dark gray T-shirt, eager to get outside and find out what Carla was up to. As he headed out the front door of the cabin, he almost reached up and straightened his damp hair, then stopped himself with a scowl. Last thing he needed was to start primping for her. When it came to Carla Reyes, he became almost more animal than man. No sense really in putting out false advertising.

The instant he got her under his hands and mouth, everything inside him—man *and* beast—went straight into feral aggression mode. She was just too much. Her taste. Her scent. The silky feel of her skin. All of it was guaranteed to turn him into a slathering animal that wanted to do things to her that would make most women run for cover—which was why he needed to get a damn grip on himself.

The last time he'd touched her, in that motel room the other night, he'd forced himself to pull back because he'd been on the verge of losing it. If he wanted to touch her again—something he wanted more than anything—he was going to have to find a way to leash that visceral, primitive part of his hunger, or he'd be sinking his fangs deep into her tight flesh, completing their bond, before he even knew what hit him. And Carla would end up skinning him alive.

Not that he would blame her, with the way things currently stood between them. Hell, at this point he'd be happy just to have her look at him without that scathing burn of fury and suspicion in her beautiful eyes. Though it was the pain that really did him in. Made him feel like his insides had been flayed and dipped in lye.

Pulling in a deep breath of the pine-scented air, he started walking a bit faster across the bustling glade, needing to be with her, close to her, even if she didn't want him there. He wasn't really in the frame of mind to fully appreciate the beauty of his surroundings, but he would have had to be blind not to notice how in the bright morning sunlight the Alley looked like something out of a freaking fairy tale, even with all the activity going on. The grass seemed greener here than anywhere else in the world, thick and lush beneath his boots, the air so crisp and clean it damn near made him lightheaded. Then there were the tall, majestic trees, thick with leafy branches, lining the perimeter, the surrounding forest brimming with life.

And yet, despite the surreal beauty of the glade, there was an air of tension and expectancy in the air that hung over those who lived here like a dark, dense storm cloud. They were doing their best to enjoy each day as it came and to be thankful for what they had, while remaining constantly mindful of the fact that everything could change in a heartbeat. That this idyllic paradise could all too easily slip into hell if they weren't vigilant.

He nodded to his sister when he caught her coming out onto her front porch, then looked around again, trying to spot a familiar head of honey-gold hair. When Carla was nowhere to be seen, he forced a grin onto his lips and made his way over to Elise. "Hey, beautiful."

She was standing on the top step, which put her only slightly above his height. Reaching down, she ruffled his unruly hair. "God, I can't get used to how huge you are now."

"I don't look that different," he muttered, going a little hot around the ears. His hair was longer than he'd ever worn it, and he'd put on more muscle in the last three years, as well as added a few battle scars. But he hadn't thought the changes were enough for others to notice. He'd obviously been wrong.

"Are you kidding?" she asked with a playful snort. "You look like a wild man."

Eli rolled his eyes. "Thanks."

"Come on," she murmured, smiling as she took his hand and pulled him up the steps. "I'll get you some more coffee. You look like you need it."

Instead of taking offense, he took a moment to study her in the morning sunlight, before saying, "And you look happy, sis."

A gentle smile touched her lips. "I am."

Eli squeezed her hand. "Good. You deserve it."

They went into the kitchen, and he let his gaze wander over the beautiful, spacious interior of the cabin as she put the coffee on. Then he took a seat at the table, feeling both at ease and nervous at the same time, his brain churning as he tried to work out what he should say…and what he shouldn't. He'd honestly never seen Elise look so happy and confident, and he didn't want to screw that up by bringing up a painful topic. Then she brought it up for him.

"You know," she murmured, setting their steaming mugs on the table and taking the chair caddy corner to his, "I never really got the chance to thank you for what you did for me." Her dark gaze was soft with emotion.

Swallowing at the knot in his throat, he rumbled, "You told me." He'd called a few times after his banishment, whenever he'd been missing his siblings too much to resist. But his calls had become less frequent over time, as it became harder to hear about life in Shadow Peak going on without him.

And each time he'd talked to them, it had just about killed him inside to keep from asking about Carla. About how she was. If she hated him. Who she was dating.

"But I never thanked you in person," his sister said with a smile. "Over the phone doesn't count."

"You don't need to thank me, El. It was my responsibility to look out for you, and I'm sorry that I didn't come back sooner. I know I've let you and Eric down."

Frowning, she said, "Eli, that isn't true. Yes, we wanted you here because we've missed you, but neither one of us would have wanted you to have to live through Dad's madness. I can't even imagine how horrific that would have been for you, given how closely you worked with him."

"But after he was dead—after the League was gone—I should have come home. Damn it, El, I should have been here to protect you from the Whiteclaw."

Looking adorably frustrated, she shook her head and said, "That's ridiculous. I think it's great that you're here to help, because God knows we need it. But you've got to stop thinking it's your duty to keep bad things from happening to Eric and me. No one expects that of you."

"I love you both," he muttered gruffly, "which *makes* it my duty."

"Well, we feel the same way about you. So I guess we can all just look out for each other. Fair?"

Some of the tension in his chest started to ease as he realized she truly didn't hold a grudge against him, and he found himself giving her a lopsided grin. "So now that both you and Eric have gotten bonded, I guess we have two new members of the family, eh?"

She slowly arched a slender auburn brow. "And what about you?"

"What about me?" he hedged, sliding his gaze away from the knowing look in her deep blue eyes as he took a drink of his coffee.

Softly, she said, "You can play coy if you want, but you should know that Wyatt told me about you and Carla. Not everything, but enough for me to know that you're life mates. And that you've had a complicated relationship for the past six years, three of which you haven't even been around for."

He flicked her a guarded look, his fingers tightening on the mug. "I don't want to talk about it, El."

"I figured as much. I just want you to know that even though I don't understand why you didn't take her with you, or come back for her, I think she would be good for you. She's an amazing woman."

"Yeah," he agreed, his voice thick. "She's something, all right."

She took a sip of her coffee, then said, "Wyatt and I sat her down this morning and must have thanked her about a hundred times. Honestly, Eli, I don't think I would have made it out of Hawkley alive if she hadn't put herself at even greater risk to give Wyatt the chance to reach me. Even Eric came over this morning and gave her a big ol' hug." She shook her head a little and gave a hard swallow. "What she did, it was one of the bravest things I've ever seen. She did everything she could to keep their attention focused on her so that I didn't get hurt."

A slight smile ghosted his lips. "She must care about you a lot, El."

Her dark eyes twinkled. "Or maybe she was thinking about you."

He grunted, taking another drink from his mug.

"I'm really hoping you'll talk to me about her, Eli." The quiet words were rough with sincerity. "I want to be able to help you, but I can't do that if I don't understand what's going on."

Steering the conversation in a slightly different direction, he leaned back in his chair and said, "Speaking of the little Bloodrunner, where is she? I thought she might be here with Wyatt."

Elise gave him a disappointed look, then sighed and gave in. "She and Wyatt are out checking on some things down in Wesley. With all the tension in the pack right now, we think a few of the younger wolves who were caught up in Dad's craziness might have slipped back into old habits. There've been a few human disappearances around Wesley, and we want to make sure they aren't the work of any rogue wolves."

A deep scowl settled between his brows. "Why the hell did Carla have to go?"

Frowning again, she said, "She's just doing her job, Eli. Don't be an ass."

"She could get hurt, damn it."

His sister looked as if she was trying not to roll her eyes at him. "This is Carla we're talking about. I get that you're protective of her, but she's a serious little badass."

His nostrils flared as he pulled in a hard breath. "Did she or did she not end up kidnapped by those bastards?"

"That was different."

"Was it? Because no matter how you look at it, she managed to get herself into a situation that put her in grave danger."

"And she got herself out of it. Seriously, Eli, what is your problem?" she demanded as she crossed her arms, her slender brows pinched. "I love you like crazy, but you're acting like a jerk."

He grunted, knowing damn well that he sounded like an ass. But he didn't know how to make her understand. He'd always worried himself sick over Carla's job, his fears only growing more intense as their connection had deepened. Now that he was back, that worry was scraping him raw inside. Made him feel like she might be stolen from him before he even had the chance to get ahold of her.

If a bloody miracle happened and she eventually agreed to let him complete the bond, how would he cope with what she did for a living? *Could* he cope with it? Would she give him any consideration at all, or dig her heels in and turn a deaf ear to his concerns?

Damn it, it was always like a chess game with her, and he didn't know how to win. Didn't know which move would be the right one to land him his queen—or what the hell he'd do with her once he got her, considering everything that stood between them. She made him feel a thousand different things at once, and he was still too wound up by her sudden appearance back in his life to make heads or tails of any of it. All he knew was that he was done with…with *this*. With feeling like the gulf between them was growing wider with every second that went by.

Elise's gaze sharpened as she studied his scowling face. "You know," she murmured, "whatever is going on between you and Carla, it hasn't exactly put Wyatt and I in an easy situation. He's protective of her, and I'm protective of you. But I'm starting to wonder if I'm on the right side in this thing."

"Leave it alone, El. You and Wyatt don't need us causing problems for you."

"Nothing is coming between us," she said in a tone that was more confident than anything he'd ever heard from her before. "We're just worried, Eli. But I have a feeling there's a lot you need to fill me in on, whether you want to or not."

"No offense, sis, but it isn't any of your business."

She turned her head a bit to the side, staring out at the thick woods that lay just beyond the kitchen window, the look on her beautiful face making his insides tighten, as if he needed to brace for an emotional blow. Then she looked at him and said, "Did you ever wonder why mother named me Elise?"

Wondering where she was going with this, and wanting to talk about anything in the world besides their mother, he gave an uncomfortable shrug. "No idea, El. I'm assuming she just liked the name."

Her lips twitched with a brief smile. "It never struck you that it was a little *too* similar to your own?"

His tension cranked a notch higher, and he mirrored her pose, crossing his arms over his chest. "What are you getting at?"

Softly, she said, "One of my earliest memories of her is the day she explained it to me. She said that Eric was her little troublemaker, but you were her rock. Strong and proud and never afraid to stand up for what was important to you, even though you were just a child. And she wanted me to be like that. She said it was never easy for women in our world, and she wanted me to have every advantage going in, so she named me Elise because she wanted me to carry a part of you with me, wherever I went."

He scrubbed his hands over his face as her quiet words wound their way through his head, then placed his fists against the tabletop and took a sharp breath. *Christ,* if his mother only knew what kind of boy he'd become after she'd left. The things he'd done to keep as much of his father's attention focused on him as he could, and not on Eric or Elise, were far from noble. He'd often acted like a bully and a thug just to keep the old man happy, and that was a shame he'd carry with him for the rest of his life.

Despite the ruthless reputation he'd earned as a high-priced mercenary, the rumors of his greed were greatly exaggerated. Yeah, he'd made a ton of cash at times, but there'd also been a lot of jobs that hadn't even come with a paycheck. More than once, he and the other guys had helped villagers who barely had enough to feed themselves, ridding the area of the bloodthirsty drug cartels who destroyed their fields and way of life. Had rescued women and children who'd been sold into the horrific sex slave industry, returning them to their homes. But Eli knew that sometimes there simply weren't enough good deeds to erase the stains on your past. Which meant he was probably a bigger fool than he'd ever realized, since he just kept on trying.

"Eli?"

Feeling as if the gritty words were being torn out of him, he forced his gaze to Elise's and said, "Don't, El. Whatever you do, *don't* be like me."

Covering one of his big, scarred hands with her soft ones, she gave him a crooked smile. "I hate to burst your bubble, but I think you're pretty damn awesome. So you'll stay my hero whether you want to or not."

He shoved his free hand through his hair, and swallowed the lump of bitterness stuck in his throat. "Damn it, honey. If you only knew."

"Knew what?" she asked, tilting her head a bit as she studied him.

He debated, wanting to unload the heavy burden of his secret after all these years once and for all, the weight of it crushing him down, but still terrified of what it would mean. Would his sister hate him? Would Eric? Would he lose them now that he'd only just come back to them?

And was the fear of that happening just another part of why he'd opted to stay away for so long? Because as long as he wasn't with them, he didn't have to fight this constant battle to keep what he'd done inside?

Needing to get the hell out of there before he said something he would no doubt regret, he pushed back from the table and stood. "Thanks for the coffee, honey, but I have to go."

She reached out and caught his hand, squeezing it until he finally looked down at her. "Eli," she murmured with concern, "whatever it is, you know I'll still love you. Right?"

He nodded as he pulled his hand from hers, then turned and walked out, no doubt leaving her with a thousand questions.

And not a single answer.

Chapter 7

After suffering two days of hell, Eli was ready to howl. He was frustrated, exhausted, and so goddamn hungry for a certain little half-breed it was driving him mad. She was doing a damn good job of avoiding him, the glimpses he occasionally got of her twisting him into knots of tension and craving. There were so many things he needed to say to her, things he needed to make her understand, more of them building up inside him with every hour that went by, but she wasn't giving him the chance.

Hell, she wasn't even willing to be in the same room with him. Which made it damn difficult to give her the explanations she'd demanded of him.

Their relationship, whatever it was at this point, had turned into one hot, tangled mess of *should haves* and *shouldn't haves,* and all he wanted was to tie her sweet little ass down and make her listen. He finally understood that there was no way forward until he did that, and while he still didn't have everything figured out in his head, the one thing he knew beyond any doubt was that he didn't want her breaking their bond. Yeah, there were a thousand and one issues they needed to work through, but that was the one thing that was non-negotiable.

"Yo, boss man!" Kyle suddenly barked, jerking Eli from his thoughts. "You heard a word I've said?"

"Doubt it," Lev murmured. They were all sitting around the kitchen table in the cabin that Eli and Kyle were sharing. Grinning like a jackass, Lev lifted his coffee mug and added, "He's too busy mentally undressing the little Runner in his dirty daydreams."

"Lev, shut up," he muttered, before looking at his second-in-command. "Sorry, Kyle. Go on with what you were saying."

Kyle leaned back in his chair. "I was telling you that the guys and I have finally ironed out a plan."

"Great. Let's hear it." He'd been waiting two damn days for this.

"First, the way we see it, there are two basic problems that we have to deal with: the fact that they have more bodies than we do, and the fact that they control the timing of their attack. There's not much we can do about the first, but the second is one we can take away from them."

His brows lifted with interest. "And how do we do that?"

Sam gave him a slow smile. "That's where the plan comes in."

Twenty minutes later, Eli agreed that what they'd

come up with was a brilliant idea that might actually succeed despite their limited numbers, and he told the guys to take it to Mason and the Runners. The five of them had been working closely with the Runners for the past few days, with the exception of Carla and Wyatt, who kept taking every "out of Alley" assignment that came up.

Thankfully, he and the guys were getting along great with the rest of the group, and the training sessions they'd been helping out with were progressing even more rapidly than they'd hoped. Everyone in the Alley was trying to keep a positive attitude, and the arrival of thirty Lycans from the Pennsylvania-based Blackstone pack, who were willing to help with security patrols, had been greatly appreciated. And there'd been a message from the Greywolf—who had actually threatened to move in on the Silvercrest's northern border in order to prevent the Whiteclaw from encroaching on their territory—that they were standing down. Apparently, the news that Eli and his group of ruthless mercenaries were now working with the Silvercrest had been enough to make the Greywolf rethink their position.

The rest of the morning was spent working out on the training fields, and then he and the guys worked with Mason and Brody to fortify defenses in the Alley. As the day wore on, he constantly searched for Carla's blond hair in the crowd of people moving around the glade, but she wasn't anywhere to be seen.

"Hey, Eli, wait up!" Kyle called out, just as Eli was climbing up the front steps of the cabin they were sharing. He didn't have the patience to deal with any more of his friend's ribbing at the moment, and was about to tell him to get lost, when Kyle said, "I thought you might want to know that she's back."

He turned so quickly he damn near took out James, who was climbing the porch steps behind him. "Sorry," he muttered, shoving past James and Lev as he hurried back down, scanning the glade. The instant he saw her on the far side, he took off.

"Carla!" he called, not caring if he looked like an idiot to those who were probably watching him.

She kept walking, and he nearly crashed into Brody and Cian, who were deep in conversation in front of Brody's cabin, as he ran across the Alley, trying to reach her before she disappeared inside Wyatt's place and locked the door again. She'd fucking done it twice already when he'd tried to get her alone.

"Stop, damn it!" he shouted, causing everyone around them to quit what they were doing and look at him. "We need to talk!"

Ignoring him, she started walking faster. Eli cursed, ready to knock the damn door down this time if he had to—and then he got the break he needed. One of the soon-to-be moms stepped out onto Carla's porch to ask her something about the thermostat in her cabin, and she was forced to stop and answer the woman's question. Breathing hard, Eli slowed down and positioned himself partially in front of her, his hungry gaze taking in every inch of her delectable form while she finished her conversation. She was dressed in a dirt-stained pair of jeans, tight black T-shirt, and black boots, her golden hair falling loose around her shoulders. It was her standard work look, and he could tell by the light sheen of sweat on her arms and face that she'd been doing something strenuous, her provocative scent even richer than normal, so good he could sense it like something warm and sweet on his tongue.

When her conversation was finished, she started to walk around him, but he grasped her arm, halting her in her tracks. She didn't even bother looking at him as she said, "Let me go, Eli."

"Not until you stop acting like a child and talk to me," he bit out, leaning in close and tightening his grip, while still being careful not to hurt her.

She pulled in a deep breath, then slowly turned her head and took a good, long look at him with those dark eyes. "I can see you're not going to be reasonable about this," she eventually murmured, forcing a note of boredom in her words that made him want to put her over his knee and spank her until she stopped acting like such a little brat. "So, fine. If you want to talk, then talk."

Eli stared down at her, lost in his hunger and craving, and suddenly couldn't think of a single goddamn thing to say. Instead, he wanted to take her down to the lush green grass, strip her bare, and make her come until she stopped being so damn mad at him. Until he'd found a way to turn her hatred into something that didn't make him feel like he was dying inside.

She crossed her arms over her chest the instant he lowered his hand, her foot tapping out an impatient rhythm against the grass, while his mind remained completely blank.

"Well?"

He ran his tongue over the front of his teeth, then got right in her face. "Why are you avoiding me?"

"It's not that hard to figure out. I told you what I wanted to hear. Until you're ready to be honest with me, which I seriously doubt is why you keep trying to do this, I have nothing to say to you."

He bit back a curse, wondering if anything he said at this point would make a difference to her. She was so damn bitter. So angry.

Sensing the curious stares coming their way, he grasped her elbow and drew her reluctant body to the side of the cabin, where they were out of view. Then he gave into the visceral urge to have her locked down, and backed her against the rustic cedar planks, caging her in with his arms as he planted his palms against the exterior wall. Holding her hostile glare, he asked, "Why did you bother to come after me, to bring me back to this place, if all you planned to do was ignore me once we got here?"

"You're seriously this upset because you think I've been ignoring you? Jesus, Eli. You ignored me for two entire days in the truck while we were driving here!"

He drew his head back in surprise. "I wasn't ignoring you."

"Like hell you weren't."

"Damn it, Rey. Why do you think I sat in the back seat for those entire two days? I hate not driving, but I wanted to be as close to you as I could be. Even if we weren't talking to each other."

"You wouldn't even look at me!" she snapped, her beautiful eyes glittering with emotion.

His voice turned guttural. "I was looking at you every goddamn time you closed your eyes or stared out your window. I just didn't want you to know it."

Taking another deep breath, she asked, "And what about at the motel? What the hell was *that?*"

"That was...complicated."

She made a sound that was half snarl, half scream, and he had to grab her again as she tried to duck under his arm.

"I was afraid of losing control!" he growled, holding her against the cabin with his big hands pressed to her shoulders. "You...you *push* me."

"Toward what?" she demanded, only to immediately shake her head in frustration. "Never mind. It doesn't matter. The only *pushing* I plan on doing is pushing you away from me, so your problems are solved."

He could feel a muscle beginning to pulse at the side of his jaw, his heart pounding to a hard, brutal rhythm. "That's not what I want and you know it."

She kept her angry gaze locked tight with his as she licked her bottom lip. "You're wrong," she argued, her breaths quickening. "I don't know *anything* where you're concerned."

Biting back a groan, he begged her with his gaze to believe in him. "You would if you would just give me a chance."

She paled as her eyes slid closed, and then she dropped her head back against the cabin with a thud that made him wince. "I told you at that shitty bar in Texas that I wasn't bringing you back for me, Eli. I brought you back for Eric and Elise, and for the pack. But not for me."

"So that's it?" he asked quietly. "You have no interest in what I do?"

She lifted her head, then slowly opened her eyes, their brown depths filled with pain. "You'll do whatever you want, same as you always have. I've learned not to care."

He moved his sharp gaze over her beautiful face,

using everything he had to read her...to see beneath her bitter words. "I call bullshit, Rey."

"What?"

Pulling in a deep breath of her warm, mouthwatering scent, he spoke in a hushed, gruff voice that was thick with hope. "I can smell the need on you. See your pulse racing at the base of your throat. Christ, baby. I can fucking *feel* how much you need this. How much you need *me*."

She glared up at him. "Unfortunately for you, my hormones don't make the decisions around here."

A low, deep laugh rumbled up from his chest, and he lowered his head, pressing his lips to the soft skin at the side of her throat. "Maybe you should let them," he murmured, licking across her hammering pulse. "Because I want nothing more than to make you addicted to me. To how I can make you feel."

Her hands settled against his shoulders, but she didn't push him away. Instead, she sank her short nails into him, that little bite of pain shooting straight to his groin. "A woman's head has to be in the game as much as her body for her to really enjoy herself, Eli."

"I know," he rasped, nipping her delicate earlobe. "And if you just give me the chance, I'll get them *both* to the right place." He lifted his head, looking her right in the eye. "Take me to your bed, Rey, and I swear I'll do everything I can to make it worth your while."

She stared back at him through her thick lashes. "I thought you wanted to talk, Eli. Not fuck."

He put his face right over hers, his big hands flexing against her shoulders. "The talking comes *after,* Rey. After I've spent hours just making you come. I'll bury my face between your sweet little thighs and lick you until you scream. I could keep my tongue busy down there for days, that's how *badly* I want you. I dream about getting you under my mouth. Feeling you beneath my lips. Drinking you in, over and over. There were too many damn things I never got the chance to do to you, and I *need* them, baby. I need them so badly it's killing me."

For an instant, he thought she was actually softening, her skin dewy and warm with color, making him want to press his mouth to those fever blushes so badly he could taste it. But then disappointment cut into him like a knife as he lifted his gaze back to her eyes. He could tell by the way they narrowed that she wasn't going to surrender so easily. "You didn't get them because you went from never touching me, to messing around with me against a freaking tree, to falling on top of me like a drunken idiot two nights later, and then leaving me!"

He ground his back teeth together, wanting so badly to argue, but what could he say? She'd spoken nothing more than the truth. After trying so hard to keep his hands to himself, only allowing a few brief kisses and touches, she'd caught him that last night when his control was shattered. He'd been hurting for Elise, for what had happened to her, filled with rage that he hadn't been able to find the other bastards who'd raped her. Had been worried about what the League would do to punish him for the kill he'd made, but unable to regret it. No, he would have done the same thing, in the same way, again…and again. But he'd drank more than he normally did that night, needing to dull the roar in his head, as well as the pain in his gut that made him ache for the feel of Carla in his arms. And then she'd knocked on his door, and his control had simply vanished, decimated beneath a crushing force of hunger so violent and savage he'd nearly taken her right there, on the hard wooden floor inside the doorway. Somehow, he'd managed to get her into his bedroom, but that was the only concession to her comfort he'd been able to make.

He'd simply needed her too badly.

At first, he'd been worried she would stop him that night, since she hadn't been happy with how he'd acted a few days before, when his control had first started to slip and he'd kissed her. Then put his hands all over her.

She'd been into the kissing...*and* the touching. Had loved it when he'd put his hand between her legs for the first time, her shirt pushed up under her chin. They'd been in the forest, surrounded by the trees and wind and rain, and he'd had her little nipple in his mouth while he'd thrust two fingers deep inside her tender sex, undone by the hot, wet feel of her. She'd been the tightest, sweetest thing he'd ever known, and when she'd pulsed around his fingers in orgasm, he'd wanted to throw his head back and howl. And once he'd finally pulled his fingers from between her silky thighs, he hadn't been able to stop himself from shoving them in his mouth, sucking off every drop of her cream. But she'd been furious at the way he'd pulled away from her when she'd reached for the button on *his* jeans, putting an end to the stolen, erotic moment, knowing damn well that if she'd put her hands on him, he'd have been inside her in an instant. Something he'd wanted more than anything, but had known he couldn't have.

So, yeah, he'd already been working on a hair trigger where she was concerned. And then, two nights later, she was there, in his house, and he hadn't been able to fight it. He'd stripped her, taken her to his bed, and shoved her thighs apart to make way for him, his chest heaving with his frantic breaths. Heart pumping, he'd worked himself inside her hot, fist-tight sheath, completely lost in the exquisite, breathtaking feel of her, and had just pierced her throat with the tips of his fangs, when his father had started banging on his front door. Terrified Stefan would realize she was there, he'd jerked away from her, leaving her in his bed with the promise to be back. He had no idea how long she'd waited, but when he'd returned from being told that the League was determining his punishment for the unsanctioned kill that he'd made, she'd been gone.

The banishment had been announced the following day, and he'd known, in that moment, that he would probably never see her again. That he'd lost everything that had ever mattered to him.

Forcing his mind back on the present and away from those gut-wrenching memories, he told her, "I wanted to finish it that night, Carla. You have no idea how *badly* I wanted that. But I tried to do the right thing."

"Which was what?" she snapped, curling her hands into fists and pressing them against his chest. "Protecting the little half-human from your big bad self? You didn't think I would have been able to handle you?"

He shook his head, hard. "I wasn't trying to protect you from me." Though he should have, considering how savage she'd made him feel. "I was trying to protect you from my father."

"Riiight." Her tone made it clear that she thought he'd just fed her the most pathetic excuse in the history of brush-offs.

Forcing his words through his clenched teeth, he said, "You *knew* him, Rey. Knew what he was capable of. I never let myself have anything that he could use as leverage against me. What do you think would have happened if he'd learned that we... That we were..."

"Jesus, Eli. Just spit it out."

His words punched from his mouth like bullets. "An item. Thing. Whatever the hell you want to call it."

A smirk curled her beautiful mouth, and she clucked her tongue. "Come on, Eli. Get real. There wasn't any chance of him ever thinking that, because I wasn't yours. Maybe nature screwed up and thought I should be, but we both know the truth. I was just the half-breed you kept pushing away. The one you were too ashamed to be seen with."

"Wrong," he bit out, shoving his fingers into her hair and holding her head in a firm grip as he pressed his forehead against hers. "You were my everything, Carla. Besides my brother and sister, the only goddamn person that mattered. The person that mattered *most*."

Before she could say anything else to piss him off, he took her mouth and filled it with his tongue, rubbing it against hers, the taste of her so incredible it nearly broke him.

"Ask me to come with you," he panted against her soft lips, his body so hard and aching with the need to be inside her he would have gotten down on his damn knees if he weren't afraid she would run from him when he did. "Invite me to your room...to your bed. *Please,* Rey. I'm *begging* you."

"Never!" she cried, the single word cracking with emotion as she wrenched her head to the side.

Beyond frustrated, he exhaled a harsh breath, then

turned away from her and paced a few yards away. Before he even knew what he was doing, he found himself smashing his fist into a towering tree trunk with so much force it would have broken his hand if he'd been human. He hit it against the rough bark, feeling his knuckles split and bleed, imagining it was his father's face since it was that bastard's fault he'd been too terrified to claim her like she'd deserved. And now, because of that, things were so screwed up, she wouldn't even give him the chance to make them right.

When he finally got himself under control and turned back around to face her, she was gone, which wasn't all that surprising. Still, a violent, guttural stream of curses burned at the back of his throat, and he braced his hands on his hips, struggling to catch his breath. What should he do now? Go after her? Follow her around like a pathetic puppy? Or the ol' tried-and-true coping mechanism of losing himself in the bottom of a bottle? If he went that route, at least he'd be able to dull this goddamn hollow feeling sucking at his insides for a short time.

Then again, given how badly he wanted her, there probably wasn't enough alcohol in the world to ease this ache.

Forcing himself to move, he walked back out into the glade, and immediately spotted a worried-looking Eric headed his way. *Shit.* How much had his brother just seen?

From the look on his dark face, too much, and Eli knew he wasn't going to like what was coming. Eric didn't even give him the chance to try and deflect him with a bullshit excuse. His brother just jerked his chin toward Elise's cabin, where they knew she was working on a training schedule for the group, and growled, *"Now."*

Eric knocked on her front door after they'd climbed the porch steps, and the moment Elise opened up, she took one look at their scowls and frowned. "In the kitchen," she murmured, noticing the blood dripping from his battered knuckles. They followed her into the sunny kitchen, and Eli slumped down into one of the chairs at the table, offering a gruff, "Thanks," when Elise handed him a damp dishtowel. He wrapped the soft cotton around his hand, then surged back to his feet, unable to sit still as he started pacing from one side of the kitchen to the other. Elise had taken a seat at the table across from where he'd been sitting, while Eric leaned against the sink with his arms crossed over his chest. But neither of them was saying a damn thing, and he ground his jaw, keeping his narrowed gaze on the floor, knowing they were watching him, trying to figure out what his problem was.

Eric was the first to break the uncomfortable silence. "So about you and Reyes?"

Eli flicked him a shuttered look. "Just leave it, Eric. I need to figure this out on my own."

His brother's dark brows were knitted with concern. "I get that, and I'm trying to be patient. To give you time to settle in after being away for so long. But I need you to answer a question for me."

"I already know what you're going to ask," he ground out, "and the answer is *yes*. She's mine."

There was nothing for a moment but the heavy sound of his boots on the kitchen floor as he paced, and then Eric gave a tired sigh. "Yeah, we kinda already figured that out. What we're wondering is…well, everything else that goes along with that. Why didn't you ever tell us? What the hell is going on between the two of you *now?*"

"Christ," he muttered, lifting his good hand and pulling it down his face.

"Did you know?" Eric pressed, unwilling to let it go. "Did you know that she was yours before you left?"

Hell yes, he'd known. Though he hadn't admitted it to her, or even to himself, he'd known for *years* before they ever even spoke to one another on that fateful night when she'd been called up to town to collect Nicole. He'd started noticing Carla when she hit her teens. Had watched her, waiting for her to grow older. And then the day had come when he could no longer keep his distance, despite all the reasons why he should. Why it would have been better for them both.

He could have walked away that night, when he'd seen her struggling with Nicole on the street, but he hadn't had the willpower. She was an adult, she was beautiful, and she was *his*. Even if he couldn't claim her, he'd wanted to be close to her. To know her. Spend time with her. It'd been torture, but he'd soaked up every single second that he spent in her company— and he'd ached for her every single moment that they were apart. Even on those nights when she'd been in her cabin down in the Alley, and he'd been up in town, with another woman underneath him, trying to ease the pain of wanting her and not having her. Of course, the meaningless sexual encounters had never worked. How could a guy enjoy sex with another woman when he couldn't get the image of the one he craved out of his head? When he kept thinking about how he'd feel if he knew she was doing the same thing with another male? What her face would look like if she were there to see him?

"Eli?" Eric prompted in a low voice.

Coming to a stop in the middle of the kitchen floor, he gave a hard swallow, then forced out a quiet, "Yeah, I knew."

His brother's deep voice was rough with surprise. "And you left her anyway?"

Lifting his head, he locked his gaze with Eric's. "I knew she was mine, but I didn't know that the bond had formed. Or at least some of it."

"*Some* of it?" Eric asked, shaking his head. "How is that even possible?"

Elise gave a soft laugh, speaking up for the first time since she'd sat down. "It's not too crazy if you think about it. I mean, Eli *is* as alpha as a Lycan can get, not to mention as pure-blooded, which means he probably has supercharged sex hormones or whatever it is that causes the bonding."

Eric waved his arms wildly, looking ridiculous. "Shit, stop!" he said to El. "Don't talk about Eli's freaking super sperm when I'm in the same room with you. That is *not* something I want to hear about."

"I didn't say super sperm," Elise argued, rolling her eyes. "I said supercharged sex hormones."

Eli used his good hand to cover his eyes, his ears hot, and wondered how he could get them to just shut up.

"And then there's Carla," Elise went on to say, obviously not ready to let the subject drop. "She's as badass as a female can get. It's not surprising the bond managed to at least partially take when you think about how potent they both are."

Eric groaned. "New topic, *now,* you little imp."

"You're such a baby," she said with another laugh, and Eli lowered his hand just in time to catch her tossing a balled-up napkin at their brother.

Eric grimaced as he batted the napkin away. "I'm not a baby. I just don't like thinking about my brother's...potency."

"Back atcha," Eli grunted. He'd just started to head back over to the table to take a seat, when a deep male voice let out a guttural string of curses right outside the kitchen window, followed by an equally pissed off sounding voice that definitely belonged to a woman. "Who the hell is that?" he asked, looking from Eric to Elise.

She stood up and peered through the slanted blinds. "Holy shit," she gasped. "It's Cian and Sayre!"

Eric frowned. "Are they arguing again?"

"Let's just say that if looks could kill, I'm pretty sure the Irishman would be pushing up daisies right about now." Shaking her head, she turned away from the window and sat back down at the table. "She just stomped off into the woods, and he stormed around the back of the cabin, probably heading back over to his place."

"What's the deal with those two, anyway?" Eli asked the question as he sat down, glad to have the focus off him and Carla for the moment.

"Who the hell knows?" Eric muttered, pushing his hands in his front pockets as he shrugged his shoulders. "He won't touch her, but he won't let any other guy get close to her, either. If he wants her, and I'm thinking he does, then he probably thinks she's too young for him."

"Isn't she?"

"Probably," Eric said again. "But then, from what

I understand from the other Runners, no one's really sure of the guy's *exact* age."

Eli lifted his brows. "Didn't he grow up with all of them?"

Eric shook his head. "He spent time here visiting when they were in their teens, but lived in Ireland most of the time. He didn't move to these mountains permanently until later."

"He can be such a smartass," Elise murmured, "but he's a gorgeous one. And that accent of his is downright sinful, which I'm sure hasn't escaped the girl's notice. But there are a lot of issues working against him, like her age, his reputation as a man-whore, and his whole 'my past is a secret' thing. And then there's the fact that her mother hates his guts. Woman turns red every time she sees him."

Eli snorted. "I wouldn't think Hennessey would let a mother get in his way."

"You know what Constance is like," Eric said with a low laugh. "That's one extremely wicked witch when she sets her mind to it."

"True," he agreed, recalling the times when she'd scared the crap out of him and his friends when he was younger and she'd caught them doing something they shouldn't be. "But Hennessey has never struck me as the kind of guy who would let something like that get to him."

"Yeah. Constance Murphy is a pain in his ass, but despite all of it, the fact is that *he's* the one making his life hard at the moment."

Nodding, Eli said, "The guy's stubborn."

Eric's voice was dry. "Sounds like someone else I know."

He shot his brother a dark look. "Different situations."

"Are they? If I had to bet, I'd say Cian's afraid of putting the girl in a dangerous situation, though no one knows what that is. But he's no doubt trying to protect her."

"Then maybe you should give the guy a break," he shot back.

"I will," Eric muttered, "just as soon as he's manned up."

Despite his foul mood, Eli couldn't help but bark out a gritty laugh. "I have a feeling Hennessey would have your damn balls if he heard you say that."

Though frustration still burned in his hard gaze, Eric's lips twitched with a grin. "He could *try*."

Glancing at the clock on the wall, Elise said, "I hate to break this up, but Wyatt will be home soon. Do you guys want to stay for dinner?"

"Chelsea's making lasagna," Eric said, pushing away from the sink, "but why don't you guys come over and join us? I know she'd love to have you over."

"That would be fun," she said with a smile.

Eric's gray gaze returned to his. "Eli?"

Thinking that Carla might come along with his sister and Wyatt, he moved back to his feet and said, "Yeah, I can make it. I just need to head over to the cabin and grab a shower."

"I'll head out with you, then," Eric said. "I need a smoke."

They hugged Elise goodbye, leaving her to get ready, then walked out onto the front porch. He started to tell Eric he'd see him later, when his brother said, "I have one more question before you run off."

He sighed, propping his shoulder against one of the wooden posts that supported the porch's roof, and watched as Eric lit the cigarette he'd taken from the pack in his pocket. He'd have wagered every penny to his name that Eric's question was about Carla, his suspicions confirmed when his brother looked him in the eye and asked, "Is she the reason you've stayed away? I mean, once you heard that Dad and the League were dead and realized you could come back home? Is she the reason why you didn't?"

"Yeah," he rasped, taking the easy way out with that oversimplified response.

Eric's pale gaze searched his with piercing intensity. "And do you love her?"

A hollow laugh punched from his chest, and he started to shove his hands in his pockets, before realizing he still had the dishtowel wrapped around his shredded knuckles.

Exhaling a silvery stream of smoke, Eric frowned. "That's not an answer, man."

He rubbed his good hand over his mouth, then gave another heavy sigh. "I've been trying to figure out how I feel about her ever since she walked back into my life and punched me in the mouth."

His brother laughed. "That sounds like Carla."

Lips twitching with a wry smile, he said, "Yeah, she's definitely got a temper on her."

"So you gonna answer the question?" Eric pressed, taking another deep drag on his cigarette.

Eli shifted his gaze over Eric's shoulder, staring out at the forest, the heavy tree limbs swaying like giant beasts in the wind, and struggled to put his thoughts in some kind of order that made sense. A few moments later, he drew in a deep breath of the fresh mountain air, and gave his brother the truth. "Yeah, I love her," he said in a low voice that thrummed with emotion. "I loved her when I left, and despite all the bullshit I started to tell myself over the years, trying to stay away, I never stopped loving her." Looking away from the sky, he took another deep breath as he settled his gaze back on Eric. "Somehow, I love her even more now. So much that it's scaring the hell out of me."

Eric's dark brows were drawn with concern. "Because you're worried you'll lose her?"

"I'm worried about all of it," he admitted gruffly, scrubbing his hand down his face. "Her safety is part of it. I hate the danger she puts herself in, like she's got some kind of death wish. But then there's the fact that she keeps claiming to want her freedom. Not to mention the strong chance that she might never be able to forgive me for leaving her or learn to love me back. That she might get tired of it all and walk away for good." *Destroying our bond and leaving me with... nothing.*

With a sharp exhale, his brother said, "I get what you're saying, Eli. I really do. But you need to stop and take a long hard look at what Carla's capable of. She's not like our mother was. She's not...fragile."

He frowned, thinking the topic of his mother was the *last* thing he wanted to come up right now.

"And secondly," Eric was saying, "do you know what I remember most from when we were younger?"

He shook his head, eyeing his brother with a careful gaze.

Jerking his chin toward him, Eric said, "The way you never gave up, man, no matter what you were up against."

"This is different," he grunted.

"Oh, yeah?" Eric murmured, lifting his brows with a challenging look. "How?"

Grimacing, he crossed his arms back over his chest and said, "I can't *make* her forgive me, Eric. I can't force her to give me a second chance."

"And have you asked for one? For a second chance?"

He rubbed the back of his neck and cursed, realizing that all he'd actually told her was that he was sorry for hurting her…and that he wanted in her bed. He'd never really gotten around to explaining what he wanted *after* that, but then, she hadn't exactly given him the opportunity to.

"Eli, if you want her, let her know. Be honest with her. You'll never know what could have been if you aren't, and you'll end up regretting it till the day you die."

"I just don't kn…" He trailed off when he suddenly caught sight of a worried-looking Sayre running back into the Alley, her pale face flushed with color and her blue-gray eyes wide with panic.

"Jeremy!" she shouted, cupping her hands around her mouth as she stood just off to the side of Elise and Wyatt's porch.

Eric tossed his cigarette aside and raced down the steps with Eli right behind him. "Sayre, what's going on?" his brother asked the girl.

She turned toward them, grabbing Eric's arm as she started talking in a rush. "There's been a…a…damn it, I don't know what to call it."

"Just take a deep breath and tell us what happened," Eric said, while the hairs on the back of Eli's neck lifted as something inside him twisted with fear.

"A woman," Sayre panted, her knuckles turning white as she gripped Eric's arm even tighter. "A White-claw female…she escaped from Hawkley and came to us for help. But she wasn't alone. She was followed here by one of their soldiers."

"Jesus," Eric hissed. "Is she all right? Is everyone okay?"

"She'll be fine. Jillian is with her in the woods. Everyone's fine. But that man…he tried to kill her…and Carla… *Ohmygod*, she was so amazing!"

Eli's head jerked back as if he'd just been clipped on the chin. "Carla? What the hell was she doing there?"

"She must have shown up just before I did. I think we were both looking for Jillian, and Carla saved her. She saved them both," Sayre told them, her big eyes shining with shock as she looked from one to the other. "She put herself between them and that maniac—"

"She *what?*" Eli roared, making the young witch flinch.

"She saved the woman and Jillian. The woman was clinging to my sister for help, and he would have killed them both, but she saved them. It was the most incredible thing I've ever seen. I would have helped her, but by the time I realized what was happening, he was already going down."

"Sayre," he croaked, a cold sweat breaking out over his face, "where is the man now?"

She brought her wide eyes back to his, and blinked up at him. "He's dead."

"Dead?"

Voice soft with awe, she nodded and said, "Carla killed him."

Chapter 8

They'd brought the woman, who appeared to be in her early thirties and was named Rachel, back to Jeremy and Jillian's cabin. All the Runners were gathered in the couple's living room, along with Eli's men, ready to hear the full story.

Sayre had offered the woman a damp washcloth, which she was using to wipe the dirt and smears of blood from her bruised, tear-streaked face as she sat in a chair that'd been placed in front of the empty fireplace. Her eyes were wide with apprehension, moving from one person to another. She looked overwhelmed and more than a little frightened, but there was also a fierce sense of determination in her dark gaze that made Eli think she just might be the real deal, instead of a spy sent to infiltrate their ranks.

Of course, that didn't make him feel any calmer about what Carla had done.

Eli had managed to plant himself right at the little Bloodrunner's side the moment she'd entered the cabin, and he was still seething with fury. The Whiteclaw she'd taken down had been a goddamn behemoth. At least six-six, with probably more than a hundred pounds on her. He didn't know what the hell she'd been thinking.

While everyone was still getting situated, he kept his narrowed gaze focused on the woman as he spoke to Carla. "Do you have any idea what that asshole could have done to you?"

He'd kept his voice low, barely above a whisper, but knew she'd heard him from the stiffening of her posture. Then she asked, "Does it matter? Fighting him was a risk I was willing to take. Do you honestly think I would have just left Jillian there to deal with him herself?"

"She's powerful. She could have handled it."

"She's also *pregnant,* you ass. And like family to me. I would *never* turn my back on someone I cared about, no matter how dangerous the situation was."

He ground his back teeth together, ready to grab her arm and drag her to someplace private where they could talk. Yeah, it was a caveman move, but he was desperate enough to use it.

"Whatever you're thinking," said a deep voice on his other side, "I wouldn't try it."

He turned his head and found Wyatt watching him with a hard, steady gaze. Before he could tell the Runner to mind his own damn business, Wyatt said, "The two of you need to sort this out later. Right now, we need to hear what this woman has to say."

He jerked his chin in agreement, knowing it was the

right move, but still too pissed off to be civil about it. A few moments later, the room finally settled down, quieting, and he realized Rachel's dark gaze was focused intently on Carla. The woman lowered the washcloth to her lap, her fingers clenched around the damp cotton, and swallowed hard before saying, "You're the female Runner, aren't you?"

From the corner of his eye, Eli watched Carla give the woman a wary nod.

Tears glistened in Rachel's eyes as she whispered a heartfelt, "Thank you. Thank you so much."

At Carla's uncertain look, the woman lifted her chin and said, "You gave me the courage to fight back and escape. We all—the other women and I—we all heard about the half-human female who bested the White-claw soldiers in Hawkley and got away. It…you…what you did, it inspired us."

"Oh, um, that's…wonderful," Carla managed to get out, though he could tell by the huskiness of her voice that she'd been floored by what the woman had just said.

Sitting beside his wife, Torrance, on the arm of one of the leather sofas, Mason said, "Rachel, what is it that you want? Is there someplace you're trying to reach?"

Strands of short black hair stuck to her battered face as she shook her head, her watery gaze shifting to the tall Runner. "I…I want to stay here. I'm seeking sanctuary," she told him. "And I'm not the only one. There are others. They just…they don't know how to get away."

"But you did?"

More tears spilled over her pale cheeks as she shook her head again. "I would have brought them with me, but I…I didn't have a plan. I just saw the opportunity, and I took it. I knew that if I didn't, I might never get another one."

"How do we know you're for real?"

"Eric, don't," Chelsea murmured at his brother's side, grasping his hand in hers. Eli had only spoken to his brother's human life mate a few times, but he liked her. She was a beautiful woman, but more than that, she was…real. And as head over heels in love with his brother as Pallaton was with his sister.

"No, it's okay," Rachel murmured, taking a deep breath. "I understand why you would be concerned, given everything that my pack has done. But I can prove that I'm for real. I can…I can give you information."

Brody spoke up for the first time from his position against the far wall, between his wife and his Bloodrunning partner, Cian. "What kind of information?"

The woman wet her lips, then said, "I know where they've stored the drugs. The ones they take to make them stronger and mask their scents."

In a soft, lilting burr, Cian asked, "And why would you help us?"

A shudder worked its way through her narrow frame, making Eli wonder just what this woman had lived through with her pack. She cleared her throat, her gaze lowered to her lap as she scraped out, "Because of Roy's greed. It's…it's like a sickness. His arrogance is spreading, and the men are…they're out of control." Pulling in another deep, ragged breath, she lifted her head and locked her shattered gaze with Carla's, as if seeking strength as she quietly added, "They…they do whatever they want, to the ones like me. With the way things are now, any female who is unmated is considered…fair game."

"Christ," Jeremy muttered, dropping his chin on top of Jillian's head, his arms wrapped around her waist as they stood together with her back to his front.

Sayre, who was staying close to the woman's side in case she was needed, said, "The man who was chasing you. Who was he?"

"My cousin," she whispered thickly, turning her head to look at Sayre. "And a bastard."

"Will they come looking for him?" Carla asked, no doubt wondering what kind of fallout they might be facing from the kill that she'd made. Everyone in the room knew that it'd been justified, considering the Lycan had been ready to kill whoever got in his way—but Eli knew Carla would blame herself if anyone ended up hurt because of what she'd done.

Answering Carla's question, Rachel said, "I…I don't think so. He worked for Roy, monitoring the pack's stock of drugs, along with a few other Lycans. That's how I know where they're stored." Her shoulders shook as she explained, "When he drinks, he talks. Or…I mean, he *did*. But he's not so important that they would waste time trying to find him. Not with everything else they have going on."

"These stocks you mentioned," Mason said, drawing her attention back to him. "What can you tell us about them?"

"They're running low on the drugs they use on the girls—the human ones. But they have a large supply of the stuff that the soldiers take, because Roy bought so much when it was first created."

Recalling how Carla had mentioned the Fed who

was working to destroy the labs where the gang-rape drugs were being produced, Eli assumed that was why they were running low. But the fact that they still had a strong supply of the "super soldier" drugs was troubling.

"And what about the drug that Sebastian took?" Eric asked.

She looked confused. "Which one is that?"

Eli had heard about the drug that Sebastian Claymore had taken the day he'd kidnapped Elise and Carla. It had enabled the Lycan to shift more of his body during the daytime than was normal, as well as increased his size and strength. At the time, Sebastian had claimed to be working on an additional drug that would allow him to completely day-shift, and either drug could prove catastrophic for the Silvercrest if they were produced in mass quantities.

With his arm around Elise's shoulders, Wyatt answered the woman's question. "It's a drug that allowed him to shift more completely during the day. Not a complete shift, but enough that it was noticeable."

She shook her head. "I don't even know about that one."

"That's good," Brody rumbled. "Hopefully his personal supply was limited."

"Rachel," Eli murmured, drawing her attention to where he stood. "Could you draw a map that leads to the exact location where the drugs are stored?"

Nodding, she said, "Yes. I just need a pen and paper."

"I'll get it," Sayre murmured, heading out of the room, and Eli looked over at his men, who were standing together against the far wall, where they'd been quietly listening. Their expressions were hard with outrage, and each one jerked their chin in assent to his silent question. He nodded, then looked round at the Runners. "We're heading out."

Carla's slender fingers bit into his arm. "Now?" she asked, staring up at him with wide eyes as he turned his head to look at her. "Where the hell are you going?"

"If we're going to make full use of the intel, then we've got to move quickly, before they shift the drugs to a new location."

Her slender brows knitted together. "Then we'll make a plan."

"There's no time," he argued. "It might take them a while to realize that Rachel and her cousin are missing, but once they do, we've lost our window of opportunity. We've got to go now, before they can move their stock."

Determination hardened her gaze. "Then I'm going with you."

Over my dead body, he thought, hating that he had to pull his arm from her grip, now that she was finally touching him. But it'd be a cold day in hell before he ever let her set foot anywhere near that godforsaken town again. She'd been lucky to make it out alive the first time, and there wasn't going to be a second one.

Wondering just how angry he was about to make her, he said, "That's not gonna happen, Reyes. The guys and I are going in alone."

"The hell you are," Eric muttered, while the other Runners seconded him.

Looking around the room, Eli frowned. "This isn't personal. It's basic logic. The guys and I are trained for this kind of op, and we're used to pulling them off alone. Mixing things up at this point is only going to make it more dangerous."

His brother's scowl deepened. "That doesn't mean we're going to let you and your men fight our battles for us, Eli. That's not how this works."

"We're not trying to fight anyone's battles," he growled, hating that they were having this argument in front of a roomful of people. "I understand what you're saying, but the reason the guys and I are here is so that the Runners don't have to do everything on their own anymore. So don't be a stubborn jackass about this. Just stand down and let us get this done before it's too late."

Eric cursed under his breath, his metallic gray eyes molten with frustration. But he didn't shove another argument back in Eli's face. Instead, he exhaled a rough breath, and muttered, "Don't think I'll let you pull this shit again. This is your one pass. You get in, you get out, and then you get the hell back here."

Eli nodded at his brother, then cut his gaze back to Carla. She stared up at him with a dazed look on her pale face, as if she was still trying to figure out how this had happened. Fighting the urge to reach out and yank her into his arms, he turned away from her and told Rachel he'd be back for the map, then followed his guys out of the cabin.

Carla stared at the front door, after Eli and his men had left, and blinked like someone coming out of a long, deep sleep. She felt like she'd been hit over the head, her thoughts disordered, her pulse roaring in her ears like an engine that'd been revved too high.

No matter how hard she'd been trying to put him

from her mind, avoiding him as she worked herself into exhaustion, her dreams had been plagued by his irresistible presence. Deliciously raw, erotic dreams of the night they'd bonded. Of their hot, sweat-misted skin sliding together as he'd kissed and licked every inch of her he could reach, while rubbing his hard, heavy erection between her thighs, against the slick cushion of her sex. His dark voice whispering things so intimate and wicked, she'd been ready to come before he'd even started to push inside her. He'd been so big, so broad and long, she'd barely been able to take him. But she'd wanted to. She'd wanted to take…and take…until he'd emptied himself into her. Until she'd taken everything he had to give. All the hunger and passion and emotion burning inside him.

Emotion she'd so foolishly hoped was love.

Only, she'd been wrong. He hadn't loved her, and she'd had to accept that. But that didn't mean she didn't care about him. That she wasn't worried for his safety, especially when *she* was the one who'd brought him to the Alley.

Unable to just stand there and let him leave her, she hurried from the room, aware of the curious way the others were watching her, and ran after him. From the height of the porch, she looked across the glade, watching as he and Kyle climbed the porch steps of the cabin they were staying in, while the other three mercs went into the other one. She knew they would be collecting their gear, and she started running as fast as she could, determined to reach Eli before he could leave the privacy of his room. The things she needed to say to him were preferably done without an audience.

Without even bothering to knock, she let herself into

the cabin and hurried across the living room, down the hallway. She had no idea which room he was using, but she tracked his mouthwatering scent to the second doorway on the left. Opening the door, she quickly stepped into the room and pressed her back against the door as it closed, then reached back and flipped the lock. He was standing by a dresser that sat against the far wall, the dishtowel that had been wrapped around his battered knuckles earlier nowhere to be seen as he checked the clip on a heavy handgun—but his attention was no longer focused on the weapon. He'd looked up the second she'd opened the door, his narrowed gaze now locked in hard and tight on her own.

Pulling her lower lip through her teeth, she took a deep, shuddering breath and said, "Are you sure about this? About what you're doing?"

He looked away from her as he tucked the gun into the back of his jeans, then grabbed a thick, complicated watch off the dresser, hooking it around his powerful wrist. "Why wouldn't I be?"

"Damn it, it could all be a setup. She could be lying!"

"My gut tells me she isn't, but either way, we're good at what we do," he said in a low voice, still not looking at her as he turned and grabbed a set of keys off the bedside table. "They're not even going to know we're there."

Frustration, and no small amount of fear, made her want to scream as she asked, "How the hell do you know that?"

He turned his head, his dark gaze locking hard on hers again with a sharp, drilling intensity, and she could physically see the satisfaction building within him, burning in those incredible blue and gray eyes. "You're actually worried about me, aren't you?"

"No!" she snapped. But it was impossible to hide the way she was shaking...trembling...her damn heart pounding so swiftly it was making her dizzy.

Looking too impossibly gorgeous to be real, he fisted his big hands at his sides and started coming toward her, around the foot of the bed, each step making her breath come just that little bit faster, until she was panting. "If you don't give a shit about me, Rey, then why do you look so terrified?"

"Don't be so damn cocky! I brought you here to help us win. Not to go off taking ridiculous chances with your life!"

"And here I was thinking you didn't care if I lived or died." He stopped right in front of her, his heavy-lidded eyes burning with molten heat as he lowered his rugged face directly over hers. To her horror, her head went back in an embarrassing sign of submission for a female wolf, seeing as how it left her throat exposed and vulnerable, and it wasn't the first time that it'd happened with him.

Before he could call her on the telling action, she growled, "Shut up," and grabbed him behind the neck, yanking his head down as she rose up on her toes, crushing her mouth against his.

With her pulse still roaring in her ears, Carla kissed him like she wanted to crawl inside him. The way he growled deep in his chest and gripped her hips with his big hands, jerking her against his hard, muscular body, only made her more desperate. It took him no more than a heartbeat to claim control of the kiss, his tongue sinking into her mouth like he owned it, stroking and rubbing, tasting every slick part of her he could reach. It was so perfect, so freaking *right,* that she wanted to push him down to the floor, rip his jeans open, and take him. She needed to take him as deep as he could go, until she was packed full of him—until she owned him completely—which was nothing more than madness, considering she didn't own him at all. Not his body or his hunger…and sure as hell not his heart, and the pain of that knowledge was enough to make her want to curl into a ball on the floor and cry like a freaking baby.

God, what am I doing? she thought, as a jolting, searing wave of panic stormed through her, constricting her lungs so tightly she almost whimpered. On the verge of a meltdown, she ripped her mouth from his and shoved hard against the same broad shoulders she'd been digging her nails into only seconds before. She only managed to move him back a few inches, but it was enough of a gap for her to wrench her body to the side, out from between him and the door.

She'd made it maybe a foot when he grabbed her arm, hauling her close again, his color high and his lips parted for the harsh, erratic rhythm of his breaths. "Where do you think you're going?"

"I…I need out of here."

"What the hell, Carla?" Instead of fury, there was something burning in his eyes that looked too much like pain, and she blinked in shock as he growled, "You don't get to kiss me like you're fucking my mouth and then just walk away."

Sucking in a sharp breath, she said, "You walked away from me first. Then again at that damn motel!"

"And I've already said I was sorry!" he roared loud

enough for them to hear on the other side of the Alley. "You have no idea how much. I just…I needed to get my shit together. And I have. God knows I'm not going to let myself ruin this a second time."

She shook her head, hating the damn tears she could feel building behind her eyes. "I wish I could believe you, but I *can't.*"

"Don't," he rasped when she tried to pull her arm from his hold. "Please, Carla. *Christ,* don't walk away from me."

"Eli—"

"Please, just stay here with me for a minute," he said as he slowly reached for her other arm.

"What do you want from me?" she whispered, closing her eyes as he pressed her against the wall, covering her front with the breathtaking feel of his body. He was hard and hot and so blasted perfect it made her want to cry.

"I just want to make you feel good," he groaned against her temple, reaching between them and ripping at the button on her jeans, then sliding down the zipper. "I just need to be close to you, Rey, 'cause I've missed you so damn much."

"No," she gasped the instant his hot fingertips grazed the waistband of her panties.

He instantly stilled. "No?"

"I…I don't know." The husky, breathless words had been spoken in a needy voice she didn't even recognize as her own. "Damn it, I can't think straight when you're touching me."

He pressed his mouth to the corner of her eyebrow, the rush of his breath against her skin striking her as deliciously intimate. "Tell me to stop, baby, and I'll stop. But if you don't, I'm going to put my fingers in your sweet little body again and make you come so hard you scream."

Knowing damn well that she couldn't resist him, even when there was every chance this was going to be something she regretted, she dug her fingers into his thick hair and pulled his mouth back to hers, kissing him with every ounce of visceral emotion that was raging inside her. With every bit of passion and fury and heartbreak he'd ever made her feel, and he made a hard, thick sound deep in his chest, his tall body shuddering against her. He gripped the back of her neck, holding her in place for his marauding mouth, and the next thing she knew the hand between her legs was inside her panties, the heat of his palm making her moan. Then his fingers separated her, sliding between the slippery folds, before two of them circled the tender opening there and pushed hard inside her. They were big enough to make her breath hitch, her body still unused to a man's touch after so many years of being alone. Long and wickedly skilled, they filled her perfectly, stretching her open as he started to plunge them in and out of her in a greedy, driving rhythm that made her breathless and achy for more. She was so wet the movement of his fingers was making slick, moist sounds in the quiet stillness of the room, but she was too lost in the way it felt to be embarrassed.

Pressing his forehead against hers, he growled, "You feel so damn perfect, it's unreal, Rey."

Then the callused pad of his thumb settled against her swollen clit, rubbing the sensitive bundle of nerves with a firm, steady pressure, and that was it. He might have left her hanging in that motel room the other night—but not this time. With a hoarse cry on her lips, she crashed into a sizzling, searing orgasm, the shattering pulses of pleasure exploding through her like an unstoppable force of nature, filling her with heat. Her head shot back as her thighs trembled, her body completely open and vulnerable to him. To whatever he wanted to give her...take from her.

He lowered his head and nipped at the side of her throat, licking his tongue over her thrashing pulse, his big hand still buried between her legs, and he kept shoving his fingers into her drenched, clutching tissues until she was gripping them so tightly he could barely move them. "God, baby, that was the hottest thing I've ever felt," he said against her shoulder, his soft hair tickling her jaw. "Only thing that could be better is feeling you do that when I'm buried inside you."

Her lips twitched with a grin that she couldn't hold back, loving the way he talked to her. The way he wasn't shy about letting her know how he felt and what he wanted—at least when it came to sex.

Still feeling languid and drowsy with pleasure, she was sad when she felt him carefully work his fingers free, then pull his hand from between her legs. Needing to see his face—to see if he looked even half as shattered as she felt—she managed to crack her eyes open just in time to catch him putting those two glistening fingers in his mouth. They were drenched in her juices, and she thought it was the most erotic thing she'd ever seen, watching him swallow her flavor down his throat, while a thick, purely male sound of appreciation rumbled up from deep in his chest.

"Christ, that's incredible," he groaned, licking between his knuckles after he'd pulled his fingers free.

"Like warm, salted caramel and cream. Rich and sweet and fucking delicious." His heavy-lidded gaze burned with hunger, and he placed his damp hand against the side of her face as he said, "I would drown in you right now if I had the time."

She blinked, too steeped in residual pulses of pleasure to understand what he meant. "Time?" *Why doesn't he have the time?*

His cock was a rigid, throbbing, impossibly thick ridge behind the fly of his jeans, and he pressed even harder against her, before giving a rough groan and taking a step back, pulling away from her. "I bloody hate it, Rey, but I've got to go. If I don't, Kyle's gonna come back here looking for me."

"Oh, God." She gasped for breath, feeling like she'd just had a bucket of ice-cold water thrown in her face. Frantically trying to sort out her jeans, she hissed, "I don't believe this! They're going to know what we were doing!"

He scowled as he crossed his arms over his wide chest, pinning her with a sharp, penetrating stare. "And what's so wrong about that?"

"Everything. Everything is wrong!" She covered her face with her hands, trying to get control, her emotions in chaos. "Damn it, I came back here to talk some sense into you. Not to…to…" Lowering her hands, she reached out and fisted them in the front of his shirt. "Please…you can't do this, Eli. It's too dangerous."

His scowl softened, but the look in his eyes remained hard and determined. Taking hold of her wrists, he said, "This is what you brought me here to do, Rey. To make a difference."

"But I didn't expect you to go waltzing into the middle of their freaking town! And in broad daylight!"

"I'm not waltzing into the middle of it. Odds are good they'll never even know we're there, and if they do, we'll handle it."

His calm, even tone just made her want to howl with frustration. "I can't do this," she said unsteadily, her throat shaking. "You have me so confused."

"Don't," he growled, sounding like a man who'd just been shoved to the end of his patience. "You don't get to give me *that*—what just happened between us—and then rip it away."

"Eli—"

The next thing she knew, his hands were gripping the sides of her head and he was taking her mouth again, ravaging it, his tongue sliding against hers in an explicit show of hunger that damn near melted her down into an embarrassing puddle of need and lust and tears on the floor.

Lifting his head, he locked his hard, narrowed gaze with hers, and said, "When I get back, we're finishing that."

"No. We—"

"It's happening, Carla." He opened the door and went into the hallway, then turned his head and cut her a smoldering, devastating look over his shoulder. "So be ready."

Chapter 9

Hours later, Eli returned to the Alley just in time to change into a clean shirt and head over to the clearing where the ceremony was taking place that night. No way in hell did he want to miss this.

He'd gotten a call from Mason on his way back from Hawkley, letting him know that there'd been a meeting. Given how things were escalating, the Runners had gone ahead and asked Max Doucet and Elliot Connors to take their Bloodrunning vows early, before their official training took place. Max, a human who'd been turned Lycan, was Brody's brother-in-law, while Elliot was a Silvercrest Lycan who'd been befriended by Max and the Runners after getting caught up in some serious trouble with Stefan's followers.

Though Eric could have had his own ceremony weeks ago, he'd decided to wait and take his oath at the same time as his friends. Elise had told him that Eric was close to both of the young men, and they'd been honored that he wanted to share their ceremony with them.

And now that ceremony would be taking place in a few minutes, in a clearing not far from the Alley.

Though the Bloodrunning Laws were no longer considered in effect, the Runners had decided that it was important to uphold tradition and mark the occasion with the proper respect, and Eli couldn't help but agree with their thinking. The Runners' oath wasn't about pack law, but about pledging one's self to the responsibilities of the job and the friends who would always have your back, no matter the circumstances, as they'd proven time and again. Though he'd never had much interaction with the Runners before, the recent days he'd spent there in the Alley had shown him that they were everything Carla had always believed them to be, and while he still hated the danger that came with her job, he was glad that she'd always had this close-knit group to look out for her. To be there for her.

God only knew her mother had never done that.

And as much as it pained him to admit it, neither had he.

As he reached the edge of the clearing, he was glad to see that the area had been lit with torches, making it easier to search for that familiar golden head of hair. Looking out over the crowd, he spotted Carla almost immediately and headed her way, surprised by how many people were there. His men were still back at the Alley, cleaning up before they came over, and he wondered what they were going to make of this. If they'd be as surprised as he was, or if they'd just take it all in stride, same as they'd been doing since their arrival. In a lot of ways, he felt that they were more comfortable there than he was—which was no one's fault but his own. Instead of the scorn he'd prepared himself to deal with from both the Bloodrunners and his pack, he'd received nothing but friendly acceptance. A fact he was still trying to wrap his head around.

Moving through the crowd, he was stopped by several of the Runners and their wives, who wanted to tell him they were glad to see he'd made it back in one piece. Thankfully, the trip he and his men had taken to Hawkley had been a success. A bloody one, it turned out, but well worth the trouble. With some well-placed explosives, they'd managed to destroy the storage building where the drugs were being kept, and made it out of the town without any injuries to their group, though they'd had to face off against two units of Whiteclaw soldiers as they made their escape.

Once they'd made it back to the Alley, Eli had been so eager to see Carla again, he hadn't even taken the time to shower. The memory of what they'd done against his bedroom wall before he'd left was burned into his brain like a brand, and he wanted her so badly it was damn near impossible to function. He'd never had such a pathetic lack of control, and he had to choke back a deep rumble of laughter and shake his head at himself, seeing as how she'd managed to make him feel like a randy teenage boy drowning in hormones when he was anything but. Hell, he'd be pushing forty in just a few years.

When he finally reached her side, he pulled in a hungry breath, just letting her warm scent soak into his system, and deliberately didn't say anything, hoping she'd be the one to speak first, so that he could gauge her mood. But aside from a slight flaring of her nostrils, she didn't so much as bat a lash at his arrival. Then someone shoved between him and the person standing on his left, and the little Runner stiffened as he was forced to press up against her side, the touch of her arm against his making him have to fight for control. But her reaction... *Shit*. He had to choke back a frustrated curse, because it was suddenly obvious as to what *she* was going to do. That she was going to keep fighting him, doing her best to resist the powerful, make-him-ache-for-her-down-in-his-bones attraction that kept pulling them together.

He could react the way he usually did, and get pissy with her. Or...he could try to play it cool for once, and see if maybe she wasn't just feeling a bit unsure after what had happened before he'd left.

Leaning down, he put his mouth close to her ear, and murmured, "Stay close to me."

"What?" She turned her head, and their faces were so close she nearly hit him in the nose. "Why?"

The corner of his mouth kicked up at the sight of her disgruntled expression. God, he really did have it bad when the woman's scowl started to strike him as adorable. Answering her question, he said, "First, because I like having you there, which shouldn't come as a surprise. And second, I believe in being cautious."

She didn't say anything more as she turned her attention back to the center of the circle that'd been marked in the ground, where Mason was standing with Eric, Max and Elliot. He didn't know if her silence meant that she'd agreed with him, or if she simply didn't want to bother with an argument, but he was glad she didn't try to storm off, and he moved to stand behind her as the crowd pressed in around them, using his body to keep her back protected.

The Lycans who were currently working as scouts with the Runners, as well as those who'd volunteered for training, had been invited tonight, and from the size of the crowd, it looked as though most of them had come. There was also a large group of teenagers there, and he recalled Jeremy explaining to him over a beer the other night that both Max and Elliot had been working with the teens who were left traumatized by the brainwashing bullshit his father had tried to pull.

Running his gaze over the gathering, it was as if he could physically *see* the bridge between the Alley and Shadow Peak being built right before his eyes. The Runners were no longer regarded as the dirty little secret that the pack needed, but didn't want to think about. Instead, they were now the soldiers who were going to lead the Silvercrest Lycans to victory or die trying, and the presence of so many pure-bloods tonight was an unmistakable show of respect that Eli was damn glad to witness.

In the face of war, it truly seemed that the pack was starting to heal the wounds that had been caused by so many years of racism, and he almost wished his old man could have been there to see it. That Stefan could have been there to witness how instead of destroying the Runners, his actions had only made them more powerful.

Mason's deep voice asking everyone for their attention drew his focus back to the circle, and he watched as Eric, Max and Elliot knelt in the grass before the tall Runner. Eli was more than a little curious about what exactly the ceremony would entail, listening with interest as Mason asked the three males to recite their Bloodrunning oaths. There was an almost dreamy, hypnotic feeling to the event, and he swayed forward just as Carla swayed back, their bodies coming together and staying that way as they watched and listened. With each of his slow, deep breaths, he was pulling more of her addictive scent into his lungs, and he couldn't stop himself from settling his hands on her narrow waist. She jolted a little at the contact, then settled, and he had to force himself not to hold her too tightly, lest he scare her away. She was as skittish as a colt when it came to letting him get close to her, and he was going to be damned before he did anything to ruin this peaceful moment.

He lowered his gaze for a few seconds, his height allowing him a breathtaking view of the front of her body, the tightness of her nipples against the cotton shirt that she wore making his mouth water, while most of the blood in his body started heading south. Knowing damn well that he was playing with fire, he forced himself to look away, shifting his attention back to the ceremony. His eyes shot wide open when he spotted Mason sliding a lethal-looking blade over his palm, blood instantly welling from the wound.

What the hell?

Before he could ask Carla what was happening, she'd pulled away from him and was walking into the circle, toward the others. He was on the verge of going after her, until he realized *all* the Runners were moving into the circle with her. One by one, they flanked Mason, then cut their palms as the blade was passed between them. He winced in sympathy for her hand, knowing that had to have hurt, though you wouldn't have known it by looking at her. She stood with her head high and her shoulders back, a proud smile on her beautiful mouth as the knife was passed to Eric. His brother used the crimson blade that'd been stained with each Runner's blood to slice his own palm, before passing it to Max, who cut his palm and then passed the blade on to Elliot, who did the same.

When the blade was offered back to Mason, he signaled for the three newly appointed Bloodrunners to stand, then announced that the ceremony had been completed. Everyone cheered until the noise could probably be heard all the way up in Shadow Peak, and then the crowd slowly began to disperse. Eli made his way through the crush as quickly as he could, heading toward Carla and his brother, and he couldn't help but notice that the women were all smiling at him as he passed by them, while the men jerked their chins in greeting, and an unfamiliar sense of rightness swept through him.

He didn't know *why* he felt at home here, but he was starting to realize that he did. He'd never been friendly with the Runners. Hell, his old man would have died before allowing it. But Eli had always held a respect for the half-breeds that he kept carefully hidden. Just as he'd done with almost every other real emotion he'd ever felt when he'd been forced to live under Stefan Drake's thumb. Which, when he thought about it, just made him a pathetic jackass who hadn't been able to make the hard choice and off the sick bastard when he'd had the chance, the way he should have done.

Instead, he'd run when given the opening, and he hadn't looked back. Not even when he realized that without him there, his father would be left to wreak havoc over the pack, and there would be no one to stop him. Eric had never truly been allowed into that inner circle of evil, so he hadn't known just how twisted Stefan had become, and Elise had simply avoided their father as much as possible. And as awful as it sounded, in the beginning, it hadn't bothered him. Hell, for the first time in his life, he'd been able to take a deep breath without feeling as if he was sucking in his father's foul spirit with every inhalation. But the feeling hadn't lasted long. As the days flowed into weeks, he'd felt more than just his abandonment of Reyes. He'd felt the pain of being cut off from his brother and sister…and yeah, even his pack. Had felt the separation from the land that had rooted its way into his blood and sweat and bones as he'd grown into a man. And yet, despite all the years he'd lived in Shadow Peak, he could honestly say that he'd never felt as connected to the town as he did to the Alley and the men and women who lived there.

Though he was as pure-blooded as a Lycan could be, he'd never truly made a place for himself in the pack. He'd been an insider on the innermost circle of pack power, thanks to his father—but an outsider all the same. Maybe that was why he fit *here,* with the rest of his rough group of friends. They were each outcasts, and yet, he would have bet anything on the fact that Kyle and the guys felt a draw to this place that was similar to his own.

Reaching the Runners, he immediately pulled Eric into a bone-crushing hug that made everyone around them laugh, including Carla, who was wrapping a strip of cloth around her wounded hand. "Congratulations, little brother. I'm damn proud of you."

"Thanks," Eric grunted, hugging him back just as hard. "That means a lot to me."

They slapped each other on the back, then stepped apart. He turned to congratulate Max and Elliot, who were both all smiles and excitement, and found Carla standing with his brother and sister when he turned back around. Pushing his hands in his pockets, he stayed back and watched her talk with his siblings, and realized that while he was gaining perspective about *his* place in the pack, when it came to the sexy little Runner, he was still...lost. But he wasn't going to let it hold him back.

He hadn't been lying when he'd told Eric that he loved her, and he knew it was a goddamn miracle that she hadn't found anyone to replace him in the last three years—that the bond had tied her to him even when he wasn't there to fight for his place by her side. If she didn't still feel something for him, he didn't think it would have worked out like this. But it had, and she was still his for the taking if he could only convince her to give him another chance.

Christ, it would probably be the most difficult, painful thing he'd ever done. But he was determined to do whatever it took.

Even if it means baring my soul to her.

Looking around this close-knit group, he could see the intimacy of the connections between the Runners and their mates. These men were rough and rugged and ruthless, and probably at one point as opposed to making themselves vulnerable as Eli was. But they'd done it. They'd been brave enough to be honest with their women, and by God, he was determined to do the same.

If the choices were between having a shot at her and losing her forever, then he'd tell her whatever she wanted to know. The good, the bad, and the ugly—though the good would definitely be in short supply. And the sooner he did it, the better, because he'd already wasted too many years. Too many damn nights spent cold and alone, when she should have been in his arms, where she belonged. Now he didn't want to lose another minute of the time they had with each other.

Moving to stand beside her again, he looked down into her beautiful eyes and asked, "Walk back with me?"

To his surprise, she nodded, and he grabbed her uninjured hand before she could pull it away, his tight hold letting her know that he wasn't going to just let her go. She sighed, but didn't drag her feet as he set off through the moonlit woods.

"I see you made it back in one piece," she murmured.

Moving a low hanging branch out of their way, he said, "We ran into a few foot soldiers on our way out, after destroying the storage facility, but they were easy to deal with." He squeezed her hand, sliding her a playful wink when she looked his way. "I promise all your favorite pieces are still in good working order."

She gave a feminine snort as she shook her head. "Nice one."

"It made you smile. That's all I was after."

"Well, then, you're an easy man to please."

He shot her a wicked look. "When it comes to you I am."

She responded with something under her breath that was lost in the wind as it swept through the trees, rustling the leaves on their branches. It was a warm night, the stars glittering in the velvety blackness of the skies like diamonds that'd been scattered across its surface, while crickets chirped in the underbrush. With each breath that he took, Eli could scent the surrounding forest, a melting blend of pine and loam and musk, and it settled him enough that he trusted himself to walk beside her without taking her to the fertile ground and claiming her then and there.

But he'd have been lying through his teeth if he'd said he wasn't thinking about it.

Coughing to clear the knot of lust in his throat, he asked, "Do you want to hit the celebration?"

"I was actually planning on just heading back to Wyatt and El's. I'm pretty beat after today."

Hearing the tiredness in her soft voice, he gave her hand another gentle squeeze. "Then I'll walk you over."

A few minutes later, they'd skirted the outside of the Alley, avoiding most of the crowd, and were climbing the front porch steps to Wyatt and Elise's cabin. Hating that it was time to say goodbye, he was surprised when she turned to him and asked, "Do you, um, want to come inside for a while? I'm sure Wyatt and Elise will spend some time celebrating with the others. Or were you planning on going for Eric?"

"He's not expecting to see me there," he said in a low voice, searching her face for signs of what she was thinking. "But I have to be honest with you, Rey. If I come inside, I won't be able to keep my hands off you."

Her eyes widened a little, then darkened, but she didn't say anything. So he didn't know what the hell to expect when she pulled her hand from his, took her keys from her pocket, and used the one Wyatt had given her to unlock the door. She stepped inside, then turned to face him. "I don't want you to leave," she told him, flicking her tongue across her plump lower lip in an endearing sign of her nerves. "But you should know that I'm not ready to have sex with you. Despite what you said before you left about finishing what we'd started, that's not what this is."

Stepping into the house, he took a deep breath as he shut the door, then slowly exhaled. Holding her dark gaze, he said, "It's killing me that you feel that way, but I'm not going to argue with you. If you need me to be patient, then I can be patient."

She started to respond, but he cut her off as he stepped forward, closing the distance between them. There was a lot he needed to say, but she didn't look like a woman who needed to have her ear talked off at the moment. No, she looked like a woman who needed to have her man take care of her, pleasuring her until she was boneless and as soft as sun-warmed taffy. And that was something he could definitely give her.

Her head tilted back as he looked down into her beautiful face, and he was glad to see the color in her cheeks as he said, "But no more pushing me away, Carla."

She swallowed, her chest rising as she pulled in a slow breath.

Cupping the side of her face in one hand, he ran his thumb over the smooth surface of her lower lip, and quietly said, "Not from this mouth." His other hand slid down her side, and then he reached between her legs, cupping her there. "And not from *this*. I'll find a way to keep some measure of control tonight, but this time I'm tasting you or I'll die."

She pulled her lower lip away from his thumb, dragging it through her teeth. "You never tried to do that before," she said in a voice that was so soft and sexy, he could literally *feel* all the blood in his body rushing south, settling thickly in his groin.

Scooping her up into his arms, Eli kept his eyes on hers as he carried her across the living room, toward the hallway. "I'd waited too long to finally get my hands on you," he explained in a rough, gravelly rumble. "Once I did, all I could think about was getting inside you and staying there. But it was always something I wanted, Rey. The first time I saw you after you'd turned eighteen, I knew *exactly* what I wanted to do to you."

Her pupils were dilated, breaths falling soft and fast from her parted lips as she pointed to the door of her room. He carried her inside, then closed it with his booted foot and asked her to turn the lock. There was a soft spill of light coming from the bathroom, falling across the bed, and his goddamn hands were shaking by the time he laid her down there, in the midst of the rumpled bedding that carried her sumptuous scent. He came down over her, caging her beneath his body, his weight braced on his forearms as he settled his hips between her open legs, pressing against her. His breath hissed through his teeth, and he ground his jaw, forcing himself to pull back, knowing damn well he was tempting fate. By some miracle, he'd managed to rein his beast in when he'd touched her that afternoon—but he knew his hold on the animal was tenuous at best. He prayed it was smart enough to know that if ever there was a time to behave itself, it was now. She wanted him, but she was skittish…and unsure…and still as angry and hurt and suspicious as she'd been since the moment she'd walked back into his life.

So tonight was going to be about making her feel good—and then tomorrow he'd go back to battle for her heart and her forgiveness and the future that he wanted so badly he could taste it.

"You're so incredibly beautiful," he whispered, lowering his head and pressing his lips against the tender base of her throat, where her pulse was fluttering madly. He groaned with pleasure when her hands dug their way into his hair, clutching at the strands. "Is your palm okay?" he asked, worried that she was in pain.

"What palm?" she murmured, making him smile as his lips coasted over her collarbone.

Ignoring the ache throbbing low in his body, he knelt between her legs and reached for the hem of her shirt, shoving it up under her chin. In the next second, he had the cups of her bra pulled down, the soft light spilling over her lush, pink-tipped breasts, and with a thick sound of hunger, he covered one of the pretty nipples with his mouth, sucking hard enough to arch her back.

"Eli… *Oh, God*," she moaned, shivering, her hands tangling in his hair as she held him to her even tighter, pushing herself against his face. Breathing hard and fast, he pulled back, releasing the swollen nipple with a wet pop, and quickly moved to the other one, lashing it with his tongue, before sucking it between his lips and hungrily working it against the roof of his mouth.

"Next time I'm doing that for hours," he groaned when he finally pulled away, kissing his way down her trembling stomach, while his hands ripped at the button on her jeans, damn near destroying the zipper as he fought to get it down. She was panting, her eyes heavy with need as she stared at him, and he almost ripped the legs of her jeans as he yanked them down and off, needing to get to her so badly he was shaking. The tiny white panties keeping him from what he wanted tore off with a sibilant hiss as he ripped them apart, and then he was *there,* and *oh, shit,* he was going to completely lose it because she was so damned *perfect.*

Unable to wait, he shoved her thighs wider, opened her with his thumbs as he leaned down, and covered her with his open mouth, a thick sound of raw pleasure burning at the back of his throat the instant his tongue touched her drenched, silky flesh. He shuddered, unable to believe it was even better than he'd imagined it would be, his greed for her like a physical thing inside him, keeping company with his wolf. He loved the way she felt against his lips and tongue, so tender and soft. Was already addicted to her taste, it was so warm and lush and sweet. He wanted to feel her come undone against his face more than he'd ever wanted any goddamn thing in his entire life, and he wasn't shy about making it happen, shoving his tongue inside that tiny opening as deep as he could go. His mouth was nothing short of ravenous as he went completely wild on her, his fingers biting into her firm thighs as he shoved her legs even farther apart, needing her completely open to him.

"What are you doing?" she gasped moments later, when he pushed up on one arm, staring hard at her flushed face as she slowly came down from a wrenching, devastating orgasm that had pulsed against his tongue like a heartbeat, her taste so intoxicating he knew he wouldn't ever be able to get enough of it. "Eli?"

His voice was low, and as guttural as a growl. "I'm watching you come undone for me, Rey."

When he pushed two thick fingers inside that narrow, slippery opening, she gasped, "It's too much."

"Like hell it is," he shot back, licking his wet lips. "It's not nearly enough."

Before she could argue, he'd lowered his head again, his open mouth covering her hot, slick folds, while his tongue rubbed her hard little clit, then plunged back inside her. Deep, dark, hungry. He was consuming her. Making her melt into thick, honeyed liquid, which just made him feast on her even more savagely, until his low, guttural groans were drowning out the sounds of the celebration taking place outside the cabin.

He could have kept his mouth on her forever. She was that perfect. That sweet. That goddamn *necessary* to him.

She came again, even harder this time, her cries deliciously hoarse as her body pulsed and pulsed, coming completely undone for him. He gentled his mouth, licking her with soft, careful strokes, while his own body hardened to the point where he feared he might burst, his blood pumping so fast through his veins he could hear it roaring in his ears.

He hoped to God that she'd changed her mind about intercourse, because if he didn't get inside her soon, there was every chance it was going to break him. Turn him into the mindless, instinctual beast that lived at his core in a transformation that could never be undone, the reason of the man lost forever beneath that primal force of madness. He'd heard of it happening to Lycans who'd been pushed to the ends of their sanity, and God only knew he could feel that point nearing, drawing closer…and closer.

"Carla," he breathed out in a harsh rasp, resting his forehead against her sleek thigh. "I *need* you."

He flinched when he felt her stiffen, instead of melting in surrender. She quickly scrambled out from beneath him, leaving him kneeling in the middle of the bed while she huddled against the headboard, her golden hair a wild tangle around her flushed face, her pleasure-hazy eyes shocked wide with panic.

"I…I can't," she whispered, shaking her head. "I told you…I'm not ready. Not for…that. Not with everything still so…so…"

He pulled in a deep breath as he gripped the back of his neck with one hand, struggling to think through the fog of hunger and craving and searing emotion that was clouding his brain. "Don't you feel it?" The next words spilling from his lips stunned him even more than they did her. "Don't you want me anymore?"

"Of course I do. Of course I feel it! But that doesn't mean I have to give into it."

"Why, Rey? Why the hell do you keep fighting it?" He moved off the bed and back to his feet, standing at the side of the mattress as he stared down at her. "I've said I was sorry, and I meant it. I screwed up and it's killing me inside. But I never meant to hurt you, and for that I am so damn *sorry*."

"It doesn't change anything, Eli."

"It could, if you would let it," he grunted, shoving a hand back through his hair in frustration.

"Look," she said after she'd taken a careful breath, seeming to brace herself. "I…I don't want to be one of those women who bitches and moans about how upset she is, but never has the guts to just say what the problem is."

He waited, alert, heart practically climbing its way up the back of his throat. "I'm listening," he scraped out.

Pulling the sheet around her body, she moved off the other side of the bed, staring back at him over the mattress. A mere distance of feet that could have been miles for the way it felt to him. "When it comes right down to it," she told him, "I don't trust you. You…you completely *shattered* me when you left. And it was so…so toxic, because I had to hold it all inside, since no one even knew about you…about us, because you'd made it pretty clear you didn't want anyone to know. Jillian figured it out…but that wasn't until much later. There was no one I could turn to. No one to hold me when I cried myself to sleep every night. It just…it ate away at me. Changed me."

"Rey—"

"No," she whispered, holding up her hand when he started to head around the foot of the bed. "Just let me get this done."

He nodded as he forced himself to stand still, his throat so tight he could barely swallow.

She wet her lips, blinked a few times, then went on. "Now you're back, and you've suddenly started talking like you want more—a second chance. And messing around is one thing. Basic biology says that we're desperate for each other because we haven't been able to scratch this itch in three years, while the bond is doing everything it can to try and pull us together. So it's obvious why we're so hot for each other. But we have nothing, no reason whatsoever, to keep going with this thing on an emotional level."

"You're wrong," he growled, hating that she felt that way. That she was even *thinking* that way, her words ripping his insides to shreds.

"Eli—"

"You want a reason, Rey? Because I have one for you. The fact that I'm falling *in love* with you all over again is a hell of a good reason."

She paled so quickly she looked like she was bleeding out. "No...that's not true. It can't be."

Unable to stop the words now that they'd finally broken free, he said, "Or maybe rediscovering is a better word. I never fell out of love with you. Not for one moment, Rey. I just buried it. Hid from it." He took a few more steps that brought him closer, hating that he wasn't holding her. "And now you're going to try to hide from it, too, because you're scared. But you should trust me when I tell you that it won't work, baby. It won't work for shit."

She lowered her head, her shoulders shaking, and he quickly made his way around the bed, desperate to reach her. But when he placed his fingers under her chin and lifted her precious face to his, the sight of the tears spilling from her eyes made him feel like acid had been poured into his veins. "Christ, don't do that," he groaned, swiping at the tears with his thumb. "Please, Rey. It's breaking my heart."

"Why? Why are you d-doing this to me?" she cried, shaking so hard her teeth were chattering. "If I'd thought you were g-going to...to do this... *Damn it*, I never would have gone after you!"

Pushing her hair back from her face, he said, "I

would have come back, anyway, Rey. That wasn't a lie. And I'm so damn sorry. For everything."

She squeezed her eyes shut, forcing more tears to spill down her cheeks. "Just tell me what you want."

Roughly, he said, "I want you to forgive me."

"Eli—"

He cut her off, his voice even rougher than before. "Because I meant it when I said that I love you, Carla. I loved you before, and I love you even more now."

"Oh, God," she breathed, her face white as she opened her eyes and stepped away from him, stumbling back. "I just...I need you to go, Eli. Please, just go."

Frustration filled him so quickly he was surprised he didn't burst with it. "That's not going to solve anything. Stop pushing me away."

She sniffed, swiping at her tears. "I'm not pushing. I just...I need some time to think."

He opened his mouth, then clamped it shut, knowing that shouting at her would solve nothing. And that's exactly what he wanted to do at that moment, his beast as angry and frustrated as the man, prowling beneath his skin; a visceral, possessive creature that wanted to break free and claim what it damn well knew belonged to them.

Jesus, maybe I do need to get out of here.

"Please, Eli. If you mean it," she whispered unsteadily, "and you want me to be able to deal with this, then you have to give me the chance to think it through. *Please.*"

It went against every single natural instinct he possessed, but he knew she was right. Staying right now wasn't going to make anything better for either one of them. Not when the only thing he could think about was completing the bond and permanently marking her little ass as *his*.

Hating the brutal knife being twisted in his chest—the knife he understood all too well that *he'd* put there—he gave her what she'd asked for, and walked out the door.

Chapter 10

Climbing out of the truck, Eli squinted against the bright rays of afternoon sunlight and looked for Carla in the crowd that had gathered to meet him and his men, as well as Brody and Cian, who had come along with them this time.

Thanks to Rachel, who was currently staying with Eric and Chelsea, their mission that afternoon had been a success. With her help and knowledge of the area and its back roads, they'd been able to pinpoint the location of a weapons stockpile in Hawkley that Roy had been putting together and form a plan for going after them. It'd been a long shot, and while they knew that what they'd found wasn't the pack's entire supply, they'd managed to drive away with a hell of a lot of guns that would now be used to protect Silvercrest lives, rather than destroy them.

Though the building they'd targeted had been on the outskirts of the town, Eli had hoped to catch a glimpse of some of the women and children who lived there, ready to take them back with them if that's what they wanted, but it was just as Rachel had said. The Whiteclaw were cocky enough to leave their munitions poorly protected, but they had the female residents of the town on lockdown, refusing to let them outdoors.

And if Bartley and his men had already arrived, then they were keeping a low profile, because they hadn't seen a single one of the mercenaries during the two ops that they'd pulled off.

"Jeremy!" he called out as soon as he caught sight of the blond Runner coming across the glade to meet them. "We need Jillian! Lev took a bullet in the shoulder!"

"On it!" the Runner called back, changing direction as he headed back toward his cabin. "Just get him over to our place!" he threw over his shoulder.

James was helping Lev out of the backseat, the blond merc murmuring something about how it must be his lucky day, seeing as how he was finally being allowed near the pretty little witches.

"By the way," Brody murmured as Lev walked past him holding a wad of cloth against his wounded shoulder. "You flirt with either Jillian or Sayre, and Jeremy's liable to kill you."

Lev's white teeth flashed in a grin. "No worries, man. I'll be an absolute angel."

Kyle snorted. "Seeing as how that's impossible, I should probably say goodbye to you now, Slivkoff."

Everyone laughed, easing some of the tension that had settled over the group when they'd learned of Lev's injury, and Eli's skin prickled with awareness when Carla finally approached him, just as he was shoving his keys into the front pocket of his jeans.

"How'd it go?" she asked, a slight flush on her cheeks as she pushed her hands in her pockets. This was the first time they'd been relatively alone since last night, the others all heading off in different directions, and he wondered if she was embarrassed about what had happened between them in her bedroom, or if that flush had something to do with what he'd told her. Or, hell, maybe she was just warm. For all he knew, she hadn't even thought about his emotional confession after he'd left her and headed back to his cabin—which had been one of the hardest goddamn things he'd ever had to do.

But as much as he wanted to be pissed at her for reacting that way, he knew that wasn't fair. Like she'd told him last night, the things he'd done in the past had killed her trust, and if he wanted her—and if he ever wanted to hear a similar declaration of love come from her own lips—then he had to be willing to put in the time and effort to rebuild it.

It wasn't something that was going to come overnight, no matter how badly he wished it could be like that, because this wasn't a damn fairy tale. But it was something he'd fight for until he'd drawn his last breath. He wasn't going to give up.

Not now. Not ever.

Shoving a hand back through his windblown hair, he held her dark gaze as he answered her question. "We got some of the weapons, but it can't be their entire stock. They've probably already distributed the heavy-duty stuff to their soldiers."

With a nod, she asked, "Is Lev going to be all right?"

A grin tugged at the corner of his mouth. "Didn't you hear him?"

She gave a soft, feminine snort. "Yeah, but from what I can tell, he *always* sounds like that."

"Don't worry about him," he murmured. "He'll be fine."

"So about the weapons. You know this kind of thing is just gonna piss them off, right?"

"I sure as hell hope it does. We're going to have our plans ready to go in the next day or two, and after learning what's happening in that town, the sooner we can give those women the chance to escape, the better."

"I agree with all that," she told him, as they both started to walk across the glade, "but was it really necessary to take such a risk? I mean, you went in broad daylight again, just the day after you destroyed their drugs supply."

"We chose the time they would least expect it," he rumbled, wondering exactly where they were headed. Not that it mattered. He'd follow her wherever she wanted to go, until she told him to get lost. And even then, he'd trail after her from behind, determined not to let her out of his sight.

She sounded more than a little peeved. "So then it's okay for you to repeatedly put your life in danger, but I'm not even meant to do my job? Do you have any idea how backward that is, Eli?"

She was obviously still pissed about their earlier argument, but he wouldn't have done a damn thing differently. She'd wanted to come with him and the guys, and he wouldn't hear of it, which hadn't exactly gone over well.

Breathing out a tired sigh, he said, "Rey, I'm covered in sweat and more than a little of Lev's blood. Can I just take a pass for a little while and argue with you about this after I've had a shower and grabbed a beer?"

"Fine."

He caught her arm as she started to walk away from him, and smiled down into her adorably disgruntled face. "You want to join me?" he asked. Just because he didn't want to fight with her didn't mean he didn't want her with him. Hell, he'd keep her glued to his side if she'd allow it. Except, of course, for when it was dangerous.

She shook her head, tugging her arm free. He expected her to stomp off, but she didn't. Instead, she made an odd little movement with her shoulder, and said, "By the way, you had a visitor while you were gone."

At the odd edge to her voice, dread settled in his gut like a dead weight. "Who the hell would visit me?" He hadn't left any friends behind when he'd been banished. Not trusting his old man, he'd never associated with any of the pack Lycans except for those who'd served his father, and he wouldn't have wanted anything to do with them now, if they'd managed to survive. Eric and Elise had been the only ones who had ever mattered to him, until Carla had come along.

"I didn't get her name," she murmured, staring off to his right instead of looking him in the eye. "But Eric confirmed that she was one of your old flames."

Oh, hell no. He wasn't letting this screw up the small amount of progress he'd managed to make. Curving his hands over her shoulders, he waited until she finally gave in and looked at him, then said, "I did *not* invite anyone to come down here, okay? I haven't even spoken to anyone in town."

"Well, you can sort that out with her."

"Are you telling me she's still here?" he asked, his tone grim.

"No. Elise got rid of her." Her mouth twisted with a smirk. "But I have a feeling she'll be back. She seemed like the tenacious sort."

"Then I'll tell her she's not welcome here."

Her brows lifted with surprise. "You don't even know who it was."

"I don't care who it was. Not. At. All."

For a split second, he was staring down into the most stunning, breathtaking look of hope on her face that he'd ever seen, before she quickly snuffed it out. "You know, I get that you're trying to say the right things here, Eli. But you could save us both the trouble and just go ahead and sleep with her."

"That's not going to happen," he ground out. "I don't even want her."

"Is that right? Because from the sound of it, you certainly wanted her before. She said the two of you were *really* close, right up until the time you left."

Christ, he just couldn't catch a break, could he? Rubbing the back of his neck, he said, "Then she was lying, Rey. I don't even know who this woman could be, which tells you how much she meant to me. But if we're going to have this conversation, let's at least take it inside."

"Fine," she said for the second time, and he clenched his jaw. He was really starting to hate that freaking word.

She followed him over to his cabin, and he was relieved they weren't going to have to do this in front of his sister and Wyatt. Once they were in the bedroom he'd taken, he turned and locked the door behind him, then leaned back against it and folded his arms over his chest.

When she finally stopped pacing at the foot of his bed and turned to look at him, he said, "Do you want to go first or should I?"

She frowned, but jerked her chin for him to start.

"Okay, then, here it is. I don't want any woman other than you, Carla. I haven't for a long time. And I would think that was fairly obvious, seeing as how I keep getting my hand down your pants every chance I get and pouring my heart out to you like a lovesick sap. Does that sound like a man looking to screw his way through the pack?"

When her frown deepened, but she didn't say anything, he asked her again. "Does it?"

"No," she muttered.

"Well, at least you're willing to admit that much to me."

"What exactly do you want out of this?" she suddenly snapped, glaring.

"Not much," he snapped back. "Just *you*."

Her voice started to rise. "You really want a half-breed? Is that what you expect me to believe?"

He drew his head back, stunned. "Where the hell did *that* come from?"

"Isn't that what this has been about right from the start? You were ashamed of me, weren't you? That's why we were always a secret!"

"That's bullshit!" Fisting his hands at his sides, he stalked toward her. "You're just grasping at straws now,

Rey," he said in a voice that was low and guttural. "I expected better from you."

"You are such an ass!"

"Because I screwed up? Yeah, I did. I know that. But I'm back and I want another chance. I bloody well *deserve* one after what I gave up for you!"

"What you gave up?" she wheezed, shaking her head. "For *me?* You're not making any sense! I didn't banish you."

"You, Rey. I gave up *you*. Don't expect me to do it again."

She blinked, staring at him as if she thought he was crazy.

"And don't ever think that I would feel the way my old man did. Yeah, I followed him. I followed him so that I could keep an eye on that bastard, and keep him away from my family as much as possible. Which included my mother. I even…" The gritty words trailed off and he shook his head, backing up a step, unable to believe he'd almost told her.

"You even what?" she asked, her voice slightly softer now, as if she sensed that something in the argument had just shifted.

He opened his mouth, but his lungs were working so hard he couldn't get anything out.

"What, Eli? What is it?"

He squeezed his eyes shut, his hands fisting and flexing at his sides, while his chest heaved like a friggin' bellows.

"Eli?"

"I was the oldest, which meant I was the one she ran to," he heard himself saying in a voice that didn't even sound like his own. "Always. Whenever he lost his shit with her, I put myself between them. I don't think Eric and Elise even remember. I tried to keep them away from it. But I knew, I *knew* he would end up killing her if she didn't get out."

"I thought your mother ran off with another man. A human one."

Wetting his lips, he finally opened his eyes, looked at her, and said, "She did."

Her slender brows pulled into a V over the delicate bridge of her nose. "I don't understand."

"I would help her sneak off sometimes, so that she could get away from it all. I guess they met during one of her trips away from the mountain. I don't know anything about him, except that he made her happy. When she told me she wanted to run away with him, I wasn't surprised."

"Oh, no," she whispered, looking heartbroken for the little boy that he'd been. "What about you and El and Eric? How could she…just leave you like that?"

He gave a small, bitter laugh that tasted like crap in his mouth. "I think by that time she saw us as more of an extension of my old man than of herself. She knew she'd never make it if she tried to take us with her. The League of Elders would have given him full permission to come after us with every resource the pack possessed. But it didn't matter. As wrong as it sounds, I was…I was *glad* she wanted to go."

Quietly, she said, "Eli, you have nothing to feel guilty for."

The sound that ripped up from his throat was deep and sarcastic. "Don't I? When she told me what she wanted, *I* got her out, because I was trying to save her. Told her to never come back, because I knew he would kill her if she did. But I didn't realize what it would mean for everyone else. Her leaving him...it just pushed him even deeper into his hate-colored madness."

"But you couldn't have known that. You were only a child."

Another bitter laugh jerked past his lips. "That's what the older pack members would always say about us. They would talk about how sad it was that we'd lost our mother when we were so young. And, Elise, yeah. She was just a little thing. But Eric and I...we were hardly little kids. He'd forced us to grow up long before we were adults."

"Do Eric and Elise know that you helped her escape?"

His eyes widened, and he could feel the blood draining from his face. "Hell no. They'd never forgive me." He took a step toward her, his breaths still coming hard and fast as he said, "And you know what the worst part is? The worst part is that I should have had the balls to end it and kill him, but I didn't, because she made me *promise* that I wouldn't hurt him. So I kept thinking someone else would do it for me, but his disease, his hatred, it spread like a damn plague. And after I was banished, I left the rest of you here to deal with it!"

Closing the distance between them, he curled his fingers around her upper arms as he leaned over her, getting right in her face as her head went back and she stared up at him with solemn eyes. "You want to know why I never told anyone about us?" he asked, forcing the words through his gritted teeth. "Because I was *afraid,* Rey. Afraid of letting myself love you. Of what my father might do to you if he found out. Of the kind of man I had become because of him. I followed him so Eric wouldn't have to, but I hated every second of it. Hated the goddamn gut-wrenching terror of what he would do to you if he found out you were *mine*.

"And the night I finally took you to my bed, he'd already been pissed because of what I'd done. Because I'd jeopardized my position in the pack by killing El's rapist. She was his own daughter, Rey. He hated her, and she was a *part* of him. So what do you think he would have done about *you?*

"From where I was standing, the banishment was a twisted kind of blessing when it happened, because there's no way in hell that I would have been able to stay away from you after finally getting my hands on you. And he would have tried to kill you for it. Then I would have killed him, which would have turned everyone who followed him against us. We would have been marked for death the second he stopped breathing. So my banishment saved your life!" he ended on a stifled roar.

"If that was true, you would have come back when you heard he was dead. Or better yet, taken me with you!" Her voice cracked, and he winced at the pain he could see filling her glistening eyes. "God, Eli. You could have at least come to me and told me goodbye."

"I *did.*" His throat was so tight he could barely force the words out. "I went to the Alley that night, Rey. I parked a mile out and walked in. No one even noticed because you guys were having some kind of birthday celebration for Jeremy. I stood out there in the damn trees and I watched you with them. With your friends. And I *knew* that as much as I loved you, and as much as I hated the goddamn danger your job put you in, the right thing to do was to let you stay with them. With your family."

"Oh, God," she sobbed, breaking away from him. With her arms wrapped around her body, she hunched forward, crying, "You had no right to make that decision for me. You were wrong!"

He swallowed, his own eyes stinging as he watched her completely fall apart. "I…I'm starting to see that. I should…have talked to you. I know that now."

She straightened and glared at him, her thick lashes drenched with tears. "You don't really love me," she said through her trembling lips. "I…I don't believe that. Either you're lying…or it's the stupid bond screwing with your emotions—with your head—now that you're back. I spent a long time thinking about it last night, and that's…that's the only explanation that makes any sense."

Feeling as if he'd been slashed open inside, he asked, "Why is it so hard for you to just believe me?"

"Why?" Her chest shook with a small, wretched laugh. "Because if you loved me, Eli, the truth is that you would have come back for me a long time ago."

At first, he couldn't get out the words he needed to say, everything jammed up inside him, locking him down. He took a deep, rattling breath, struggling for his damn voice, and somehow managed to tell her, "I was afraid it was too late." Pulling a shaky hand down his face, he stepped close to her again, wanting so damn badly to take her into his arms and crush her against his body. "Christ, I was so afraid you wouldn't want me anymore. Makes me sound like a pussy, but it's the truth. I didn't know if you were feeling the same pull. Was afraid of what I would do when I saw you.

What if you'd found someone else? I was always too worried to ask about you whenever I talked to Eric or Elise. I talked to them less and less over the years, not wanting to know. I swear I've lived with that same cold burn of fear every goddamn day since you became a woman and I realized how badly I wanted you, and it was even worse after I left.

"And maybe…" He shoved a hand back through his hair again, then shook his head. "Hell, maybe I felt like I had to protect you from me. From all the things I'd done for that bastard. Even with him dead, I would have still been the same person."

"You really think I would have cared?" she asked in that tear-drenched voice that was killing him.

Working his jaw, he said, "You *should*."

Her chin went up, a rush of angry color burning in her cheeks. "Well, I wouldn't have, because you survived him, Eli. You didn't let him break you. You might have acted like his thug, but you survived him and became the man you are today. A man I could have loved if you hadn't already broken my heart."

"Rey," he groaned, reaching for her.

"Don't," she snapped, stumbling back from him. "Don't touch me. I can't think when you do that."

"And I can't *not* touch you," he rasped, catching her with one arm wrapped around her waist, the other lifting as he pushed her hair back from her face, "because you're the only thing in this world that I want."

"Eli—"

"Christ, Carla. *Listen* to me. What I told you last night, it was the truth."

She started to shake her head, but he gripped the back of it, holding her still.

Pressing his forehead against hers, he said, "If you won't believe my words, then trust what your body is telling you. Because *sex* doesn't feel like this. Sometimes it feels good, sometimes even fun—but it doesn't feel goddamn *necessary*."

"It's the bond," she cried.

Lifting his head, he stared deep into her beautiful eyes, and said, "Bullshit. It's your heart, Rey. And I want it so badly it's killing me."

She blinked, and then, without any warning, she suddenly grabbed him like she had in this same room yesterday, and crushed her mouth against his. He took her with him as he stumbled back, falling onto the bed, and she straddled his hips, rubbing herself against his already hardening body. Hunger rolled up his spine in a thick, searing wave, and he cursed the layers of clothing separating them. Breaking away from the kiss, he sucked in air, ready to beg her for what he wanted, but the words dried up on his tongue when she scooted back and shoved up his shirt, kissing the center of his chest, right over the thundering beat of his heart. He pulled in a sharp breath as he ripped the shirt over his head, and every muscle in his body tensed with anticipation as her mouth traveled lower, trailing biting kisses across his torso, around his navel, until she was nuzzling his happy trail with her nose and ripping at the buttons on his fly, the worn denim straining over the heavy bulk of his erection.

"What?" he gasped, half convinced he must have hit his head somehow and was imagining this. "What are you doing?"

"You're always touching me," she panted, kneeing his thighs apart as she tugged down his boxers and jeans. Wrapping her hand around the thick base of his cock, she looked up at him through her lashes, her voice even huskier as she said, "You're always making it about me. About my pleasure. But this time, it's going to be about you, Eli."

Bracing his booted feet on the bed, he reached down and shoved his boxers and jeans a little lower, his face so friggin' hot he knew he had to have turned bright red. But he had Carla's feminine little hand wrapped as far as it could go around his massive hard-on, her lush mouth hovering over the slick, swollen head, and he was pretty sure his heart was getting ready to pound its way right out of his chest. He looked too brutal to ever go inside that perfect mouth of hers—but then, he had a strong feeling he was going to look right there, too. As if it was where he belonged, his body close to hers, letting her do whatever the hell she wanted to him.

Then she took him between her lips, inside the moist heat of her mouth, stroking him with her tongue, and the sensation was so shockingly intense that he shouted.

Needing to see every carnal, mind-shattering second of this, Eli let his knees fall open and braced himself on an elbow, his other hand gripping her hair and lifting it away so that he had an unobstructed view of her going down on him. Of that hot little mouth hungrily sucking him deep, damn near sending his eyes rolling back in his head.

"I'm going over," he growled just moments later, warning her, but she didn't move away. Moaning around his aching shaft, she sucked him even deeper, and he fell back to the bed with another guttural, visceral shout on his lips as the climax ripped through him, so explosive his back literally arched off the mattress. He shoved his fingers into her soft hair, holding her to him as it went on and on, the sexy sounds she made only driving him further over the edge, until he was shaking and cursing and willing to bet everything he owned on the fact that she'd almost killed him with the pleasure.

Son of a bitch, he thought, throwing his arm over his eyes as he tried to catch his breath. If he'd come that fast when he was younger, he'd have been embarrassed as hell. But this was Carla, the woman who turned him inside out, who turned him on like no other had ever even come close to doing, and he figured he was lucky he'd actually lasted as long as he had.

While he lay there trying to make sure he wasn't in the middle of a heart attack, she pulled her head back, releasing him from the hot, wet suction of her mouth, and rested her forehead against his lower abdomen. Her body shook with a fine vibration, her shoulders lifting and falling with her rapid breaths.

"Carla, that was unreal. I didn't even know it was possible to come that hard. Or that it could feel that friggin' incredible."

He felt a smile curl her lips. "That's because I lo—"

She instantly froze, whatever she'd been about to say choked off before he could catch it, her breaths coming so quickly he worried she was going to hyperventilate.

"Rey?"

"I...I need to go," she whispered, the soft words unsteady as she scrambled off the side of the bed.

"What?" He knew he sounded out of it, but he was still groggy as hell from the violence of his release. "What are you talking about?"

Pushing her hair back from her face, she turned toward the door. "I'm sorry, but I just realized that Wyatt's, um, waiting for me. He said he needed to talk to me."

"Wait!" he growled, jerking into a sitting position. "Jesus, Carla, just stop for a second and look at me!"

She whipped her head to the side as she flicked open the lock on the door, glancing at him over her shoulder, and he felt like he'd been punched in the gut.

He could see the fear on her beautiful face as clearly as if it'd been lit up like a neon sign.

"Damn it, don't do this," he choked out. "Don't run out on me again."

"I've never run out on you," she argued, twisting the handle. "I might have asked you to stop, or to leave, but I've never run away. And I'm not running now. I just... I have...I have to go," she said in a carefully controlled tone, before hurrying out of the room.

By the time he'd yanked his jeans over his hips and made it onto the front porch, she was already halfway across the Alley. He ran after her, not caring what he looked like—just a crazy half-dressed man with wild hair who was cursing a blue streak. But he forced himself to stop when she ran inside Elise and Wyatt's cabin, knowing damn well they were at home. He could see the colored lights from their TV flashing across the living room window. Yeah, he could force his way inside, but where was that going to get him? In an argument with Wyatt? The usually easygoing Runner had already made it perfectly clear how protective he was when it came to the woman he thought of as a sister. The only person who meant more to him was Eli's own sister, and he scowled, not wanting to make this situation any more difficult for Elise.

Shit. He would have to get to Carla another way. Maybe wait until everyone went to sleep that night and sneak in through her bedroom window, the way he'd considered doing before. But what if Wyatt set an alarm? He didn't care if he made a jackass of himself by setting it off, but Carla would probably want to kill him if he ended up putting everyone in a panic.

Figuring he'd just keep calling her cell phone until she picked up, he turned and headed back to his cabin. Just as he was about to climb the porch steps, he caught the raised voices coming from the side of the cabin, and went back down to take a look and make sure everything was okay. But the instant he walked around the corner, he realized it was the Irishman and the little witch who seemed to be driving the guy crazy.

"You go off on a walk with that guy again, Sayre, and there won't be enough of him left to bury," the Runner was snarling in a low voice, the rough words vibrating with fury.

"Why are you doing this?" she hissed, sounding on the verge of tears. "What the hell is it to you who I go out with?"

"He's got a reputation. All he's interested in is getting between your legs."

Eli didn't know who they were talking about, but he hoped to God it wasn't one of his guys. The last thing they needed was trouble with any of the Runners—especially this one.

"Hah!" she shouted, stomping her foot against the grass. "That sounds like *you* and pretty much every woman you ever come across!"

"Don't," Hennessey growled, grabbing her by her upper arms. "This isn't about me. It's about—"

"Oh, just shut up," she snapped, cutting him off as she jerked away from him. "And stay away from me, Cian. I mean it. I'm tired of this stupid mind game you keep playing. You don't want me, but you don't want anyone else to want me, either? It's sick! Just leave me alone!"

She stormed off around the back of the neighboring cabin, and the Runner stared after her, his big hands fisted at his sides. He looked like a man who was having to physically restrain himself from doing something that he knew he shouldn't, and then he suddenly turned around, stalking forward with his head down, while a guttural string of curses fell from his lips.

"You've got a problem on your hands with that one," Eli said, before the guy could mow him down.

Drawing to a stop, Cian's head shot up, his grim expression twisting into an even darker scowl. "And you don't?" he muttered, obviously talking about Carla.

Scrubbing his jaw, he said, "Reyes is just being stubborn."

The Runner slowly arched one of his ebony brows. "Is that what you call a woman willing to risk her life to end her bond with you?"

He flinched at those softly spoken words, feeling as if he'd just been kicked in the stomach. "What did you say?"

Pulling a pack of cigarettes from his pocket, the Irishman took one out as he murmured, "There aren't many secrets here in the Alley, Drake. You'd do well to remember that."

Eli took an aggressive step forward, his hands curling into fists. "Why the hell did you say she was willing to risk her life?"

Lighting his cigarette, Cian took a long drag, then slowly exhaled as he locked his shuttered gaze with Eli's. "You know how our world works," he said in a low, lilting rasp. "How nature works. One rarely gets something for nothing. There's always a risk, and some are greater than others. What matters is what we're willing to gamble with to get what we want."

"Are you telling me her life would be in danger if Jillian breaks the bond?" he growled, feeling a muscle begin to pulse at the side of his jaw.

Cian slid him a chilling look. "I'm saying it might damn well kill her."

He swallowed as he locked his jaw, thinking *Christ. Oh, Christ.* How desperate must Carla be if she was willing to take that kind of risk?

As desperate as my mother was?

He flinched again, that particular thought striking his body like a physical blow. It was *that* jarring and painful. He wanted so badly to quiet the voices in his head, but it was impossible to stop the destructive train of his thoughts. Because if she was willing to go that far, was there anything he could do, anything at all he could say, that would ever get through to her?

Wasn't that what kept me away from her these past months? The fear that she'd already scarred me from her heart?

Damn it, he needed out of this place. And he needed a bottle.

Turning away from the Irishman, Eli figured it was time that he finally made his way back home.

Chapter 11

Twenty-four hours later, Eli still hadn't returned from wherever he'd run off to. After their argument, Carla had stood at the window in Wyatt and Elise's guest room and watched him drive one of the mercs' big black trucks out of the Alley. And he hadn't been back since.

I should be relieved. It's what I wanted.

True. The only problem was that relief was the last thing she was feeling.

She hadn't wanted to run out on him, after sharing something so incredible, but she'd panicked when the word "love" had almost slipped from her lips. She might have finally come to terms with the fact that she was madly, desperately in love with him, but that didn't mean she was ready to tell him. Just because he'd said the words to her didn't mean it was smart to say them back. Not until she understood *why* he'd said them… and was sure of his feelings.

Because she really did fear that it might have more to do with the bond than it did with his heart.

But what about the things he said about his mom and his dad and how he felt about me?

Then again, am I just meant to forget that he supposedly decided to leave me behind for my own good, without even giving me the choice? Without even talking to me about it or telling me goodbye?

Damn it, she didn't know how to process everything that was churning round and round in her head, and the result was a cracking headache that she hadn't been able to shake for hours now. She wanted to crawl into bed and sleep for a week, the session she'd worked with Wyatt that day on the training fields making her as physically exhausted as she was mentally, but she was due over at Jillian's in twenty minutes for dinner, and she still needed to freshen up. So a nap was unfortunately not in the picture.

Fifteen minutes later, she'd managed to grab a quick shower, throw on a pair of leather sandals, clean jeans, and a slouchy gray top, as well as put on a little blush and lip gloss. Wyatt and Elise were over at her cabin, having dinner with the women who were living there at the moment, so she pulled her keys from her pocket as she stepped out onto the porch, intending to lock the door behind her. But she froze the minute she looked up and realized she wasn't alone.

They were all there, the Runners and their mates, standing around the front of the cabin, watching her with careful gazes, as if this was some kind of intervention. A wild burst of laughter almost rumbled up with that thought, and she wondered when her life had become like a crazy TV sitcom.

"Did I suddenly become insanely popular," she murmured, arching her brows, "or did you guys need something?"

Eric climbed up the porch steps, his handsome face set in a chilling expression of anger. "Go. Get. Him," he said in a low, guttural voice. "Now."

"What?"

"Eli went up to Shadow Peak yesterday, and spent the night at my place, where he apparently decided it was a good idea to get shit-faced. I want you to get your ass up there and bring him back."

Her eyes narrowed, and she could feel her own temper simmering at his tone. "Why me?"

"Because you're the one who put him there," Eric growled, and she was a little surprised that no one, not even Wyatt, took exception to the Runner's tone. Jesus, did they all blame her? Were they all on Eli's side?

Crossing her arms over her chest, she said, "You can't put this on me, Eric. That isn't fair."

"Why shouldn't I? He's done nothing but follow you around since he got back, trying to get you to give him the time of day, and all you do is make him feel like shit. Accuse him of stuff he hasn't even done. If I thought there was a chance in hell he could find someone else, I'd tell him to get out there and do it. But he's hung up on you, because the two of you friggin' belong with each other. So fix it and get him back down here!"

"Eric," his wife murmured, sounding concerned.

"Not now, Chelse. I've been patient, but this is getting ridiculous." He got right in Carla's face, and lowered his voice. "I watched him go through shit with my old man while growing up, doing everything he could to keep that bastard happy, never getting anything back for it. I won't watch him go through the same thing with you."

She flinched, reeling on the inside as Eric's harsh words worked their way through her system. Was he seriously comparing her to their crazy psycho father? What the hell?

And why was she even bothering to argue with him about this when she actually *wanted* to go up to town and check on Eli? She'd have been lying if she'd said she wasn't worried about him. But then, she was also worried about what she might find when she got there.

"Are you sure he doesn't have company?"

Eric gave her a stunned look, then laughed. Shaking his head, he said, "God, I wish I could tell you that he had a woman with him. It would serve you right, Reyes. But he's at my place, and he's alone."

She'd known that Eric still had his house up in Shadow Peak, though he and Chelsea never stayed there. When she'd asked Elise about it, his sister had said that the couple was thinking of selling the house once things had settled down. But this was hardly the time to be worrying about real estate.

Since Carla was already dressed and had her keys with her, she left Eric and the others standing around the cabin after murmuring a few words to them and headed straight for her car. The short drive to Shadow Peak took forever, thanks to the security checkpoints she had to go through. She knew it was just her imagination, but she felt like she was being judged by every single person she came into contact with, as if she were walking around with a scarlet RB on her forehead that apparently stood for Raving Bitch. It hardly seemed fair, seeing as how none of these Lycans knew the full story, but such was the nature of gossip.

She was familiar with where Eric lived, and was parking on the curb in front of the attractive two-story just a few minutes after reaching the town. Her gaze flicked to where the black truck was parked in the driveway as she turned off the engine, telling her Eli was definitely there. Curling her hands around the steering wheel, she lowered her head, banging her forehead against the leather wheel, then stopped and raised her head again, looking around. There were so many scouts posted now, there was no telling who was watching her from the thickening darkness. Were they waiting to see if he slammed the door in her face? At the moment, she was feeling a bit as if it might be deserved, which made her scowl.

Forcing herself out of the car, she shut the door and headed up to the house, climbing the porch steps and then knocking on the door. The powerful, smoky scent of whiskey was the first thing that hit her nose when he ripped the door open, followed immediately by the richer, deeper scent that was completely his. A heady, erotic blend of soap and salt and the wild outdoors. Wearing nothing more than a faded pair of jeans, he stared down at her through hooded eyes that were thankfully focused, despite the scent of the alcohol. His jaw worked a few times, and then he muttered, "What are you doing here, Reyes?"

"Thanks to your brother," she murmured, "I've been sent to collect you."

"Ah. Of course you have. God knows you wouldn't have come after me on your own." He turned and headed back into the living room, leaving her to walk in and shut the door herself.

After glancing at the disheveled room, the coffee table littered with bottles and a blanket hanging halfway off the sofa, she looked at him and arched one of her brows. "Been having fun up here?"

He slid her a shuttered look as he sat on the arm of the sofa, his muscular arms folded over his broad, beautiful chest, the golden skin gleaming beneath the soft glow of the track lighting. "You'd like to think that, wouldn't you?" he replied, his tone flat. "To have something that would give you even more of a reason to hate me."

She stiffened, something in his tone setting her even further on edge. "I don't hate you, Eli."

"Sure you don't," he drawled with a mocking smile on his sensual lips.

She rubbed her forehead, wondering what his problem was. As well as hers. She couldn't seem to get close to him without saying whatever she could think of to piss him off.

"Believe it or not, Rey, no one's been here but me." At the look she cut him, he said, "Use your nose, little wolf. Come over here and sniff the blanket I've been sleeping under. Sniff any friggin' surface in the house you want. You won't find what you're looking for."

"Why?" she asked softly, blurting the question out before she had the sense to stop herself.

His gaze narrowed in on her face, the long lashes making it difficult to read the look in his eyes. "Are you asking me why I haven't been busy screwing my way through the pack?"

Her response was simple and to the point. "Yes."

She couldn't help but watch the way his biceps bulged as he lifted an arm, hooking his hand around the back of his neck. His breath left his lungs on a rough exhalation, and he said, "I haven't had sex with anyone because the woman I want hasn't been on the top of this bloody mountain with me." Lowering his arm, he held her gaze like he never meant to let it go, and continued speaking through his gritted teeth. "I haven't had another woman, Carla. Not since you. Hell, I haven't had one since long before that night we were together."

For a few dizzying seconds, all she could do was stare at him in shock, unable to believe he was actually trying this with her. God, did he think she was a fool? A naïve little idiot who would believe anything he told her, if it was what he thought she wanted to hear? "Don't. Even. Try. It," she seethed, so angry she was shaking.

He rolled one of those hard, muscular shoulders as he moved to his feet and turned away from her. He walked to the front window, bracing a hand against the top of the frame as he stared out into the starless night. "Get pissed, Rey. It doesn't matter what you do or what you believe. You can't change the truth."

"I'll never believe you."

"Christ, that's almost funny." His head dropped back on those mouthwatering shoulders as he laughed. "You believe everything that *isn't* true, but not what is."

"Fine, then answer me this. What about the blonde in the dive bar when I found you?"

The hand he had braced on the top of the window frame curled into a fist. She listened as he took a few hard, deep breaths, watching the muscles in his sleek back flex with the movement, and then he said, "She'd dropped into my lap, trying to flirt, when she passed out in my arms. Since I couldn't have cared less about her, I let her sleep there."

"You actually expect me to believe that nonsense?"

He turned around as he pushed his hands in his pockets, the masculine pose making him look like something that women would plaster all over their bedroom walls and drool over. Tall, dark, and outrageously delicious, with his piercing eyes and that wild hair, a dark covering of stubble shadowing the hard angle of his jaw. Taking a step toward her, he growled, "Would it make you believe me if I completely humiliate myself for you? What would you think if I told you that I was desperate for even that small, pathetic bit of comfort, after so many years of missing you until I felt like my insides had been scraped raw? That I'd sat there, drinking my whiskey, trying like hell to pretend that it was *you* I was holding?"

"I don't...I can't..."

With his gruff words drowning in frustration, he took another step closer to her and muttered, "I don't know why you think this would affect me any differently than it would you. How eager have you been to find some other male to rut between your legs?"

Her chest shook with a hollow, heavy laugh. "I was so angry with you that I *wanted* to. I wanted to find someone."

"Don't." His nostrils flared as he took a sharp breath, his deep voice little more than a snarl. "I don't want to hear it."

As quickly as her anger had come, it vanished, leaving her feeling deflated, like a balloon that had sprung a leak. "It...it doesn't matter. I couldn't go through with it. No one...I just...there was no one after you," she finished lamely, her voice so small it made her cringe.

For a moment, she thought he was going to close the distance between them and take her into his arms. But then he turned around again and stalked back to the window, his tall body hard with tension. "It was the same for me," he said quietly.

"I find that so hard to believe," she whispered. "I mean, you could have had any woman you wanted."

Seconds ticked by as he stood there before the large window, staring out at the darkened street, while she fought the urge to go to him and wrap her arms around him, pressing her cheek against his warm back...simply holding him as tightly as she could. Pretending, just for a moment, that she wasn't broken inside and the past had never happened. That they could start fresh, without any of the pain and fear and resentment.

Finally, he broke the silence, his deep voice rough with emotion. "There were a few times, when I was lonely, that I thought it might help to find another woman. Times when I tried damn hard to put you out of my mind. Wishing I could just rip you out for good.

"When I left here, I told myself that when the time came that I wanted sex again, I would approach it with the sense of detachment it deserved. A bodily function that had to be fed, nothing more. And when it was done, I would move on, wiping it from my mind. I wouldn't think about what I'd lost. And I sure as hell wouldn't waste time wishing for things that could never be mine."

He turned a little to the side as he slumped against the edge of the window frame, his profile so stark it could have been carved out of granite. "But I could never go through with it. I would find a woman, talk to her, drink with her. But when it came time to get down to it, not only were my body and heart unwilling, all I could think about was the look that would be on your face if you saw me touching someone else." Shaking his head, he gave a bitter laugh. "Guess that was stupid, though, seeing as how you already hated my guts. It's not like falling into bed with some woman I didn't even want could have made you hate me more."

She knew she needed to address this idea he had that she hated him, but she was still too stunned by the realization that was slowly sinking into her. "My God, you're serious, aren't you?"

Turning around, he crossed his arms over his chest, his gaze becoming darker as it locked with hers. "Why do you think my friends are always laughing at me, giving me a hard time about you? They've never seen me act like this over a woman."

She shook her head a little, still trying to wrap her brain around it. "The night I found you, in that bar, Sam said you were always so freaking *nice* to women."

The look he slid her was equal parts exasperation and fury. "Nice to them, Rey. As in wanting them to be safe, but not giving a shit about them beyond that." He scrubbed a hand over his face as a gruff laugh jerked from his lips. "But it was all a pathetic joke, wasn't it? Because we both know you don't really give a shit about what I do or who I do it with. Why would you, when deep down inside you can't stand me?"

"Why do you keep saying that? I thought you believed that I was madly in love with you? That we belonged together?"

His gaze lowered, dropping to the floor, while he drew in a deep breath of air that shuddered on his exhale. Then he said three simple words: "Cian told me."

Feeling more than a little confused, she asked, "He told you what?"

His dark gaze shot back to hers, burning with emotion. "About the bond breaking. About how dangerous it is for the one who's seeking it."

She wheezed as she took a step back, everything suddenly snapping into place with a lot of noise and reverberation, like a series of gunshots going off in her head. "Is that…is that why you're here?"

He rubbed his eyes with his thumb and forefinger, lips parted for breaths that were getting rougher by the second. "Yeah. I just needed…to think."

Carla heard the catch in his deep voice, and felt as if something dark and heavy was falling over her, like a cold rain. She honestly hadn't thought it would matter to him one way or another, or maybe she just hadn't let herself consider how he would feel about the risk she would be taking. Either way, it was clear to her now that her willingness to endanger her own life to destroy their bond was something that had hurt him deeply. Was *still* hurting him.

"Eli," she whispered, so confused she couldn't make heads or tails of any of the powerful emotions tearing through her. Moving like someone in a dream, she felt her feet covering the distance between them, and then she was standing right in front of him, her head going back so that she could keep her eyes on his beautiful face. Wetting her lower lip, she said, "I'm not doing this to hurt you."

He stared so hard and deep into her watery gaze,

she felt like he was seeing right inside her. "I'm sorry, Rey. So fucking sorry, for everything, for all of it." The sincerity in his rough voice made her ache. "I never wanted to hurt you. That was the *last* goddamn thing that I wanted."

Her throat shook, melting, and she found herself lifting her hands to his face, her thumbs stroking over his flushed cheekbones. "It's really true," she murmured, an unmistakable note of awe in her voice that she didn't even try to hide. "You haven't been with anyone. I can see the truth in your eyes."

"It's about damn time you can see something," he groaned, and she didn't know if she was the one who lifted up or if he was the one who leaned down, but their mouths were suddenly crashing against each other and they were kissing as if they needed the other's taste to breathe...live...survive. He tasted sumptuous, like whiskey and hot, addicting male. A taste she knew she'd never be able to get enough of. That she'd go to her grave craving, no matter how many years she ended up having on this earth.

And then the raw, aggressive tenor of the kiss changed, their mouths gentling as it melted into something soft and lush and heartbreakingly poignant. Every stroke of his tongue was conveying something so much deeper than pleasure, as if he was pouring his very soul into the touch of his mouth against hers. His hands threaded through her hair, holding the sides of her head as he slanted his mouth over hers, stroking and licking and nipping, his warm breaths pelting against her lips as they shared the same air.

"You drive me so damn crazy," he rasped, wrapping one arm around her lower back as he drew her up against him, his body already hard and thick with need. Pressing his lips to the side of her throat, he said, "No one else has ever had the power to make me so angry, and yet, I've never been as happy as I am when I'm with you, Rey. Even when you're snapping at me, all I can think about is holding you and getting inside you and making you come, again and again, until you're steeped in so much pleasure all you can do is melt and shiver and smile up at me."

She gave a soft laugh, loving the feel of him under her hands as she stroked his shoulders, the muscles so firm and hard beneath his hot skin. "Not that it doesn't sound fun, but I swear you don't have to go to that much trouble just for a smile."

"Feels like it," he muttered, kissing his way up to her ear and then nipping at the delicate lobe, while his hands settled on her hips, holding her against him.

"Am I really that crabby?" she asked, grimacing on the inside.

"Just with me. You're all smiles with your friends. And hell, you smile all the time at mine, as well." His head suddenly shot up, a worried look on his gorgeous face as he said, "Has Lev been flirting with you since I came up here?"

"What? No," she murmured, running her fingers through his soft, thick hair, loving that she was able to touch him. "There's no need to be jealous, Eli. I'm not attracted to Lev. He's just a big ol' teddy bear. To be honest, he kinda reminds me of Brody."

"A teddy bear?" he choked out, sounding skeptical. "That's not how most women view Slivkoff."

Her eyebrows slowly lifted. "Well, I'm not most women."

He leaned back and let his hot gaze roam down her body, before giving a low, rumbling groan. "Don't I know it."

She smiled at that—one of those soft, beautiful smiles that made him want to throw her over his shoulder and keep her forever—and Eli could feel the fever inside him rising even higher. As if she could tell just how much power she had over him, she flattened her hands against his abs and started pushing him across the room, until his back hit the front wall of the house, to the right of the window. His heart started pounding like a friggin' jackhammer as she smoothed her soft little hands over his heaving chest, the smile on her lips becoming downright wicked as she leaned forward and pressed her parted lips against his left nipple, flicking the pebbled flesh with her tongue. His breath sucked in on a gasp, and her smile got bigger as she trailed her lips lower, her hands reaching for the top button on his jeans.

"Damn it, baby, don't," he groaned, gripping her wrists and drawing them away from his body, his cock so achingly hard he was surprised he hadn't burst through the zipper.

She pulled her head back and looked up at him, that succulent lower lip—the one he wanted to devote hours to tasting—caught in her teeth. "What? You didn't like the way I give head?"

A stunned laugh jerked up from his chest. "Not like it? I friggin' loved it."

"Then why are you stopping me?" she asked, pulling a little at her captured wrists. The wolf in him gave a low, aggressive growl, loving the sight of her caught and trapped, and he mentally shoved the animal back, determined to keep it under tight control. No way was he giving it an inch, knowing it would have its fangs buried deep in her slender throat the first chance it got, and they were nowhere near that point yet. Not when she was still thinking to sever their connection in an act that could very well end her life.

His heart stuttered at the thought, and he forced it from his mind, since it was only going to twist him up inside and lead to another argument. And there would be plenty of time for that later, when she wasn't looking at him in a way she hadn't looked at him since she'd walked back into his life and punched him in the mouth, her eyes soft and warm and full of desire.

Moving his hands from her wrists to her ass, he lifted her off the floor, her body locked against his as her legs wrapped around his waist. "I stopped you because as much as I loved what you did to me," he said in response to her question, turning so that she was the one pressed against the wall, "I didn't get my fix last night."

"Your fix?" she said with a smirk. "That makes you sound like an addict."

"For you I am. That's what I feel like when it comes to your body and the way it tastes."

She snuffled a soft, shy laugh, and he smiled, loving that happy sound on her lips.

"God, I can't get enough of you," he muttered against her mouth, kissing each corner, before touching his tongue to hers. "Not these lips…not any part of you, Rey. I want to lay you down, strip you bare, and lick every beautiful inch of you for hours on end."

"Will I get the chance to do the same to you?" she whispered, curling a hand around the back of his neck.

"God, yes," he breathed out. "As long as you want, baby."

He took her mouth then with every bit of emotion burning inside him, pouring everything he felt for her into the lush, drugging kiss. It was hot and wet and blisteringly perfect, her tender mouth moving against his, and he was in heaven until she suddenly started pushing at his shoulders. The instant he lifted his mouth, she turned her head to the side, and he gnashed his teeth in frustration, his beast surging up inside him, wanting to throw back its head and howl. She was doing it again—pushing him away—and he set her back on her feet before jerking away from her. Lifting his arms, he clasped his hands together behind his neck and clenched his jaw, not trusting what might come out of his mouth at that moment. Then he heard the noises out on the street, and realized *that* was the problem—the reason why she'd pushed him away. "Christ," he scraped out, shaking his head. "I don't believe this. No one's luck can be this shit."

"Eli, what's going on?"

"I don't know," he muttered, lowering his arms as he headed toward the front door. "But I might kill someone if it doesn't turn out to be the end of the world."

Stepping out onto the front porch, he looked over the group of Lycans running down the street, heading toward the woods at the far end. He recognized Charles Decker, the Lycan who'd been leading the scouting party that had helped them during the ambush, at the back of the group.

"What is it?" Carla asked, coming out onto the porch with him.

"Not sure." Sliding her a careful look, he said, "Will you wait for me here if I go talk to Decker?"

"I'm not helpless, Eli," she said with a sigh, shaking her head a little. "I could just go with you and we could find out *together*."

Shoving his hair back from his face, he held her gaze and tried not to sound like an overbearing jackass. "I know you're tough as hell, Rey. But until I know what's happened—what we're dealing with—I'd feel better if you'd stay near the house."

She looked like she wanted to argue—but then her gaze slid away from his and she casually shrugged her shoulders. "You'd better hurry," she murmured, jerking her chin toward the street, which was empty, the Lycans all gathered at the far end now, just at the thick edge of the trees.

With a silent, frustrated string of curses on his lips, he turned away from her and headed down the porch steps, knowing there was little to no chance she was still going to be there when he got back. Hoping like hell for a miracle and that she'd actually stay, even if it was only so they could talk, he jogged down to the end of the street, where Charles was listening to a report from two red-faced scouts. The younger men were hunched over with their hands on their knees, trying to catch their breath as they spoke.

"What's going on?" Eli asked as he joined the group.

Charles jerked his chin toward the trees, and Eli followed behind him as they walked about ten yards or so into the woods, until they reached a small clearing, where another group of scouts was busy discussing what sounded like a possible infringement on Silvercrest pack land by several Whiteclaw soldiers.

"We think it's a false alarm," Charles told him. "Sounds like it might have been a couple of Whiteclaw teenage boys meeting up in the woods with a few Silvercrest girls. But we have to double-check every part of the border now to make sure it wasn't a ploy meant to draw our attention away from something more sinister."

"Have you called in help from the Alley yet?"

With a nod, Charles said, "I just got off the phone with Mason a few minutes ago. He's already mobilized five different scouting groups and put them on it."

"Do you need any help?" he asked, thinking he could call his men up and they could join the scouting parties, but Charles shook his head.

"You and your guys have been going non-stop since you got here," the Lycan said, giving him a friendly clap on the shoulder. "This is one you can sit out for now. But I'm sure Mason will call you if it turns out to be something more than we're expecting."

He talked with the Lycan for a few more moments, satisfied that they had the situation under control, then turned to head back. When he emerged from the woods and looked down the street, toward Eric's house, he wasn't surprised at what he saw. Carla had run. But he didn't think it was because she didn't want him. Climbing up the porch steps, Eli gripped the back of his neck, and struggled to grasp on to the hope that it just might be because she *did*. That she'd run because she was finally starting to see that he was for real. That they had a chance, if she would just make the choice to fight for it.

He might have lost her tonight, but tomorrow was a new day, and he was going to do everything he could to get this right.

If he wanted to land his queen in this backbreaking game of emotional chess being played between them, then he needed to rethink his strategy. And he needed to do it fast, before he ran out of time and she slipped from his grasp. Not just for a day…or a month…or another three miserable godforsaken years.

But forever.

Chapter 12

After spending the day with Wyatt at the training camps, Carla wanted nothing more than to soak her tired body in a hot bath and enjoy a glass of wine. Then she wanted to drag her aching muscles to bed early, and sleep so deeply that she didn't even dream.

Lately, dreams had become a dangerous playing field for her mind. As treacherous a landscape as her memories of the night Eli had forged the tenuous bond that linked them. She kept thinking of how deeply she'd been able to feel his need that night, as well as the pain he felt for what had happened to his sister. His fury for the ones responsible, and for the one he'd killed so viciously. He'd needed comfort. Had needed *her*.

She'd felt that same need pouring from him last night, when he'd taken her into his arms and held her so tightly, his powerful body tremoring with desire.

Was she just a fool, doomed to fall prey to a man who had brought her so much pain? Or was the fool the one who turned a blind eye to her own heart? Who never learned to forgive?

She didn't know. All she knew was that she fell further under his spell each time he touched her, which was the last thing that she needed.

Determined to distract her mind from thinking about him, she mentally worked through her day as she made her way on foot through the heavily secured woods, and found her frown only deepening. She and Wyatt, who had been a pain and tried to talk to her about Eli the entire damn day, had worked with a group of women who wanted to learn combat skills that could be used when the Whiteclaw finally mounted their attack—but the female Lycans had been woefully uneducated when it came to even the most basic fighting techniques. She hated the idea of telling them they couldn't fight, and yet, it wasn't right to send them up against soldiers who fought as dirty and deadly as the Whiteclaw did. So there were definitely going to be some hard decisions to make in that regard.

Reaching the edge of the trees, she came into the Alley behind Jeremy and Jillian's cabin, and headed around the side, toward the open glade. The instant she rounded their front porch, she caught sight of a tall male talking to Eric on the far side of the Alley, and immediately recognized those broad shoulders and the dark, shaggy hair as Eli's. She knew there was a part of her that had been hoping he would return, and yet, there was an equally strong part that had been terrified of that very thing.

As if he could feel the sensual weight of her stare,

he slowly turned around, found her with his gaze, and started walking toward her. Mere heartbeats later, he was right in front of her, and she could only stare back at him, a little in awe. He looked so gorgeous, standing there with the falling sun burning at his back, his hands shoved deep in his pockets, as if he were afraid he might reach for her if he didn't keep them hidden. "I've moved back into the cabin."

"Why?"

He cocked his head a bit to the side at her simple question, his gaze deep and piercing as he stared down at her, making her feel as though he was trying to read her. Read her more intimately than any other person ever had. Then he quietly said, "Because I don't want to be that far away from you."

She shivered and pressed her trembling lips together, almost afraid of what might slip from her mouth in response.

Lowering his lashes a little, he asked, "So why did you run off last night?"

Squinting against the glimmering rays of sunshine, her face warm from the heat and the intense way he was watching her, she said, "I texted Wyatt and he told me what was going on. I thought I should get back in case I was needed, and I…I guess I just figured that the moment was…um, gone."

"Yeah, I guess it kind of was," he admitted with a slight nod, his dark hair blowing in the breeze. "But I still would have liked to have you there, even if it was just to talk, Rey. Hell, I'd have been happy just to chill in front of the TV with you or to go to sleep. Whatever you would've wanted."

She wet her lips with a nervous flick of her tongue, her pulse rushing. "I…I should have said goodbye."

He lifted his hand, tucking a windblown strand of her hair behind her ear, but didn't say anything.

"Eli, I…I know we need to talk. About a lot of things. But I'm exhausted. I…I didn't sleep much last night, after I left you, and it's been a long day. Do we have to do this now?"

"No," he said in that low, delicious voice that always made her melt, his blue eyes locked on her so tightly she couldn't have looked away from him to save her life. "I just wanted to tell you that I'll do it."

"What?" she mouthed, blinking up at him in shock. It was the last thing that she'd expected him to say, and though he'd been vague, she knew *exactly* what he was talking about.

His eyes gleamed. "If Jillian promises to do everything in her power to make it safe for you, and you're still sure that it's what you want, then after the battle, I'll do it. I'll cut you loose."

She drew an unsteady breath, amazed at the burning sensation in her chest, as if he'd just stabbed her there with a lethal blade. If he truly felt like he'd *claimed* to feel about her, why would he give in? Did this mean she'd been right? Or that she'd merely succeeded in destroying something that should have been unbelievably beautiful?

Knowing she needed to say something, she somehow managed to murmur, "Th-thank you."

"Please, don't do that." His voice was still soft, but with a hard edge of raw emotion that made her breath freeze in her lungs. "It's ripping my goddamn heart out, Rey. So whatever you do, don't thank me."

She swallowed, unsure of what to do as she watched him shove one of those big hands back through his disheveled hair. Then he gave a hard sigh and braced both his hands on his lean hips as he turned his head, staring off to the side, into the distant line of trees.

Forcing the words up from the burning depths of her chest, she finally managed to ask, "What changed your mind?"

He took a deep breath, then slowly let it out. "If it's what you want, I don't want to disappoint you. Not again. I've already done enough of that to last a lifetime."

She licked her lips again, unable to tell if she was flushed or pale, her body both hot and cold at the same time. "Thank you," she repeated, even though he'd asked her not to, and hating the way the words tasted on her tongue. Or maybe she simply hated what she was thanking him for.

But I can't complain, can I? Not when I'm the one who asked for this.

Bringing his head forward again, he trapped her in the place where she stood with nothing more than a look. "But you should know I'm staying close."

She blinked, understanding there was a hell of a lot more to those words than their surface value. "What do you mean?"

His hooded gaze burned with primal, visceral determination. "I'll do it. But only on the grounds that until this thing is over, I'm your shadow."

Blinking up at him, she said, "I...I can live with that."

He seemed a little surprised, and maybe even wary,

that she'd agreed without an argument. But it didn't stop him from saying, "There's more."

She nodded, waiting, unable to look away.

Crossing his arms over his chest, he looked her right in the eye, and said, "You should know up front that I'm going to do everything in my power to change your mind. About…about a lot of things."

Eli watched the slight shiver that moved over Carla's slender frame, her soft lips parting on a gasp, but she didn't say anything. Her throat worked as she swallowed again, then gave him a nearly imperceptible nod. He'd been expecting a hell of an argument when he put those words out there, and couldn't help but breathe a sigh of relief that she wasn't going to get into it with him now.

From the dark smudges under her eyes, he could see how tired she was. He felt the same, the previous night spent lying on Eric's sofa and staring up at the ceiling, lost in his thoughts. He hadn't been able to shake the tension grinding through his muscles ever since she'd left him, but it was currently easing with each second that passed by. Now that he was with her, he could finally take a deep breath again, and he savored the way her scent filled his lungs, unable to get enough of it, the heat only making it more wild and lush.

Lowering his arms to his sides, he held her gaze as he asked, "Will you let me help you tonight?"

She slid him a wary look. "Help me how?"

"You're just as beautiful as you always are," he murmured, while a wry grin tugged at the corner of his mouth. "But, honey, you look about ready to fall on your face any second now. Let me bring you back to my cabin."

She looked stunned, and more than a little tempted. But her tone was still cautious as she said, "And do what?"

He pushed his hands in his pockets again and tried like hell to look innocent, when he was fairly positive he'd never looked that way a day in his life. "Run you a bath. Feed you dinner. I'll pamper you all night long if you'll let me. I just want to spend time with you, Rey."

"Won't Kyle be there?"

He shook his head. "He's gone until tomorrow morning. He and Lev have headed into Virginia to meet up with one of our East Coast suppliers about securing another batch of weapons."

Aside from the scare last night, things had been strangely quiet in regards to the Whiteclaw—especially considering the raids they'd made against their drugs and their weapons—and Eli and the others couldn't help but assume that things were going to happen sooner rather than later.

He could tell she was torn about what to do, but he gave her the time to come to the decision on her own, wanting her to choose him tonight over being alone. *Needing* her to do that.

"All right," she finally murmured, the soft words making him smile.

"No need to look so wary, Rey. I'll be golden, I promise. Scout's honor."

She snuffled a quiet laugh under her breath. "I know damn well you were never a scout."

Eli grinned. "Wasn't for lack of trying. One of my friend's dads put together a troop when we were little, thinking it would be good for us, and he ended up kicking me out. Said I wasn't good at playing with others."

She shook her head as she smirked. "I'll bet."

"Hey, be nice. I was crushed. They got to go on all these kickass fieldtrips to places like DC and the beach, while I was left at home, cutting the grass."

Her eyes glinted with humor, and maybe even a little bit of sadness. "Aw. Now I *am* feeling sorry for you. Cutting grass sucks."

He laughed, then jerked his chin toward the cabin he and Kyle were sharing. "Come on. I promised you some pampering."

True to his word, Eli told her to sit on his bed and wait while he ran her a hot, steaming bath. The cabin had been furnished and stocked when they'd arrived, and he was glad to find some aromatherapy bath gel under the sink, a thick foam building up on the surface of the water as he poured a healthy amount under the tap.

"It's all yours," he told her when he came back into the bedroom, catching her holding one of his worn T-shirts against her upper chest. He arched a brow at her, and she blushed at being caught with his shirt so close to her face, as if she'd been sniffing it before he'd come in, searching for his scent.

Coughing to clear the lump of lust in his throat, he rubbed the back of his neck and said, "I'll just go, um, get some food on while you relax in your bath." Then he got the hell out of there, not trusting himself to stay and watch her undress, knowing it would be too much for him and shatter his control. And he was determined to do this right. To make it through one night with her, just enjoying her company, without everything falling apart on them.

He wasn't much of a cook, but he put some frozen pizzas into the oven while she took her bath, doing his best to keep his mind on his task…and not on what she looked like in all those bubbles, her beautiful body slick and wet and warm.

"Get a grip, jackass," he muttered under his breath. "It's gonna be a long night. You can't screw this up."

She grinned when she came into the kitchen dressed in one of his big T-shirts and saw the freshly baked pizzas he'd just set out on the table, between the two place settings he'd put together. A flush covered her smooth cheeks as she took a seat at the table, and he would have given anything to know if she was just warm from the bath, or if her reaction had something to do with the hungry sideways glances she kept stealing at his bare chest. The oven had made the kitchen warm, and he'd ditched his shirt, boots and socks in an attempt to cool off a little.

"You still like pizza, right?" he asked, forcing himself not to stare at the way his shirt had ridden up on her bare thighs when she'd sat down. Christ, was she wearing anything underneath it? He stole a quick peek at her chest and had to choke back a low, appreciative growl at the sight of her hard little nipples pressing against the soft cotton. Yeah, definitely no bra.

How the hell am I going to make it through this without lunging across the table and ripping that shirt right off her?

Before he could come up with an answer, she said, "I love it."

Sounding more than a little distracted, he asked, "What?"

She tucked her damp hair behind her ears, looking so much like the girl he'd first talked to all those years ago. "You asked if I still like pizza, and I said that I love it."

"Ah, right. Good," he rumbled, turning toward the fridge. He took two bottles of beer out, twisted the caps off, and placed them on the table as he sat down.

"So if Kyle's with Lev," she said, grabbing one of the slices of pepperoni and cheese and putting it on her plate, "where are the other guys tonight?"

He took three slices of the spicy beef, saying, "They're up in Shadow Peak with Brody and Cian, double checking all the security checkpoints we have set up around the town."

She took a sip of her beer, then picked up her pizza, her cheeks still flushed with that lovely warmth that made him want to kiss her until she forgot her own name. "They've been awesome at helping," she murmured. "You all have. I don't know what we would have done without you."

"Yeah, they're a good bunch of guys."

She finished chewing the bite she'd taken, then said, "You know, you never have told me how you all ended up together."

Carla watched as he finished off his first slice, then washed it down with a hefty swallow of beer. When he set the bottle back down on the table, he leaned back in his chair and locked his beautiful gaze with hers. "When I left, I didn't have a friggin' clue what to do or where to go. I was sitting in this dive bar down in

Wesley, getting drunk, when this news program came on the TV, talking about how skilled soldiers could make a lot of money working as mercenaries down in South America." His lips twitched with a wry grin. "It was one of those journalistic exposés meant to showcase how dangerous the area was becoming, but all I saw was an opportunity. So I bought a plane ticket and headed down."

Grabbing the beer again, he tilted the bottle up to his lips, then went on with his story while she listened and ate. "And they were right about the money, as well as the danger. But I was feeling so reckless at that point that I just didn't care. I was on my third job when I ran into Kyle, Sam and James. They'd had some trouble with their packs and had decided to do the same thing I'd done. So we started working together, and a month later, we'd recruited Lev, who was living in Colombia at the time. The five of us have been working together ever since."

"You got lucky, all of you, to find each other the way that you did."

Fiddling with the label on his bottle, he said, "Yeah, I've never really thought about it like that, but I guess you're right." He took a deep breath, then slowly let it out as he lifted his gaze back to hers. "If I had to be away from here, I was damn lucky to have those guys watching my back."

"They look up to you."

"Don't know why," he drawled, setting the bottle down and reaching for another slice of pizza. "I think it's just that I'm the oldest."

"No. You're a natural leader, Eli. You always have

been. You just never had a chance to do anything about it when you were here before."

He shrugged, then took a bite of his pizza, looking uncomfortable with the praise as he chewed.

"So you and the guys started your new life as mercs," she murmured, before taking another sip of her beer. "Was it hard?"

"Hell, yeah," he said with a grin. "But there were times when we made damn good money at it. And then, if it was something we believed needed to be done, there were times when we didn't make a penny."

"So I was right!" She smirked in response to his curious look. "You know, the whole Merry Men thing. I had you pegged!"

He arched a brow. "You got a thing about men in tights, Rey?"

"Maybe," she murmured, teasing him. She didn't really, though she was fairly certain she'd find Eli hot in *anything* he wore, even if it was hosiery.

They shared a quiet laugh, then settled into a comfortable silence while they finished off the pizza, and he went to the fridge to get them both another beer. When he sat back down, twisted the cap off her bottle, and handed it to her, she leaned back in her chair and said, "So the guys…they're different, aren't they? I mean, I sense that they're Lycans. But…there's more, isn't there?"

He leaned back and tilted his bottle to his lips, then gave a rough sigh. Holding her gaze, he said, "I don't ever want to keep anything from you, Rey, but I'm afraid that's not my secret to tell."

She nodded, respecting that, since it meant he was a good friend. After a moment, she asked, "Were you ever close to dying? I mean, when you were out on a job?"

"Just once. Last year. We got caught up in a nasty turf war between two rival cartels, and I still can't believe we made it out alive. James and Sam took bullets in the arms and legs, and I got caught with a god-awful machete blade across my back."

She lurched forward in her seat so quickly she nearly spilled her beer all over the place. "Jesus Christ, Eli. Let me see."

He pushed back from the table and turned in his chair, showing her the left side of his back. She blinked, unable to believe she hadn't noticed it before, the long, raised scar cutting from the top of his shoulder blade down to the lower edge of his ribs. In that heartbreaking moment, she realized just how lucky she was to have found him in that shitty Texas bar that night. He could have so easily been lost to her over the past three years. Stolen away from her before she ever had the chance to get to know him again...or fall into love and lust with him even deeper than she'd been before.

There were some things she wasn't willing to leave this world without experiencing, and having this man, taking him into her body again and feeling him become a part of her, was one of them.

He watched her with a sharp, heavy-lidded gaze as she pushed her chair back and moved to her feet, coming around the side of the table. When she knelt on the floor beside him, he inhaled with a sharp breath that turned into a raw, guttural growl the instant she leaned forward and pressed a tender kiss against the middle of the scar. "Eli?" she whispered against his hot skin.

"Yeah?" he grated, his deep voice rough and low and deliciously husky.

She pressed her lips an inch higher. "Take me to bed?"

He went so still he wasn't even breathing. "You mean that?"

"Yes," she told him, leaning back and looking up at his hard, beautiful face. "In fact, I don't think I've ever meant anything more."

Chapter 13

The next thing Carla knew, she was in Eli's arms and his long legs were rapidly covering the distance between the kitchen and the bedroom. He kicked the bedroom door shut behind him, then quickly walked to the bed and practically tossed her into the center. She bounced with a startled gasp, glaring when she caught sight of his wicked grin. Then she realized his hot gaze had moved lower, to where her legs had parted and his shirt had ridden up, the pink, already slick folds between her legs completely exposed.

"Jesus," he rasped, his eyes gleaming with a hot, hungry glow as he started to reach for her.

"No, wait!" she blurted, propping herself up on her elbows. "If this is gonna happen, I want to see you. All of you, Eli. I want to watch you get naked for me."

His eyes widened a bit with surprise. "You want to watch me strip?"

When she bit her lower lip and nodded, he said, "I will if you will."

She slowly arched her brows as she drew her knees up, but didn't pull them together, leaving herself open to him. "I think you're already seeing everything there is to see."

The slow, provocative smile that curved his mouth was almost too beautiful to be real. "Lose the shirt, Rey. I don't want a single thing covering you but me."

Breathless with lust, she sat up and drew the shirt over her head, tossing it to the foot of the bed. Her breasts felt heavy and full, her nipples almost painfully tight, and she loved the way he consumed her with that searing, heavy-lidded gaze as he pulled in a deep, ragged breath of air.

"God, that's beautiful," he groaned, his breath hissing through his teeth as he exhaled.

She jerked her chin at him. "Lose the jeans, Eli."

When he bit his lower lip and undid his top button, revealing more of the taut, hair-dusted skin of his abdomen, it was so freaking sexy she almost forgot how to breathe. She watched with rapt attention as he slowly undid the fly and started shoving the jeans down to his thighs, each glimpse of skin making it obvious he wasn't wearing anything underneath. He shot her a smoldering look through his lashes as he pushed the jeans completely off, kicking them free. Then he stood before her completely bare, with his hands fisted at his sides, his chest rising and falling with each of his harsh, heavy breaths.

Carla had never had the chance to visually soak him in and look her fill before, so she was doing it now. "Don't move," she whispered, holding up her hand when he would have drawn nearer. "Stand still. Let me look at you."

A hard tremor shot through him, and he tightened his fists until thick veins popped up beneath his skin on the backs of his wrists and his masculine forearms. "I'll…try," he muttered in a tone so low and rough it made her smile.

Catching her lower lip in her teeth, she swept her greedy gaze over him, undone by the broad shoulders and hard chest. The muscular arms and legs, and the ridged, mouthwatering abdomen. The dark trail of hair that swirled around his navel, then led down to that thick, beautiful, brutal-looking cock…and below that, the dusky testicles, heavy and weighted, drawn tight with need. He made a low, thick sound as she stared at them, her hot gaze sliding up again, to the broad root nestled in that dark, curling hair. She followed every heavy inch of his fully erect shaft, the width and length of him enough to make her wonder how he ever managed to get it inside a woman.

Lifting her gaze back to his dark, scorching one, she said, "Okay, you can move now," and he was on her before she could so much as gasp, his powerful body pushing her back to the bed. His head lowered over her full breasts, his big hands holding them up in offering, and he breathed on one pink, swollen tip, the warmth of his breath making her crazy.

"I've needed these in my mouth again so badly," he groaned, squeezing her breasts together, her nipples so pink they were almost red. With a guttural sound rumbling up from his chest, he closed his mouth over one, and the blistering heat and wetness, the hungry strokes of his tongue, it all made her cry out from an intense wave of pleasure. She was holding his shaggy hair so tightly it had to hurt, pulling him even harder against her, while his mouth did things to her nipple that could all too easily make her orgasm. Just from his mouth on her breast, which seemed so…impossible.

She trembled, trying to think…to reason, but she knew she couldn't blame her stunning reaction on the partial bond that they shared. Yes, it was there, pulsing and throbbing between them like a living, breathing thing, but there was *more* to it than that. More emotion…more need. Was this what the other couples in the Alley felt? If so, she was amazed they ever managed to crawl out of bed and get anything done.

When he pushed her legs wider with his knee and settled in the cradle of her thighs, rubbing that hot, textured shaft against the sensitive folds of her sex, he lifted his head, looked her right in the eye, and quietly asked, "Are you giving in because you think it will get rid of me?"

"Do you really think that?" she murmured, sinking her nails into his shoulders as she pulled him against her, wanting to feel his weight pressing down on her, surrounding her.

"No," he rasped, bracing himself on his elbows, "but I'd take you anyway. I'll take you any way I can— *oh, hell.*"

Her eyes went wide. "What? What's wrong?"

"I don't have any condoms," he groaned, closing his eyes as he winced. "They're still in my bag, and I took it up to town with me. Damn thing is still out in the truck."

A frown started to work its way onto her mouth. "You were carrying around condoms?"

His eyes snapped open at her tone, and he shook his head once, hard. "For *you*. It's a new pack, Rey. Hasn't even been opened yet."

Her breath whooshed out of her lungs in a sharp burst of relief, and he shook his head a little again as he smirked, reading her like an open book.

"Wait right here for me, okay?" he whispered, leaning down and pressing a tender kiss to her lips. "I'll run out to the truck and get them."

"You don't have to," she said, running her fingers through his thick hair. "I'm covered as far as birth control goes. So we're, um, good. You know, if you want to…to just—"

"Hell, yes, I want to," he said so forcefully it made her dissolve into a girlish burst of giggles.

Eli closed his eyes again, taking a moment to simply soak in that beautiful sound. God, he hadn't heard her laugh nearly enough in the time that he'd known her, and he vowed to himself then and there that if she would just take a chance on him, he'd spend the rest of his life doing everything in his power to make her happy. To make her smile and laugh just like this.

But right now, he needed to make her moan.

Unable to wait a second longer, he opened his eyes and reached down, positioning the head of his rigid shaft at her warm, tender entrance. Then he started to push inside, thinking he'd be able to sink in all the way, so desperate to feel her clasping him in her wet heat that he was shaking with the need. But he froze almost immediately, his body caught in the hold of a terrible tension.

"What's wrong?" she gasped, gripping his biceps as she blinked up at him.

"I don't want to hurt you," he said in a raw voice, struggling so hard to keep control that he could barely get the words out. "Christ. You're *tighter* than a virgin, Rey."

The color in her face started to get brighter, and she wet her lips with a nervous swipe of her tongue. "It's, um, been…a long time for me. You know…other than the one time we were together."

He sucked in a sharp breath, his gaze locked tight on hers. "How long?"

She turned pink, her breaths quickening as she lowered her heavy gaze to his chin and whispered, "Since before that first night when we talked six years ago. The night you helped me with Nicole."

His eyes shot wide, his pulse rocketing.

Voice as strained as her expression, she said, "I… couldn't. There was no one…no one who…" The words trailed off, and she lifted her troubled gaze back to his. "You obviously didn't have the same problem."

No, he'd tried for months after that night to screw her out of his system with the pack females who were always ready to welcome him between their thighs. But he'd felt nothing with them. Not a goddamn thing.

"It didn't work. I might have gone to bed with those other women…but I didn't feel them, Rey. Didn't see them." He dropped his forehead against hers, and closed his eyes, determined to keep his focus for the moment on his words and not on how incredible she felt, her plush sheath holding the first few inches of his cock in a way that promised to blow his friggin' mind when he was buried deep inside her. Gritting his teeth, he said, "I stopped sleeping around when I finally accepted that it didn't matter a damn to me, who was under me. All I could see or hear or think about was you. I never touched another pack female from that night on."

"When was that?" she asked in a voice so soft he could barely hear her.

He pulled in a deep breath, and forced himself to pull his head back and look her in the eye as he said, "Nine months before I left."

She stiffened beneath him, the tips of her nails digging into his skin a little in her surprise. "And while you were gone?" she asked huskily.

Brushing his lips against her soft ones, he whispered, "You know the answer to that already."

"Eli, I—"

He cut her off, saying, "I'll answer any damn question you want, Rey. Just later, *please*." A trickle of sweat slipped down the side of his face, his muscles trembling under his hot skin as he fought to keep still and not pound himself into her, deep and hard and thick. "Because if I don't get inside you soon, I'm pretty sure my heart is gonna stop."

"You're the one who quit moving." Her grip on his shoulders gentled, a deep groan vibrating in his chest when she swept those soft fingertips down his rigid arms, his biceps bulging beneath his skin. "I didn't ask you to."

"Trying. To be. Considerate here," he bit out between his rough breaths, unable to hold back any longer. His hips rolled forward, pushing him another inch deeper into that hot, slick heaven, and he swore under his breath at how incredible it felt, her soft gasp making him need to thrust and thrust, working against her resistance until he'd hit the end of her. "And it isn't easy," he growled, fisting the sheets in his hands as he shook the sweat from his eyes, "seeing as how I was ready to lose it the second I got inside you."

She suddenly pushed against his shoulders, her legs moving against his, and the next thing he knew he was on his back and she was straddling him, pushing down on him with steady pressure, her eyes dark and hot as she bit her lip, and he went deep…*deeper,* as she took him inch by inch, until not even a sliver of space existed between them. She made a soft, provocative sound that was insanely sexy, the look on her face as she leaned forward and braced her hands against his chest, her head back, nearly making him come then and there.

"Oh, Christ," he groaned, holding her hips in a death grip. "You're gonna turn me inside out, aren't you?"

She stared down at him, her beautiful mouth curving with a small, sensual smile. "Could I?"

"You could do anything you wanted. Any damn thing you wanted, and I'd be at your mercy."

With that gorgeous smile still on her lips, she held his blistering gaze and started to move, the voluptuous pulse of her hips as she rose and fell on him so good he didn't know how he'd ever survived without it. Her mouthwatering scent was rising with the heat of her beautiful little body, her lithe muscles working beneath her silky skin as she broke him down with pleasure, taking him apart piece by piece. He felt his gums burn with heat as his fangs started to drop, his beast prowling beneath his surface. His knees drew up as his back arched off the bed, his grip on her hips so tight he worried he would leave marks, and he gnashed his teeth, determined to keep from ruining the best goddamn moment of his life.

"You're destroying me," he ground out, falling so completely into her shimmering gaze he didn't think he would ever climb back out again. "I don't know how much longer I can hold myself back, Rey."

She gave a soft siren's laugh that only made his blood pump harder. "Then just let go."

"You're already so swollen, and I don't want to make it worse. Don't want to make you...Damn it, I want you to *love* it with me, Rey." His voice was so guttural it barely sounded human. "I want you coming back for *more,* addicted to it. I don't want to hurt you."

"You won't. You won't hurt me," she breathed out, leaning over him and nipping his lower lip with her teeth. "I'm not that breakable, Eli."

He growled, undone, swiftly rolling until he had her trapped beneath him again, his body buried hard and thick inside her. With his damp face right over hers, he watched her eyes glitter with a dark, possessive, primitive hunger that matched his own as he drew back and then gave her a hard, hammering thrust that shoved him even deeper than he'd been before. He loved the way she held him so tightly, but he needed her soft and melting with pleasure if he wanted to be able to ride her the way he craved. And God only knew he could never get enough of her mouthwatering taste. So he forced himself to pull out, knelt between her sprawled thighs, and lifted her hips as he lowered his head between her legs.

She gasped as he shoved his face against her drenched flesh, eating at her plump sex with all the raw, gnawing hunger that was burning inside him. She was so soft and sweet and deliciously slick, the tight clench of her sheath around his tongue as it plunged inside her making him growl like an animal. He heard a throaty cry break from her throat as she crashed, coming so hard he could feel the breathtaking power of the climax as it tore through her. He pressed his face even harder against her as she pulsed and quivered, the sounds she made driving him wild, while he went at her like a man who'd been starved for her taste for a lifetime, until he couldn't wait a moment more.

"Again," he growled, bracing himself on his arms and slamming his cock inside her so hard it drove her up the bed. "I need you to come again, Rey. I need to feel it on me."

She gripped his bunched shoulders and arched beneath him, pressing her breasts against his sweat-covered chest as he came down over her and started thrusting in hard, powerful lunges that were getting faster…and faster, taking her the way he'd been dying to for so many heartbreaking years.

"Oh, God, Eli. I'm there!" she cried, her silky sex clutching him like a hot, wet mouth, milking him as she came.

"That's it," he growled, throwing his head back as his own release thundered through him with the stunning force of a storm, completely destroying him as he pulsed and pulsed, pouring himself inside her until he started to wonder if it was ever going to end. Not that he wanted it to. What he wanted was to keep thrusting inside her while he buried his face against the smooth, tender curve of her shoulder, but he didn't dare, know-

ing he couldn't risk letting his fangs get anywhere close
to her throat.

"Damn, baby, I think you killed me," he groaned,
when he could finally find his voice again. His hips
were still gently rocking against hers, his arms shaking
as he hung his head forward, trying to catch his breath.

"Mmm...sorry about that," she practically purred,
and he felt a grin tugging at the corner of his mouth.
She sounded like a woman who'd been well and thor-
oughly taken, and he knew there was only one thing
that could have made it better. Something he hoped
like hell they were closer to now that they'd shared
something so incredible.

"Don't ever be sorry," he told her, finally lowering
his mouth so that he could kiss her soft, pink lips as
he carefully pulled himself from her tight clasp. "I'll
happily die again and again if it means getting more
of this."

Touching her as gently as he could, he lifted her
boneless body up higher on the bed, until her head was
resting on the pillows, then moved onto his side and
reached down for the quilt, pulling it over her.

"You don't want more now?" she asked, looking a
little surprised. And maybe even a bit disappointed.

"I *always* want you, Rey. But I can wait," he told
her, reaching out and pushing her hair back from her
flushed face. "I don't want to make you too sore."

She smirked up at him. "You're not worried about
making me sore, just not *too* sore?"

"Hey, I'm a guy," he said huskily, leaning down
again and brushing his lips across her smiling ones.
"I love the thought of you walking around tomorrow,
feeling how hard I took you every time you take a step."

"Barbarian," she teased, making him grin as she playfully smacked him on the shoulder.

Your barbarian, he thought. *Always yours...*

He could feel his body stirring, already hardening again, and knew he needed to put some space between them while he still could. Rolling into a sitting position on the far side of the bed, he grabbed a pillow and the afghan that was tangled up in the bottom of the quilt, then laid them on the floor, switched off the bedside light, and forced himself to lie down. A second later, her beautiful face peeked over the edge of the mattress, her bright eyes shining with laughter in the silvery wash of moonlight streaming in through the window. "You got something against the bed? Or is it me?"

Putting his hands behind his head so he wouldn't be tempted to reach up and grab her, pulling her down there to join him, he said, "I'm not sleeping in a bed with you until things between us are completely settled."

Her golden hair fell over the side of the mattress as she cocked her head a bit to the side, her expression curious. "Why?"

Because he was afraid that he would wake up, hazy with sleep, and reach for her. His need for her was so intense that he didn't trust what he would do in those foggy moments of consciousness. Sink his fangs into her and complete the bond, once and for all? It was so damn tempting, and yet, he knew it would be the kiss of death for any chances they might have of a future together, if he did it before she was ready.

Watching her carefully, he said, "When you're ready to give me what I want, you won't be able to keep me from sleeping beside you."

She blinked, and he could see the exact moment when she understood what he was saying. With a quick breath, and a flick of her tongue over her lower lip, she said, "You don't trust yourself, do you? You don't trust yourself not to bite me."

"I've told you what I want, Rey."

He had...and more than once. But as she stared down at him with that soft, shell-shocked expression on her lovely face, the look in her eyes a mesmerizing blend of emotions, Eli realized that for the first time, the little Runner was *finally* starting to believe that he meant it.

Chapter 14

God, I've been such a fool.

That was the painful, embarrassing thought that kept spinning its way through Carla's head as she sat in Mason and Torrance's living room the following morning, trying to listen to the plans being made. She'd meant to stay smart and focused on what was good for her—but her lust and lovesick heart had finally gotten the better of her, and now her disappointment was crushing.

Was what happened between us all for this? Was he just trying to get things to work out the way he wanted them to? To make me so crazy over him, I'd do whatever he wanted?

As if he knew she'd be feeling skittish after waking in his bed, Eli had already left the cabin by the time she'd blinked her eyes open, a little stunned to realize what she'd done. That she'd given in to her desire and made love to him. And it had definitely been making love. She'd had sex before, and while nice, it didn't come anywhere close to what had taken place between her and the manipulative, gorgeous, too-freaking-sexy-for-his-own-good alpha.

Had she honestly thought she had a good idea of what truly emotional, hunger-driven mating would be like? Hah! She hadn't had a clue.

She didn't know if all Lycan males were like that, like *him*. He was the only one she'd ever allowed to get close to her in a physical way—the only one she'd ever wanted. But she'd have been lying through her teeth if she'd said she hadn't loved it. His strength. His aggression. The raw, primal savagery of his sexual hunger. A hunger he kept telling her was only for her. For her…and no other. And, God, how badly she'd wanted to believe him.

But now, after what he'd just said, and in front of everyone? She shook her head, wondering if she would always be nothing more than a fool when it came to this man.

When she'd climbed out of his bed, terrified by the warm glow of happiness burning in the center of her chest, she'd been desperate for the time to stand beneath a hot shower and make sense of her buzzing, complicated emotions, but there hadn't been any. Dressing in her clothes from the day before, she'd hurried over to Wyatt and Elise's, only to have her partner catch her coming in through the door. Instead of teasing her about her night out, he'd told her they were late for a meeting at Mason's. The next thing she knew, she was standing in a roomful of friends, her emotions still

on edge. And the sight of Eli standing on the other side
of the room had made her heart pound so hard that it
hurt. He'd looked up, locking that intense, smoldering
gaze on her face, and though the set of his mouth had
been a little grim, it was still so beautiful that she'd
wanted to kiss him until he was all she could taste and
hear and see. She'd flushed, and he'd just kept staring,
the fiend, even when everyone had started to notice.

She'd already known that their night together
wouldn't be a secret. That kind of news traveled fast
in the Alley, but that didn't mean he'd had to be so blatant about it. The way he'd stared at her—so hard and
possessive—had made his thoughts clear to everyone
around them, and she'd felt herself blushing all the way
to the roots of her hair.

When she'd caught Wyatt smirking at her, she'd
stomped on his toes with her booted foot, enjoying the
low grunt of pain that'd slipped past his lips. "You're
mean," he'd grumbled.

"Don't forget it," she'd muttered in response, determined not to look in Eli's direction again. But it
hadn't mattered. She'd still felt the weight of his searing, possessive gaze on her, and damn it, it'd felt good.
So perfect and right that she couldn't help remember-
ing the dream she'd had during the night, when she'd
been cuddled up in his sheets, his mouthwatering scent
surrounding her.

She'd dreamed about their wedding day, of all
things. Of a day when they would stand before their
family and friends and pledge their love to one another. A day she'd been an idiot to even think about,
considering the words that had left his lips when he'd
looked at Mason a moment ago and said, "Before we

get started, I want to say what I'm sure a lot of you are thinking, but haven't felt right about bringing up. So I'm doing it now. I know we need as many bodies going into battle as we can get, but I feel pretty strongly about the fact that the women shouldn't fight. Not just the ones who are only just learning some combat skills, but *any* of them. After seeing firsthand what the Whiteclaw are capable of, it's just too dangerous." Without looking at her, he'd crossed his arms over his chest and gruffly added, "And before anyone argues that there are women in this room who are more than capable of going into battle, that might be. But it still doesn't mean that they should."

Her jaw had dropped as she'd stared at him, unable to believe those words had actually just come from his mouth. And she was so staggered by them, her heart feeling like it was being crushed in her chest, that it'd taken her a moment to realize the meeting was still going on around her.

Fighting hard to concentrate, she narrowed her burning gaze on Mason, and tried to listen. He was saying something about how they needed to be prepared for the fact that some of the Whiteclaw might have their own supplies of the "super soldier" drugs, which they would undoubtedly be saving for the attack, but she was only half hearing him. The majority of her brain was still focused on what Eli had said, and what it meant for them. He'd never made it a secret, how he felt about her job. Now his words had confirmed that he didn't want her fighting alongside the men she'd been fighting beside her entire adult life, which was exactly where she belonged.

If he couldn't see that, then he didn't actually know her at all. So where the hell did that leave them?

It was obvious that important plans were being made, but she didn't have a clue what they were, unable to get past the shock of hearing Eli say what he had in front of everyone. In front of the men she'd worked with for so long. She couldn't have been more insulted if he'd stood there and told them all that he thought she was a pathetic weakling who couldn't be trusted to do her job. Because that's what it'd felt like, and she felt so betrayed she was terrified she was going to burst into tears before she could get out of there.

The instant Mason called an end to the meeting, she shoved past Wyatt, who was trying to say something to her, and ran like she had the devil on her ass. It took her only moments to reach Wyatt and El's cabin, and she stormed through the living room, down the hall, ready to slam the door behind her when she reached the guest room—only to find that Eli was right behind her as she turned.

"Get out!" she snarled, shoving hard at his chest as she tried to push him back into the hallway. But the bastard didn't budge.

"I'm not going anywhere until we've talked," he said in a low, calm tone that grated on her nerves so badly she wanted to scream. Spinning away from him, she paced at the foot of the bed, breathing hard and fast, glaring at him from the corner of her eye as he shut the door, then leaned back against it, watching her with a hooded, cautious gaze.

Finally, she stopped pacing and braced her hands on her hips as she turned to face him. "What the hell was that in there?" she demanded, flinging the words at him.

Crossing his arms over his chest, he worked his jaw a few times before he answered the question. "I was only saying what I thought needed to be said."

"Ohmygod! Are you honestly that stupid?" she seethed, so angry she wanted to cry. But she was going to be damned before she spilled any more tears in front of him. "Or maybe you're just too blind to see what an ass you're being. Is that it?"

His lips pressed together in a hard, grim line, but his eyes gave him away. He didn't regret what he'd said. Not even a little. He actually believed that crap!

Breathing in rough, uneven bursts, she said, "You're always trying to protect me. But guess what? I don't need your protection, Eli. What I've always needed was your love. I needed you to stand by me. To fight for me. And you didn't. You ran. You didn't stand by me before, and you're *still* not standing by me. So I'm done!"

Eyes burning with a raw, molten gleam, he growled, "I did love you, damn it."

She shook her head. "If that's true, then you didn't love me enough."

"Christ, woman. I've said I'm sorry for leaving so many times," he ground out, lowering his arms to his sides as he pushed away from the door. "I've told you that I'm more in love with you now than ever, and I already loved you more than I ever imagined was possible. What more do you want from me, Rey?"

"I want something I can obviously never have!" she shouted, completely losing control. Of everything. Her emotions. Her fears. The entire goddamn situation. "So I'll take being free, instead. I want to tear you out!"

He took another step forward, and a muscle started to pulse in his cheek with a rhythmic, telling tic. "You didn't feel like that last night."

"That was sex," she snapped. "You of all people should know the difference."

"I know it was the best, most incredible sex I've ever had," he shot back, and she could see his wolf burning in his eyes, the icy blue now as dark and turbulent as a storm. "There isn't even a close second."

She glared, thinking he might literally drive her mad.

"I know I want it again. I haven't—" He broke off, seeming to struggle with what to say, then growled, "I'm—not—done. I'll *never* be done."

Fighting the urge to stomp her foot like a child, she screamed, "God, Eli! You can make me so angry! No one's ever made me as angry as you do." She lifted her arms, pressing the insides of her wrists to her temples, her voice breaking with emotion. "I *hate* it. Hate feeling like that about you, but you need to listen to me. Please. Just listen." Pressing one of her hands over her pounding heart, she said, "I *love* what I do. It's not just a job to me. It's a part of who I am, and that's never going to change. If you loved me like you say you do, then you would understand that. Which means more than the fact that you don't love me. You don't even *know* me."

"That's not true."

"Are you saying you wouldn't want me to quit? That if we completed the bond, you'd be supportive of what I do?"

He opened his mouth, then snapped it shut again, his nostrils flaring as he pulled in a deep breath. Then he muttered, "I need to go and meet with Elliot and Max. In a few hours, we'll know whether or not it's a go tonight."

"That soon?" she gasped.

His dark brows drew together in a scowl. "Weren't you listening at the meeting?"

She shook her head. "No. I was too upset."

His scowl deepened, and he said, "If Max and Elliot have gotten the rumor mill going at full speed, then it looks like we'll be putting the plan into action not long after sundown."

She nodded, thinking that part of the mercs' plan was brilliant. In fact, the entire plan was genius. And who better to spread gossip than a bunch of gabbing teenage girls who were still in contact with other Whiteclaw teens? But how the hell had she managed not to hear that they might be going to war in a mere matter of hours?

"There must be a thousand things to do," she said distractedly, her thoughts spinning as she lowered her gaze. And there clearly wasn't any time for anger or arguments at the moment. Not when there was so much to get done and to organize. And despite what anyone else might say or think, she *was* going to be in that town fighting beside her Bloodrunning brothers. It would take more than Eli Drake to stop her. It'd take a freaking act of God, and even then she'd fight tooth and nail to make sure she was there when she was needed. "We can finish this later," she added, careful to keep her expression neutral as she lifted her gaze back to his. "You need to go, and I should go and find Wyatt."

Instead of turning and leaving, he stepped even closer, locking her in his hard, penetrating stare, and quietly said, "When we go to war—whether it's tonight or tomorrow or the night after that—I'm *begging* you, Rey, please don't fight in town. Please stay here and help look after the others."

Tears burned at the backs of her eyes, but she refused to let them fall. "Why?" she whispered, her chest heaving with emotion. "Why do you think I'm so weak?"

"God, Rey. I don't think you're weak," he groaned, lifting a hand to the side of her face and stroking her skin with his thumb. "I just...I don't want to lose you. Is it so wrong to want to protect something I care about more than I care about my own life?"

Clutching his powerful wrist in her hands, she stared up at him and said, "It is when you keep comparing her to something she's not. I'm not your mother, Eli. I don't need your protection. I just need your love. And your faith."

"I *have* faith in you," he growled, his frustration bleeding through the guttural words. "But that doesn't mean I'm not terrified of losing you."

"You've trusted me with your lust, even though you were worried it would be too much for me. Can't you trust me to be strong and smart enough for my job?"

"I wish to hell that I could, Rey. But it terrifies me. I *hate* it," he scraped out, "and I don't know how to make that change."

"I don't know, either," she said in a throaty voice that was thick with tears. "I just know that this isn't healthy. We can't do this, no matter how we feel about each other."

He looked at her so hard and intensely that she felt like he was trying to change her mind with the sheer force of his will, his eyes dark and angry and troubled, his throat working as he swallowed. But she could tell he had no idea what to say to her.

Pushing his hand away from her face, she let go of his wrist and stepped back from him. "Later, Eli. We can sort things out later. But *now* is not the time."

He worked his jaw again, looking like a man who'd been pushed far beyond his limits, then turned and walked away, slamming the door behind him.

The instant she was alone, Carla covered her face with her hands, breathing hard, and all she could smell was *him*. His scent covered her, inside and out, and she wondered if she would ever be free of it.

The day went by in a blur of tension and frantic activity, and twelve hours later, as she pulled in a deep breath of the nighttime air, she realized that her head was finally clear of Eli's scent.

But that was only because the night smelled like death. And Shadow Peak looked like a warzone.

Keeping to the shadows, Carla surveyed the scene before her with a pounding heart. The night winds howled through the quiet town, eerie and hollow, like the lamenting cry of a banshee. As a trickle of sweat slipped its way down her spine beneath her tight, long-sleeved black top, the thick, meaty scent of blood filled her nose from the drenched street that currently resembled a crimson river. Voices from the street carried easily in the silence as the wind took a brief respite, and she heard someone say, "It's just as the call said. All that talk of the Silvercrest pack coming together was just a trick to try and put us off, and now the idiots have slaughtered themselves."

She moved closer to the corner of the building she

was hiding in the shadow of, eyeing the two males standing among the bodies. They were human, and she recognized them both from the descriptions Kyle had given her of Jack Bartley and his second-in-command, Joe Mackey.

"It's disappointing," Bartley muttered, nudging a body with the toe of his boot. "I was looking forward to seeing their fall."

"Me, too. But now Claymore has gotten what he wanted without shedding a single drop of Whiteclaw blood. That's going to do wonders for our reputation."

"There is that," Bartley drawled, before giving a low laugh. "But he'll die if he thinks this means he no longer owes me our final payment."

Mackey grunted his agreement, then asked, "So what do we do now?"

Voice thick with disgust, Bartley said, "We bring in the soldiers and let them get to work. It will take forever to deal with this mess. Bloody mongrels."

Flexing her hands at her sides, Carla had to physically restrain herself from lunging into the street and ripping the merc's throat out, knowing she had to bide her time. One false move and everything would be ruined.

A few minutes passed, and then the Whiteclaw soldiers poured into the town square that lay at the end of the street, cursing and muttering to each other. Peeking around the edge of the building, she watched as Roy Claymore climbed the steps leading up to the Town Hall, and felt bile rise in the back of her throat as he looked out over the crowd and shouted, "Shadow Peak is ours!"

The crowd cheered, and then Roy yelled out, "Rid

the streets of the filth and pile the bodies on the south field, where we'll burn them at tomorrow's celebration!"

Another raucous cheer went up, and her pulse slowed to a hard, thudding beat, the way it always did just before she engaged the enemy.

When Kyle had first brought the mercs' plan to the Runners' attention, he'd told them, "The control of information is key." And he'd been right. By controlling what was going out of Shadow Peak via the rumor mill, they'd set the stage, spreading tales of a growing dissention within the town. An escalating tension between those who supported the Runners and those who didn't, that tension supposedly exacerbated by the arrival of Eli and his fellow mercenaries.

Taking deep, controlled breaths, she watched the Whiteclaw soldiers make their way through the piles of bodies that covered the streets, and waited for the signal that Eric would give from the top of the Town Hall. She counted down the seconds in her head, and then the first signal came—a low, warbling whistle—and she undid the safety on the automatic machine gun strapped over her shoulder. Then she heard the second signal, and she lifted the weapon as she stepped out of the alleyway where she'd been hiding, spraying the Whiteclaw with bullets. At the same time, the blood-covered Lycans lying on the ground who had pretended to be dead rolled onto their backs, weapons at the ready, and fired from below.

Many of those Lycans were women who had wanted to defend their town, but didn't have enough training to effectively fight with their fangs and claws. But as Mason had told the group during another meeting they'd had that afternoon, even if the women weren't properly trained in hand-to-hand combat, they could still do a hell of a lot of damage with the right kind of gun, in the right kind of situation, and he'd had a good point. Eli hadn't been happy with the decision, but he hadn't gone against the Runner. Instead, he'd used his expertise to create the safest situation that he could for the women under the circumstances, and she was hopeful that they would have limited casualties.

Hating the violence, but understanding that it was necessary when one group had to protect itself from another, Carla kept firing as wave after wave of Whiteclaw soldiers, many of who had clearly taken the "super soldier" drugs, swarmed into the streets. She could sense Eli somewhere near her left side, and she knew he was purposefully staying close to her. But as long as he didn't interfere with her job tonight, she wasn't going to complain. An argument right now would only get someone killed.

When her machine gun fired the last of its bullets, she tossed it to the ground. A quick glance at her watch told her that the women in the street would soon be making a run for the security of the buildings, where they would hide while those who had been trained in physical combat dealt with the second phase of the battle. They'd already taken down a good portion of the enemy, but the fight was far from over, and the soldiers who had been wounded by the bullets now needed to be killed.

Stepping back into the alleyway, Carla quickly did a weapons check on the blades she'd secured to her body, turning away from the group of mercs who were with her as they stripped down. Though she'd decided to fight in her human form, since she would be able to use a variety of weapons as well as her claws and fangs, the men would be fighting as werewolves, and she glanced over her shoulder just as Eli and the others allowed the shift to wash over their expanding forms. Bones cracked as fur rippled over their skin in a mesmerizing display of power, muscles increasing to nearly twice their original size. When the transformations were complete, they would stand at nearly seven feet in height, with wolf-shaped heads, lethal, claw-tipped hands, and long, deadly fangs that gleamed in the silvery moonlight.

Of course, that was what she'd *assumed* would happen, given her knowledge of Lycan transformations. But when Lev, Kyle, Sam and James completed their shifts, she realized they were even taller than Eli and the other Silvercrest males who were coming to join them, and she could only gape in shock.

"Um, Eli," she croaked, blinking her eyes in astonishment. "What *the hell* are they?"

Eli reached out and gently pushed her chin up with a claw-tipped hand, a crooked grin on his wolf's muzzle-shaped mouth as he said, "Not the time, Rey."

"Uh, right," she murmured, shaking her head.

"Stay close," he told her, not giving her time to argue as he turned and headed back out to the street. The others followed behind them, and it didn't take long before they were embroiled in battle, the Lycans they were going up against a mix of ones who'd been enhanced by the "super soldier" drugs, and ones who thankfully hadn't. Most of Bartley's men, it seemed, had been taken out in the initial wave of the attack, and Eli was grateful as hell to his guys for coming up with such a brilliant plan.

"Sam," he said in the deep, guttural voice of his beast, "watch your right. They're coming in hard and heavy from the next street over."

"Got it covered, boss man," Sam replied, sounding like he was actually enjoying the fight, and Eli figured once a mercenary, always a mercenary. Or maybe his friend just liked kicking bad guy ass and helping those who needed it, the same as he did. Either way, Eli was glad to have Sam and the guys there, and if they survived this, he was going to make sure he told them how much their loyalty meant to him.

Carla was fighting beside him, and like the night they'd been ambushed on their way up to the Alley, they were working together in perfect synchronicity. It should have made him feel better, but he was still raw inside with fear over the danger she'd put herself in by coming here. He knew she was still seriously pissed off at him, but damn it, he'd only done what he'd felt was right. What he'd felt he *had* to do, because he loved her and couldn't imagine ever losing her.

A little farther down the street, he noticed Cian working his way closer and closer to Sayre, who was fighting with a skill that was remarkable in an eighteen-year-old. But then, Sayre was more than your average girl, her powers apparently some of the strongest that either her mother or sister had ever seen in a witch. But Cian clearly wasn't any more comfortable with her fighting than Eli was by Carla's determination to be there.

When three burly Whiteclaw soldiers charged Sayre all at once, the Irishman roared for her to run for cover as he tore through the Lycans in a deadly flurry of claws and snapping jaws that was truly impressive. Well, to anyone but the witch. She shouted at the Runner to leave her alone, going so far as trying to use her power to hold him back when Cian snarled that he was getting her out of there. But to her obvious shock, the Irishman stormed right through the crackling wall of light she'd raised between them, hooking his arm around her waist and leaping onto the top of an RV that'd been left parked against a tall building on the far side of the street.

Eli could have sworn he saw Constance Murphy give the Runner a nod of thanks, or maybe even approval. But then her attention was drawn away by a fallen Silvercrest Lycan who needed her help, leaving Cian to deal with a furious Sayre all on his own. She growled something at him that Eli couldn't hear, but the Runner stiffened and growled something right back, before jumping off the top of the RV and ripping any of the Whiteclaw who tried to get near it to pieces, while a still enraged Sayre looked as though she wouldn't mind blasting him with another shot of light from her hands.

Yeah, the Runner definitely had his hands full with that one, and he almost felt sorry for the guy, until Eli realized that he was in the exact same boat. Because *his* woman was also a serious little badass. And as he finally took a moment to stop letting his fear control him, and really *watched* her in action, he saw that Carla Reyes was truly breathtaking when she fought...and he was a major, shit-for-brains jackass.

Christ, I'm an idiot.

He might have been slow on the uptake, but he was

starting to see that he'd been wrong to worry so much. It didn't mean that he *wouldn't* worry, because he loved her and would always put her safety above his and anyone else's. But he knew a natural warrior when he saw one. In truth, the realization had been creeping up on him for days, though he hadn't wanted to acknowledge it. And his men had been hammering it home, none of them shy about telling him that it'd been a dumb move he'd pulled on her during the meeting at Mason's that morning. But it wasn't until right then, until that very moment, that it truly sank in. That he saw what they had all been telling him.

She was a friggin' goddess on the battlefield, gorgeous and deadly and seriously skilled, and he needed to get a grip, because that wasn't ever going to change.

When another heavy wave of the enemy suddenly poured into the street, Mason and Elliot quickly joined them, and the fighting became brutal. "Reyes, fall back!" Mason shouted, tearing his claws through one soldier's throat, before breaking another's knee. "This is getting too intense!"

She shot the Runner a blistering glare as she took down one opponent and then immediately engaged another. "What the hell, Mase?"

"I mean it, honey," Mason grunted, cutting her a worried look. "These assholes know they've lost, which means they're desperate."

Knowing he needed to speak up, Eli said, "Mason, it's okay, man. I know you mean well, but she's where she's meant to be."

Both Runners turned their heads toward him the instant the soldiers they were fighting fell, their shocked expressions almost identical. Mason recovered first, growling for her to be careful, then got back into the fight. It took Carla a little longer to recover, but she finally shook herself out of her daze, took a deep breath, and then gave Eli a tender look of thanks that he swore he could feel reach all the way down to his soul.

"You ready?" he asked, a wry grin tugging at the corner of his mouth.

Carla blinked, thinking that crooked grin of his was about the most beautiful thing she'd ever seen on a sexy-as-sin Lycan.

"What?" he asked, when he caught the way she was looking at him.

"I can't believe you just did that."

He had the audacity to shrug one of those massive, muscular shoulders, as if he didn't know what the big deal was. "Why wouldn't I? In case you hadn't noticed, you're a serious little ass kicker."

I will not smile...I will not smile...I will not smile. She repeated the words over and over in her head, still too hurt by what he'd done to forgive him that easily.

As if he sensed the confusing rush of emotions she was feeling, he winced and said, "I'm sorry, Rey. In case you hadn't noticed, I've been a blind, stupid son of a bitch."

Not knowing what to make of the change in him, she shook her head a little to clear it and got ready to get back in the fight. But a few moments later, when she saw the group of Whiteclaw soldiers who had just come around the corner up ahead, she knew what she needed to do. "Hey, Eli?" she called out, drawing his attention.

He hurried to her side, as if he'd just been waiting

for her to call him closer. "You okay?" he asked, his bright eyes narrowed with concern.

"I'm good," she told him, gesturing toward the Lycans. "I just thought you might want to help me take out those assholes over there. They're the ones who knocked me around when I was in Hawkley."

"With pleasure," he growled, flexing his deadly claws at his sides. Together, they fought the soldiers, easily taking them down, working with that same startling precision and intuition that they'd used before. By the time the bastards who'd beaten her had fallen, more Silvercrest fighters, along with many of the Runners, were making their way into the street, since it had been set as their primary meeting point before the battle that had waged across the entire town had started. From what she could hear everyone saying, it sounded as if those Whiteclaw soldiers who were still standing were abandoning the attack and making a run for it.

Looking over the group, Eli spotted Jeremy, who had returned to his human form and was dressed in a torn pair of jeans, and asked, "Where are my brother and sister?"

Using his forearm to wipe the specks of blood from his face, Jeremy said, "They're helping Wyatt and Brody search for Roy. The last thing we want is for that asshole to slink away."

"I'm not going anywhere!" a belligerent voice called out from the far end of the street.

Turning around, Carla stared at the Lycan who'd spoken, thinking he was the most unattractive male she'd ever seen in wolf form, his fur a dingy gray and his head too small for his shoulders. "It's Roy. He's here," she said, and the mercs around her growled with aggression, while Eli simply watched Claymore with a cold, deadly gaze.

Walking across the fallen bodies of his soldiers as if they were nothing more than dirt, the monster responsible for all this bloodshed looked over the gathering of Silvercrest wolves and snarled, "I want the bitch Runner who brought the goddamn mercs here to help you. Give her to me, and we'll leave."

"You're leaving anyway, just not on your feet," Jeremy growled from Eli's side. "Because you have a hell of a lot to answer for, you twisted bastard."

"That's the problem with you Silvercrest," the Lycan sneered. "You let emotion get in the way of everything."

Instead of charging forward and taking Claymore's head off, the way she'd fully expected him to do, Eli turned his head and looked at her, holding her sharp gaze with his. Speaking in the wolf's garbled, gravelly voice, he asked, "You gonna let me take this one?"

"If you want him, go for it."

The instant the words left her mouth, she felt the change coming over him, and knew precisely what it meant.

Eli's *dark wolf*—that most deadly, primitive part of him that could only be created by a bloodline as powerful as the one he and his siblings shared—was awakening.

She'd heard it said that a dark wolf could only fully awaken, embracing its total power, once it had found its true life mate. Like so many things in nature, the rule was meant to keep balance, since it was a dark wolf's need for its mate that was meant to temper its savage, visceral aggression.

However, the rule no longer applied when that aggression was being channeled toward someone who had threatened the wolf's woman. In that event, all bets were off, and the threat was destroyed by any means necessary.

And that was just what Eli was getting ready to do.

Yes, in this case, Carla was perfectly capable of defending herself. But she freaking loved that Eli felt so protective of her that he was taking the shape of his dark wolf *now*.

Eyes burning with emotion, he looked down at her and said, "This doesn't mean that I don't believe in you. It only means that I love the hell out of you."

With those incredible words buzzing through her head, she jerked her chin toward Claymore, silently telling Eli to get on with it, and he gave a low, wicked laugh that struck her as impossibly sexy, even in these dangerous, deadly circumstances. Though the danger and death at this point were all for Roy.

There was an aura around Eli as he prowled forward, a power pulsing like a physical force that you could feel in the air, and it made her shiver as it swept over her skin. Everyone around them was watching in awe, including his fellow mercenaries, who she would have guessed had never seen a dark wolf in action before, though they would have surely heard of them. He stood even taller than he had just moments ago, his body more muscular, while his eyes burned a deep, mesmerizing shade of amber. And when he started to fight, leaping through the air and catching Roy around the neck, slamming him into the side of a building, it was clear that Claymore didn't stand a chance. The older Lycan might have experience on his side, but he was no match for Eli's ferocity, speed and strength. His body was like a blur as he punched and clawed and kicked, and within mere moments the encounter was over.

When Roy finally fell, his head no longer connected to his shoulders, Eli turned and locked his hooded, burning gaze with hers. Then he gave her a slow, sexy smile, and the crowd erupted in cheers.

The battle had reached its end, and the Silvercrest were victorious.

Chapter 15

Six days later, Carla stood on her front porch, watching Eli and his men hard at work at the far end of the glade. They'd cleared the area of trees, and looked to be putting in some kind of series of foundations, but she couldn't be sure without going down there and checking it out firsthand.

And that was something she wasn't prepared to do, her panic now at an all-time high.

The days after the battle had been difficult, and she knew it would take time for normal life to resume. The pack mourned the loss of those who'd fallen, while holding those who'd survived a little closer to their hearts. And though there was a lot of work still to be done in those parts of the town that had been hit the hardest, they had made their stand and shown the Lycan nation that they weren't to be trifled with. Not unless you were looking to have your ass kicked. She knew they had Eli and his men to thank for so much of their success, and she'd personally spoken to each one of the mercenaries and expressed her gratitude.

Well, except for Eli.

Despite how he'd stood up for her during the battle, she'd been avoiding him. She hadn't even gone after him about the bond breaking, since Jillian and her mother and sister had exhausted themselves after the fighting, using their powers to heal the wounded. Jilly needed to recoup her energy now, especially in light of the small life she was carrying, so Carla hadn't even broached the subject.

And, yeah, she knew she was running scared by not talking to Eli, but damn it, she was just so…so terrified of what would happen when he finally grew tired of this place and left her again. Despite everything that he'd said, all the beautiful things that he'd told her, she couldn't get past her fear that that's exactly how this would all play out.

And strangely enough, Eli wasn't pushing the issue. There'd been no stolen kisses…no tries for sex…no pleas for her understanding. She saw him often, but they were always in a group of people. And things had simply been crazy busy since the war, so he probably hadn't had the time to seek her out on his own, especially with all the work he and the mercs had been doing.

Either that, or this was some kind of new battle plan he was waging against her. One that had her twisted in knots…and thinking about him constantly. Was he just wearing her down, waiting for the moment when she would snap and go running after him?

A few women had come down from town to see him—including the one who'd tried to visit him before—but he'd sent each one of them away, and apparently asked them not to return. She knew because his friends loved talking about it in front of her, as if the idea of Eli having to constantly tell his former lovers to get lost was the funniest thing they'd ever seen. On the surface, she was afraid to read too much into it. But deep down in her heart, Carla couldn't help but fall for him a little harder each time she heard that he'd sent another woman from his past back home, hoping that it meant he was saving himself for her. That he knew what he wanted, but just hadn't managed to secure the deal.

Not that it would make any difference in the end, considering she fully expected him to bail. But it was still something that she cherished, fool that she was.

Another loud noise came from the far end of the glade, drawing her attention back to the area, and she glared. What the hell were they doing down there, anyway?

Damn it, she was *done* wondering. She was going to go down there and find out for herself once and for all!

Starting down the porch steps, she saw Jeremy carrying what looked like the box for a crib into his and Jillian's cabin, which made her think of the dinner she'd had with all her girlfriends a few nights ago. Every single one of them, with the exception of Jilly, had been chatting about how they were trying to conceive. Even Elise, who had only been bonded with Wyatt for a short time, was giving it a go.

As Carla had watched their faces and listened to their excitement, she couldn't help but be happy for them and wish them all the best. And knowing their mates, she had a feeling they'd all be knocked up before the end of the summer. Which meant that it wouldn't be long before little rugrats were taking over the Alley, and she was looking forward to being the awesome aunt that all the kids adored. She would put her freaking heart and soul into spoiling those munchkins rotten.

But as thrilled as she was for her friends, it hurt that she didn't have any chance of bringing her own baby dreams to life. Not that she was ready now, mind you. But she'd always wanted to have a big family someday. When she'd been younger, those dreams had always revolved around Eli. And now...*no*, she thought, shaking her head. She wasn't following that dangerous train of thought, knowing damn well that she wouldn't be able to handle where it led.

Fired with an even greater sense of frustration, Carla cursed under her breath as she walked through the crisp blades of grass in her bare feet, the guttural sound catching Max's attention as he walked by. Sliding her an easy smile, he said, "Hey, Reyes. Those foundations for the cabins the mercs are building look pretty awesome, don't they? I think it's so cool that they're staying."

In that moment, she was pretty sure that her heart had just stopped. "What did you say?"

Max lifted his brows, looking a bit concerned as he took in her stunned expression. "That they're staying?"

"So then...they're building...you mean the cabins are for..." She broke off, unable to go on, shaking so hard her teeth had started to chatter.

Jesus Christ, she couldn't believe it. They were

building cabins. For *all* of them. Freaking cabins for
them to use on a permanent basis.

Oh, hell, no.

He wasn't going to pull this on her. Give her foolish
hope and then leave nothing but a pile of rubble behind him in the place where her heart had once been.

Dodging anyone who got in her way, she stomped
across the clearing, not even bothering to say goodbye
to Max, who was no doubt watching her like she was
a crazy woman. But, damn it, that's what she felt like.
She knew something weird had been going on with Eli
and the others, but she'd never expected *this*. Never!
And she couldn't believe that none of her friends had
told her. What was this? A freaking conspiracy?

Before she could reach the place where Eli and the
others were working, he came around the side of the
cabin he was still staying in with Kyle, a sudden grin
on his lips when he caught sight of her. "Hey, Reyes.
What's up?" he asked, his tone so deliberately casual
it made her want to bite him.

When she didn't respond, just stood there seething and glowering at him, he nodded his head toward
the cabin. "You want to come in and take a look at the
plans for the place I'm building?"

Her nostrils flared as she pulled in a rattling breath,
but she managed a thick, "Yeah," and followed him
up the porch steps, through the door, and back to his
room. The detailed blueprints had been laid out over
his bed, and after looking them over, she turned her
head to stare at him. He stood only a few feet away, at
the foot of the bed, his hooded gaze locked in hard and
tight on her flushed face. "Is this…is this some kind

of joke?" she pretty much wheezed, since she couldn't get enough air into her lungs.

"A joke?" He rubbed a hand over his stubble-darkened jaw as he shook his head, and said, "No."

"Then why?" Breathing in rough, choppy bursts, her pulse roaring in her ears, she said, "Please, just tell me why you're doing this, Eli."

With a wry arch of an eyebrow, he asked, "You sure you want to know?"

She nodded, her throat so tight she could barely swallow.

He closed his eyes for a moment, took a deep breath, and when he opened them, they were burning with so much brilliant emotion it made her light-headed. Then she heard that deep, bone-melting voice of his say, "Because you might not want to be mine right now, but it doesn't mean I'm not yours, Rey."

"No," she whispered, her eyes stinging. "You were *never* mine."

His voice was soft, and so damn delicious. "Hell, yes, I was. I always have been. From the first time I ever set eyes on you." Shaking his head again, he said, "I was just too afraid to admit it."

She blinked, wondering why his face was swimming out of focus. "I know you, Eli. You're not afraid of anything."

"You know that's not true, Rey, because I've been terrified of a lot of things." He came around the foot of the bed until he stood right in front of her, then reached out, swiping something hot and salty from the corner of her mouth. "But I'm also man enough to admit when I'm wrong. And I was so wrong, sweetheart. About…about so many things. But never about how I feel about you."

"It doesn't matter," she said unsteadily. "It's…it's too late."

Taking her face in his big, warm hands, he kept his glittering gaze focused hard on hers. "Carla, listen to me. It's never too late, baby. You're just feeling scared, and trust me, I know how hard that is. But I'm not giving up on you. *Ever*."

Sniffing, she whispered, "This won't work, Eli."

"It *will*. When we're husband and wife, completely bonded, it will be the most incredible thing that's ever happened to me, and I will do whatever it takes to make you happy."

"Oh, God." She knew the look of shock on her face had to be priceless. "You want us to get *married?*"

"That's what this has all been about," he murmured, his voice getting huskier. "I want you. Not for a moment, Rey. I want what's *mine*. I want it forever." He threaded his fingers through her hair, pulling her head back as he lowered his face over hers, so impossibly gorgeous she couldn't think straight. "And you know what else? I know you love me. You aren't ready to tell me, but I *know* it's there inside you, and one day, you're going to give me the words." His dark eyes gleamed with emotion. "I have enough faith in that happening for both of us, Rey. Whatever it takes, I'm going to wear you down."

"You're mad," she gasped, unable to stop the tears spilling over her lashes.

A beautiful grin tugged at the corner of his mouth. "Maybe. God knows you won't make it easy on me. But I'll see this through. I have to. I can't accept any other outcome."

"You don't get to make that decision."

"Yeah, well, you don't get to decide everything, either," he drawled with a quiet, rugged laugh. "We need to do it together."

Stepping back from him, she swiped at the tears on her face. "You won't stay. Not for long. You'll be bored out of your mind before that cabin is ever even built."

His shoulders lifted in a casual shrug. "I'm sorry you believe that, but I guess you just don't know me as well as you think you do. Because as long as you're here, then I am, too."

She shoved her hair back with shaking hands, her voice thick with panic as she snapped, "Fine, whatever. I...I've got to go now."

"Then go, Rey. But I'd like to see you tomorrow."

Despite her words, she didn't leave. She didn't even move. She just stood there staring at him, while her heart pounded so forcefully in her chest it felt like it was trying to escape.

"See something you need?" he asked after a moment, hooking his thumbs in his pockets, acting as if he had all the time in the world to wait her out.

She licked her lips with a nervous flick of her tongue. "I...I feel tricked."

His lips twitched with another one of those sinful, crooked smiles. "I think the word you were actually going for was needed. Or loved. Worshiped. Adored." Raising his eyebrows, he asked, "Should I go on?"

"Oh, God, you *are* crazy."

"Crazy about *you,*" he muttered softly, suddenly grabbing her and pulling her against him. His arms wrapped around her like steel bands, holding her close, while his mouth caught her startled gasp, his tongue thrusting past her lips as if he had every right to put it there, and she forgot all about resisting him. His hot, addictive taste pulled a helpless moan from her as she wrapped her hands around the back of his neck, holding him to her, the soft strands of his hair tickling her skin.

Muttering a thick, guttural curse, he lifted her and carried her across the floor until he could push her against the wall, trapping her there, grinding against her as she wrapped her legs around his waist. "I want to be *here*," he growled against her lips, and she wished she wasn't wearing her stupid jeans. "Live here. I want to be inside you again so badly I can taste it."

Shoving her fingers into his thick hair, she arched against him and cried, "Just do it, damn it!"

He groaned like a man who was desperate for his woman, but he didn't start ripping her clothes off. Instead, he pressed a tender kiss to the corner of her trembling mouth, and rasped, "I want to, baby, but I can't."

"What?"

Staring deep into her wide eyes, he slowly shook his head. "It's not gonna happen, Rey. Not until you're willing to give me everything."

She blinked, unable to believe what she was hearing. "Are you freaking serious?"

He set her back on her feet and took a step back, the gray cotton of his shirt stretching tight across his broad shoulders as he pushed his hands in his pockets. "I know how this works," he murmured. "If I keep giving it up, you're going to lose all respect for me, right?"

"You manipulative son of a bitch," she growled, fisting her hands at her sides. The bastard had gotten her all worked up, and completely played her!

He arched his brows, looking as if he was trying hard not to smile. "Sexual frustration makes you cranky, Rey."

"Not for long it doesn't," she snapped, the words rushing from her mouth in a surge of anger before she could hold them back.

His arm shot out, stopping her forward progress as she tried to storm around him, heading for the door. He waited until she turned her head to pin him with a sharp glare, and then he said, "Before you go causing trouble, there's something you should know."

"What?" she snapped.

"I'll kill any man who touches you."

She snorted. "Including your own men?"

He held her hostile gaze as he lowered his hand. "Anyone, Rey. So keep that in mind."

She sighed, knowing damn well that she was only bluffing. She didn't want anyone but him, and the cocky jackass knew it. Crossing her arms over her chest, she turned to face him. "So your men, they're staying, as well?"

"Does it matter?" he asked, his neutral tone giving nothing away.

"I'm not complaining. They're good men. But what the hell are they going to do here?"

"What they've always done. Just not all over the world. They're going to focus on the Eastern seaboard, which makes this a prime location for a permanent base. Something they've never had. But it means they'll have a chance for stability. Hell, they might even start families."

A quiet laugh fell from her lips. "Wow, then you've all lost your minds," she murmured, knowing she sounded like a bitch. But that's what fear could do to a person. Make you too afraid to even be honest with yourself, much less the man you loved with every single miserable part of your soul.

"Keep telling yourself that if it makes it easier," he said, the tender look in his dark eyes nearly breaking her down. "I'm prepared to wait you out, however long it takes. Just remember that I'm here, Rey. Waiting for you. And thinking about you every single moment of every day."

She started to pace from one side of the room to the other, knowing she should leave, but unable to just make herself do it. She couldn't get past the gut-wrenching feeling that if she walked out that door right now, it would be the biggest mistake of her life.

Finally, she stopped and whirled toward him, her chest heaving with her sharp breaths as she asked, "And just why is your cabin so big?"

He gave another one of those relaxed, easygoing shrugs. "I'm a big man."

She glared, biting her tongue, while her mind churned the question over and over in her head.

With a knowing grin on his perfect lips, he waited for her to say something more. To point out the obvious. And it didn't take long for her to crack.

Pointing at the blueprints still laid out over his bed, she said, "So you have like…what? *Five* bedrooms planned? What's that about? Are you planning on having a harem, Eli?"

"More like a family," he murmured, keeping his beautiful eyes locked tight on hers. "*Our* family, Rey."

"What?" she mouthed, frozen in place with shock, while her heart tried to climb its way into her throat.

He gave her a greedy, smoldering look, as if to say that he knew just how deeply his words had touched her, reaching those secret tender places where her dreams lived, because he felt the same way. Dreams she'd been terrified for so long would never come true.

Softly, he said, "You heard me, baby."

Oh...oh, God. In that blinding, breathtaking moment, she could finally see it—*feel it*—what it would be like to build that wonderful, incredible life with him, and it was the most magnificent feeling in the world.

Her throat tight with emotion, she whispered, "You're such a liar, Drake."

"It's not a lie," he said roughly, giving her a fierce look of determination. "I've never meant anything more."

"Not about this." She lowered her gaze so that he couldn't spot the happiness that was surging through her before she was ready for him to. "I'm talking about the bond. You never had any intention of breaking it, did you?"

She heard him exhale a ragged breath. "Not without one hell of a fight."

The sensation in her chest was so warm and sweet she was surprised she hadn't melted, and in an aching voice, she said, "You really do love me, don't you, Eli?"

He made a hard, thick sound, as if he'd finally realized he *had* her, and when she looked back up at him, she could actually see the tears in his eyes. God, was there anything more seductive than a badass alpha willing to cry?

Reaching out and yanking her close again, he buried his face in her hair, his body shaking with a visceral wave of emotion. "I love you more than you could ever possibly understand, Rey. And I'll never regret anything more than letting my old man take you from me for all those years, when we could have been together. Not just the ones while I was gone, but the ones before that, when you belonged with me and I was just too damn scared to do anything about it. I was such a stupid jackass."

He lifted his head, connecting that bright gaze with hers, and he held her head in his hands as he growled, "I've missed you so damn much. It was killing me inside a little each day, not having you in my life. In my arms. Not being able to tell you how much I love you. How deeply I will *always* love you."

"Damn it, you are *such* an ass for making me cry again," she sniffled through her tears, leaning up on her toes to press her trembling lips to his. He groaned as he quickly deepened the kiss, his arms locking around her, lifting her off her feet as he crushed her against his body.

"God, I need you," he said in a guttural burst of words, turning and laying her down on the bed, the blueprints crinkling beneath them as he came down over her, putting his face close to hers. "I need you to be *mine,* to be my *wife,* Rey, because there isn't any part of you that I don't love. I love your strength and your mind and your wicked sense of humor. I even love that you're a little badass, because it means I can do whatever the hell I want to your beautiful body and you'll be able to take it."

She arched against him, rubbing her breasts against his chest as she gripped the hem of his shirt and tried to rip it off him. They struggled for a moment, panting and giving breathless moans of excitement as they tore at each other's clothes, until they were both blessedly naked, her legs spreading wide for him as he rubbed his heavy erection against her sensitive folds. "Tell me, Eli. What are the things you want to do?"

His eyes scorched as he braced himself on straight

arms and looked her over. "Everything," he said in a dark, velvety rasp that made her shiver. "I want to do every single thing there is to do to you, Rey."

"I want that, too," she gasped, lowering her gaze as she reached between them and curled her hand around his impressive length, the plump tip so swollen and succulent it made her mouth water. Did other women think this part of their male was so beautiful? She didn't know. She only knew that she loved looking at him, tasting him, holding him inside her. Loved the weight and the veined ridges and the sleek skin. Loved how powerful it was and what he could do with it. The intimacy and the trust she felt from him when she held him like this, stroking him with her hand.

Leaning down and pressing his forehead against hers, he groaned, "Christ, you really are trying to kill me."

"No," she whispered, lifting up and running her lips across the stubbled edge of his jaw. "But I love making you crazy."

"You do...I am...and I can't wait," he growled, reaching down and positioning himself at her entrance. "I need inside you, Rey."

"Then get inside me," she said, smiling up at him as he lifted his head and stared down at her with those smoldering, thick-lashed eyes. "It's where you belong."

His expression tightened with lust as he slowly started to thrust, working himself in deeper...and deeper, while his lips parted for his jagged breaths. He seemed even bigger than he'd been before, and it wasn't easy for him to get inside her, even though she was drenched with need. Then he was *there,* hitting the end of her, both of them breathing hard and fast, their mouths coming together in a kiss that was raw and wet and deliciously wild. His body started to move in a hard, shattering, devastating rhythm, and as wonderful as it'd been with him before, this was... different. Richer, and more intimate, as if something that had already been the best had somehow become even better, and in that blinding, poignant moment, Carla realized that she no longer wanted to forget their past, because it had taught her the valuable lesson to never take love for granted. To be brave and say what needed to be said.

"Eli?" she whispered against his mouth.

He lifted his head and locked her in his dark gaze, while his body kept thrusting deeply into hers, so thick and hot and hard that she was already completely addicted to the feel of him. "Yeah, baby?"

Clutching his broad, muscular shoulders, she said, "I just wanted to tell you that I love you."

He froze, lips parted and eyes gleaming, and she felt his cock get even harder...thicker, throbbing inside her. She'd stunned him, but it was clear from the look on his face and the reaction of his body that he'd *liked* what she'd said. The words had completely wrecked him, and she couldn't help but smile.

"I do. I've loved you forever," she told him, cupping his gorgeous face in her trembling hands. "I always will. And I should have told you that years ago. But I'll always say it for as many years as we have to come. I'll say it until you're sick of hearing it."

"That," he breathed out shakily, "will *never* happen."

Tilting her head to the side, she wrapped a hand around the back of his strong neck, and pulled him down to her as she said, "I'm *ready,* Eli. Show me how much you want me."

He made a rough sound that was so much more animal than man, and it drove her wild, knowing that she affected him so deeply. Even the most primal, possessive parts of him. He fisted his hand in her hair, holding her head tight, and she shivered when she felt the soft warmth of his breath against her sensitive flesh. He flicked his tongue against the smooth column of her throat, moaning with pleasure at her taste, and then she felt the hot slide of his fangs. He dragged them across her tender skin, teasing her, making her writhe, until she reached down and grabbed his magnificent ass, pulling him even deeper inside her. He shuddered as he gave a raw, guttural growl that was smothered against her throat, then drove his fangs deep, and it was so freaking good that she screamed.

Holding him to her, she opened her heart and soul to the beauty of the emotions that were flooding into her—to the love and tenderness, so protective and everlasting, combined with a greedy hunger that was so fierce and ravenous she could only shiver in rapture—and she wrapped her arms and her legs around him as tightly as she could. She was undone by the beauty of the bond as it built between them, twining their hearts and souls together until they couldn't ever be torn apart. She could feel his throat working as he swallowed the rich spill of her blood, his body driving into hers with all the raw, primal ferocity of their connection, until they were both gasping and shuddering. And then they were both crashing into a dark, savage pleasure that completely consumed them, and everything in her world went warm and soft and black.

She didn't know how much time had passed when she finally came back to her senses, but Eli was still inside her, and her lips curved as she blinked her eyes open, finding his gorgeous face right above her.

"There's that beautiful smile," he said huskily, nuzzling his nose against hers, and she could feel her smile growing, spreading through every part of her. Pulling his head back, he stared down at her with a breathtaking gaze that was molten with love. "I've waited a lifetime to see you look at me this way, Rey."

"You know, as badly as it hurt, I'd do it all again," she told him, her own eyes burning with tears.

"Do what?"

Sniffing, she said, "Relive every moment of pain, of anguish, that I've gone through. I'd do it all again if it meant we got to this point. Because it was so worth it, Eli. *You're* worth it."

"God, I love you so much," he groaned. "I love you more each day, woman, and it scares the hell out of me, because I don't know how to hold it all inside."

"Don't. You can trust me with it. I'll keep it safe, because I'm never letting you go," she whispered, pulling him down for another tender, soul-searing kiss, the moment so perfect and right she wanted to freeze it in her mind for the rest of eternity.

They'd completed their bond, her man was buried deep in her body, and she was wrapped up tight in his arms.

After all this time, they were both exactly where they were meant to be.

Epilogue

One week later...

Standing on Carla's front porch, Eli looked out over the twilight-colored Alley, watching the preparations being made for Elise and Wyatt's wedding, which would take place in two days. His life was more blessed than he could have ever imagined it would be—and he knew, without any doubt, that it was only going to get better. He had his woman, his family, and a new sense of purpose to fill his days...while his nights were for Carla alone. And, God, were they incredible.

Someone called out a greeting to him, and he waved with his free hand, a cold beer in the other, looking forward to the event that had the entire Alley buzzing with excitement. Though the glade had seen its fair share of weddings lately, this one would be different, because it would no longer be just their small group of friends and family. For the first time in history, after the ceremony took place in the Alley, there would be a reception held up in Shadow Peak, since the townspeople had insisted on taking part in the celebration. The social divide between the Alley and Shadow Peak had been all but laid to waste after the war, and those who hadn't been willing to accept the change and move forward with an open mind had been invited to leave and make their homes elsewhere.

But while they'd lost some members, they'd gained others. After the battle, the Bloodrunners had offered sanctuary to the women and children from the Whiteclaw pack who had wanted a new beginning, and the town, for the most part, had accepted them. Were there still some assholes who would never change or learn? Of course there were. Nothing was ever going to be perfect, because this wasn't a bloody fairy tale. But things were finally on the right track for the Silvercrest, and he knew the coming years would only see greater changes that brought *everyone* on the mountain closer together.

Instead of creating hatred, his father's legacy had accomplished the complete opposite of what he'd wanted, and none of them were happier to see that happen than Eli was.

Once the Whiteclaw had been defeated, Eli had taken Eric and Elise aside one night and confessed about the help he'd given their mother. They'd been angry, just not over what he'd expected. Instead of blaming Eli for what he'd done, they'd been pissed at him for not trusting them with the truth…and for not having the faith in them to understand. It'd been an emotional moment for the three of them, but it'd brought them closer together than they'd been since they were kids, and he'd slept lighter that night for having the burden off his chest.

Then he and Carla had finally gotten the new beginning they deserved, and sleep had been the last thing on Eli's mind. They'd been holed up in her cabin the entire week, and the bed was pretty much shredded, seeing as how his wolf had definitely wanted to come out and play now that they'd finally claimed their mate.

No matter how wild Eli got with her, she never feared him. If anything, the little hellcat reveled in his absolute need for her, pushing him harder, demanding everything he had to give her, including the parts of himself he hadn't thought anyone would ever want or accept.

The way Eli saw it, a person could easily go through life living with fear, letting it strangle them. Fear of someone they loved getting hurt. Fear that they weren't good enough. Of loss. Heartbreak. They could let that fear hobble them—or realize that all it really meant was that they had something worth keeping...worth *loving*. Some*one* worth giving the very best parts of themselves and finally letting the fear go. So that's what he'd done during the battle. And though it'd taken her a bit longer to realize, he could have sworn he'd felt Carla do the same on the day she'd come to him and they'd bonded.

That had been the best damn moment of his life, and he'd be grateful for it, for *her,* until the day he died.

As if she could sense that he was thinking about her, Carla came out onto the porch with him, snuggling up against his side as they watched the flurry of activity together. They'd offered to pitch in, but everyone had shooed them away, telling them to take some time to simply enjoy their bonding. They'd definitely done as they were told, and Eli was wearing the claw marks on his back to prove it.

And he was sure as hell wearing them with pride.

Of course, in another month, he'd be wearing something else that his mate had given him: a ring on his finger, on the day they had their own wedding there in the Alley. A wedding that his men had insisted on planning the reception for, which made him grin just thinking about it. With that lot, there was no telling what they might cook up. Eli only knew it was sure to be the party of the decade, and he couldn't wait to experience it with Carla right by his side, where she always belonged.

He was about to ask her if she wanted him to grill some steaks, when Jeremy came over and invited them to dinner with him and Jillian. They accepted the invitation, enjoying the evening they spent with the couple, and then Carla took him home and had her wicked way with him. He'd fallen asleep in her arms, and found himself waking up hours later with a damn grin on his face. At first, he didn't know what had roused him, and then he realized someone was tapping on the bedroom window.

What the hell?

Rolling out of bed while being careful not to wake her, he raised the blinds and found Lev standing outside in the moonlight. "What's going on?" Eli asked, after lifting the window.

Lev jerked his chin toward Cian's cabin. "I thought you might like to know that the Irishman's running."

With a scowl, he muttered, "Why should I care if he's going for a run?"

Shaking his head, the merc said, "He's packing, Eli. As in *leaving*."

"What? You mean…?"

Crossing his arms over his chest, Lev nodded. "That's exactly what I mean."

It took Eli only seconds to throw on a pair of jeans and head outside. Lev was nowhere to be seen, leaving him to deal with the situation on his own, and he choked back a curse, thinking he'd have to thank the jackass for that later.

He hadn't seen how things had worked out on the night of the battle between Cian and Sayre, but it'd become clear to everyone in the Alley that the Runner and the witch were doing everything they could to avoid each other in the days since. Eli had thought that meant the Irishman had finally come to terms with his feelings for the young woman. But he'd apparently been wrong.

Making his way down the porch steps, he walked through the damp blades of grass, toward the Land Rover parked beside Cian's cabin. The Runner was leaning into the backseat through an open door, and it was clear that the interior of the car had been filled to the brim with the guy's belongings.

"What the hell are you doing, Hennessey?"

With a cigarette hanging from the corner of his mouth, the Irishman turned toward him and frowned. "You're a clever bloke," he drawled. "Give it a guess."

Working his jaw, he said, "All right. Then let me ask you this. *Why?*"

"I just need a break from things for a bit," the Runner offered in a bored tone that Eli knew damn well was forced.

"Bullshit," he grunted, jerking his chin toward the loaded Land Rover. "You're not packing a bag. That's damn near everything you own in there."

Cian leaned back against the open door, and took a sharp pull on his cigarette as he held it between his thumb and forefinger. "All right. I *can't* stay here," he bit out, exhaling the smoke on an angry, frustrated breath.

"Because of Sayre?" When the Irishman's head jerked back, his silver eyes gleaming, Eli said, "Don't look so surprised. We're not blind. We've all figured it out."

"You haven't figured out shit," the Runner snarled, curling his upper lip.

"She's your life mate?"

Cian didn't respond at first. He took another deep drag on the cigarette, the tip gleaming like a demon's eye in the moonlit darkness. The silence stretched out, punctuated only by their breaths and the wind whipping through the leaf-draped branches, until he quietly growled, "She's nothing but a little girl."

"I call bullshit again."

Throwing the cigarette butt on the ground, the Runner pushed away from the door. "Damn it, the *best* thing I can do for her is to get the hell out of her life."

Eli gave an irritated shake of his head. "You might think that, but I'd be willing to bet that you're *wrong*. And you have no idea what you're setting yourself up for. You're gonna hurt out there," he predicted, pointing his finger toward the road that led out of the Alley, "because there's a big ass difference between screwing around and being with the one woman who matters."

Cian's mouth curled in a slow, chilling smile. "Trust me, I know."

"Then don't be a jackass! You can't run from fate, man. Take that from someone who *knows*. Even when you try to convince yourself that leaving is the right thing to do, it's nothing but a goddamn lie. And it all comes back to bite you hard in the ass when it finally catches up to you."

Shifting his turbulent gaze to the interior of the Land Rover, Cian said, "That's a chance I've got to take."

"You could try taking a chance on her instead," he argued.

"No. She's not the problem."

"And you are?" he grunted, watching the Runner shut the door to the backseat, then open the driver's door and climb behind the wheel.

Cutting him a sharp look from the corner of his eye, Cian said, "I'm something you've never even known."

And with those soft, ominous words ringing in the air, the Irishman slammed his door, cranked the engine, and drove away, disappearing into the night.

* * * * *

MILLS & BOON®

Why not subscribe?
Never miss a title and save money too!

Here's what's available to you if you join the exclusive **Mills & Boon Book Club** today:

- ✦ *Titles up to a month ahead of the shops*
- ✦ *Amazing discounts*
- ✦ *Free P&P*
- ✦ *Earn Bonus Book points that can be redeemed against other titles and gifts*
- ✦ *Choose from monthly or pre-paid plans*

Still want more?
Well, if you join today we'll even give you
50% OFF your first parcel!

So visit **www.millsandboon.co.uk/subs**
or call **Customer Relations** on **020 8288 2888**
to be a part of this exclusive Book Club!

MILLS & BOON®

Why shop at millsandboon.co.uk?

Each year, thousands of romance readers find their perfect read at millsandboon.co.uk. That's because we're passionate about bringing you the very best romantic fiction. Here are some of the advantages of shopping at www.millsandboon.co.uk:

* **Get new books first**—you'll be able to buy your favourite books one month before they hit the shops

* **Get exclusive discounts**—you'll also be able to buy our specially created monthly collections, with up to 50% off the RRP

* **Find your favourite authors**—latest news, interviews and new releases for all your favourite authors and series on our website, plus ideas for what to try next

* **Join in**—once you've bought your favourite books, don't forget to register with us to rate, review and join in the discussions

Visit **www.millsandboon.co.uk**
for all this and more today!

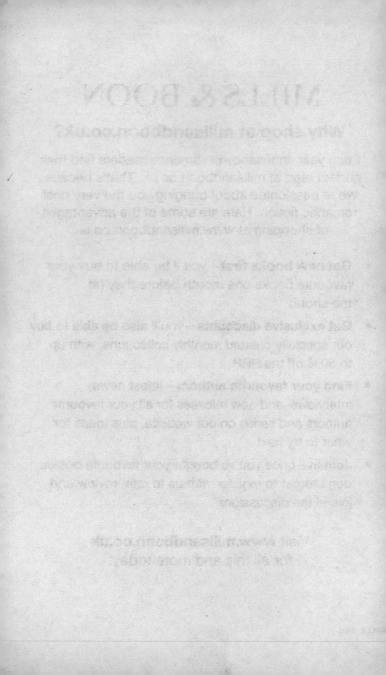